*Everything was perfect.
Until it wasn't.*

THE
PERFECTS

PRAISE FOR THE PERFECTS

I finally popped my Rachel Van Dyken book cherry and what a yummy delight it was! The Perfects is heartbreakingly beautiful and brilliantly told. All the WOW! I wholeheartedly felt this shatteringly stunning saga of soulmates, survival, sacrifice and second chances at love and life.

—Karen Mc, Bookalicious Babes Blog (BBB)

Intense, heartbreaking and tender, MB and Ambroses' story gave me all the feels. With an original and unexpected plotline, this book delves deep and forces you to leave your comfort zone. Filled with hurt, struggle and redemption, the shared experience with the characters is both unsettling and cathartic unlike any book I've read before.

—Stital, Goodreads Reviewer

The angst is like no other, it had me at breaking point, my emotions were on a knifes edge, heart in the mouth, I wouldn't have had it any other way.

—Julie Workman, Bookaholic Sisters Blog

Rachel Van Dyken has mind-blowing talent and can make you laugh and cry on the same page. With turmoil and love hanging in the balance The Perfects is an emotional wave that you just might drown in. 5-Perfect stars for The Perfects by Rachel Van Dyken.

—Celeste, Goodreads Reviewer

The Perfects is a heart-wrenching story about two people finding their forever with the one who sees the raw imperfections and loves one another all the more for it. explosive chemistry, a sassy heroine, an alpha-hole(ish) hero, clever banter, heartbreakingly raw emotions, and red-hot steam.

—Melissa, Book Boyfriend and Husband Make Three

The Perfects is Rachel Van Dyken's newest standalone and it's different than anything I have read by her and I am here for it. It's an addictive, raw, beautiful, and heartbreaking story."

—Sandra Shipman, Two Book Pushers

5 heart wrenching stars! Just wow! This book was everything! So many twists and turns, heartbreak, destruction, love and devotion. Your heart will break for Belle. You will fall in love with Ambrose (and Quinn), but it will take a hot second. RVDs banter and wittiness in back, and I'm here for it all.

—Angie Schexnaildre, NOLA504nerds

The journey that both these characters go on gives all the feels, breaks your heart, fixes it but then hurts your heart again only for the journey to recover from the free falls that were on its path and gives you the HEA you soul craved throughout the whole experience.

—Vanessa, Goodreads Reviewer

WOW! This is my first RVD book and I am in love! To say I didn't know what to expect just does not put into perspective what I just read.

—Sheyla Avalos, Goodreads Reviewer

This book has angst, heartbreak, secrets, drama, friendship, found family and spice. It will have you in all your feels and have you invested from the first chapter! This is one of my top reads of the year!

—Trish, Goodreads Reviewer

I love how Rachel Van Dyken gives me a fresh story from a different angle in every new book. The Perfects was a mix of brutal angst, heart stopping drama, forbidden love, complicated feels and so much twisted passion. This new adult romance delivered complex characters with never ending secrets and heartaching emotions.

—PP's Bookshelf

This story really pushes you and forces you to look deeper at not just the characters but the whole situation! Which is what I love about it! I love a story that takes you to places you are unsure about. I love a book that is more than words on paper but a cathartic experience that has be going through it all along side the characters!

—Patricia Rohrs, words we love by blog

THE
PERFECTS

RACHEL VAN DYKEN

A NOTE ON CONTENT

Some of you like to know if there is anything in a book that may be difficult for you to read. Some real-life issues are discussed/portrayed within these pages.
If you would like to see what they are, please flip to the very last page or scan the QR Code

CONTENT GUIDANCE

As always, thank you for reading!

DEDICATION

*If I put in all the people that helped with this book, this
dedication would be way too long.
I'm so thankful. So thankful to the readers, other authors, my
team, and just everyone who encouraged me as I wrote this.
I also have a confession—I did, in fact, drink Red Bull.
Wow, that felt good to confess.
Love you all ♥*

PART 1

CHAPTER ONE

Ambrose

I hate being rich.

This is the only phrase getting repeated in my head over and over again as I stomp through the halls of my high school.

Senior year is supposed to be the time of your life; instead, I'm throwing around fake smiles, fake fist bumps, and even the random high five to people all because I'm student body president—and because my dad's famous.

And I'm not talking like he owns a billion furniture stores or he's a politician… no, he doesn't have a restaurant franchise.

He just owns the town, the same town I live in, the same town named after our family, God help us, and the same town that's been established as the safest place to live in Idaho four years running!

What an accomplishment. A round of applause, everyone!

He keeps his fucking trophies on the mantle in the living room, you know, next to the key to the city and our perfect little family photo.

Ask me if I'm smiling in it.

He comes from at least a century of a fuck-ton of money which means we're basically untouchable and that I have to have a sorry-ass smile on my face whenever I'm out in public because the last thing I need to do is make the great McCree family look bad.

I'm pretty sure I've made one mistake in my whole life—I ate candy in public, and my dad got mad because my tongue got all red before a press conference.

Yeah, that was it.

That was my one mistake.

Forget smoking weed, getting drunk in public, and wanting to develop a serious addiction to anything that will help me escape. How would I even find the time at this point in my life?

Everything is perfect.

Literally everything.

Except it isn't.

The only thing I have going for me is that everyone thinks I'm this untouchable asshole prick who sleeps in a different pair of Jordans every night just because he can.

The guys want to be me.

The girls worship me.

And I'm set for life.

Blah, blah, fucking, blah.

So, why do I want to jump off a ten-story building and see how fast the blood leaves my body every single time I have I walk into this high school?

I need to be done with it—with all of it.

God, I can't wait until college.

At least then I can have a tiny bit of separation from the pressure of it all. I force another smile as I walk into English Lit and take my seat in the back corner next to the window, where I spend at least an hour watching birds fly around and thinking how fucking jealous I am that they're outside and I'm inside.

At least I have lacrosse practice after this, and I'll be allowed outside of prison.

I'm paying basically zero attention when my phone starts blowing up. I frown down at it and see a group text from some of my teammates.

> Mel: Bro, you holding out on us?
>
> Astin: I mean, seriously—how lucky are you? Fucking prince of potato town and all that.
>
> Me: I have zero clue what you guys are talking about.
>
> Mel: Bulllllllllllshit. I just saw the article. Byron sent it over like two minutes ago.

Byron Big B has been added to the conversation.

> Astin: Bro, tell him!
>
> Byron Big B: Dude, you're getting a new roommate! Or shall I say, princess? And I agree with the guys, bullshit you didn't know. I mean, it's all over the afternoon news; twitter's blowing up with pictures of her and your parents all over town.
>
> Me: She? Who is she? And what the hell are you talking about?

They send me a link to an article. I click on it just as one of the office aides knocks on the classroom door and lets themselves in with a note for Mr. Stick-up-his-ass, also known as my English Lit teacher—Mr. Wilder.

He frowns down at the note and then looks directly at me. "Ambrose, you're needed in the office; grab your things."

Part of me's thinking day just got better, and then I think back on the group text and wonder if this walk down the hall will be more like death row than a prison escape.

My mom's waiting for me at the school office; her eyes are blurry with unshed tears—she's not allowed to cry in public, but I can tell she wants to.

"Mom?" I frown at her.

She stands, puts on her black Chanel sunglasses, and adjusts her all-black Lululemon outfit.

She's wearing a ring on almost every finger, and the filler in her lips has yet to go down enough for her not to look like a Kardashian.

She's beautiful—and I have nothing against a woman doing things to her body, have at it. I just wish that the confidence came from something other than spending money on looking like someone else.

Her dark hair is slicked back into a tight bun. "Honey, something's happened. We need to go to the house."

Panic seizes my chest. "Is it Dad?"

"No," she says quickly.

"Grandpa?"

"We'll talk in the car." Is all she says when we leave the office. I'm a little bit shook up as we make it to the red Lambo SUV she drives around.

She still refuses to let me drive any of the sports cars to school ever since crashing my brand-new BMW last year after taking a corner too fast.

How was I supposed to know there would be a stupid rabbit out of nowhere?

We drive through Eagle and into the Boise foothills, and she still says nothing as we drive around the mountain and to the black front security gate to our house.

"Mom." My voice cracks. "What's going on?"

"My sister—your aunt was in an accident. She didn't make it." Her voice is hoarse. "As you know she couldn't have kids and had just decided to start fostering a young girl."

"Okay…" My mind is spinning. Is this what the guys were talking about?

"Anyway…" She sniffles and pulls around the driveway. "If we don't take her in—she goes back into the system, and she's lived a very rough life, you don't have any siblings."

I'm stunned stupid. What the hell? "Charity," I say. "We're doing charity so Dad looks good. Why am I not surprised?"

She cuts the engine. "You know how much I loved my sister."

"You saw her twice a year." I point out. "Last time you fought over which plastic surgeon was better, and she threw wine in your face."

"She wasn't herself." Mom looks away. "Your dad pulled a few strings, and we were able to cut through some red tape and take her in."

"Does the long-lost princess have a name?" I sneer like the asshole I am.

Mom grabs her purse and checks her lipstick. "Mary-Belle."

I roll my eyes. "Of course it is."

"Be nice." Mom snaps. "She's a little… overwhelmed."

I look over at my three-story mansion with its seven waterfalls, strategically parked sports cars, and brick driveway and shake my head. "No. Shit."

CHAPTER TWO

Mary-Belle

I'm petrified I'm going to break something.

I knew when Sarah took me in that she had money, and quite honestly, I didn't care at the time because I was so done carrying around a black trash bag from house to house and getting leered at by some of the men I was forced to live with.

Some were great.

But I always had my guard up, you just never know, and after one bad experience, you tend to brace yourself for another and another until all you have are shields up like a damn Star Trek episode while the Klingons go full phasers

I may also be a huge Trekkie with zero shame, but the example still works.

I'm holding a brand-new iPhone in my right hand, staring down at it and trying not to look up all the news stories they warned would come out about me.

I'm the shiny new charity case.

With her shiny new phone.

And I get to go to a shiny new private school on top of that—starting tomorrow—with what I can only imagine has some of the most stuck-up people on the planet attending.

People who don't know what it's like to starve.

Or what it's like to sleep with the lights on, just in case.

I twirl my long blonde braid to keep my other hand occupied and take a deep breath as Mr. McCree paces in front of me on his phone.

I hear phrases like. "Money is no object. Get it done. I want it delivered now." And then he's covering up the phone and asking if I like pink.

I almost laugh but shrug instead.

My foster mom is dead, and I'm sitting with a black trash bag at my feet. And he wants to know if I like pink.

Can't I just say a bed would be nice, maybe a pillow so I can scream into it and then cry?

I keep a polite smile on my face as he talks. And freeze up when the front door opens and footsteps sound.

I don't know why but the hairs on the back of my arms stand on end as the smell of expensive cologne wafts by me.

He salutes his dad before going to the immaculate kitchen, grabbing a water, and looking toward me.

I find a small amount of satisfaction in the fact that he chokes a bit as we make eye contact.

And his eyes are—beautiful.

A glassy dark blue that seems to almost reflect my exact same panic. His hair color is a shade of amber and gold that makes him look like the prince he is, and of course, it's shaved high up on the sides with potentially perfect man bun execution if he wanted.

He looks like a younger version of David Beckham.

He's wearing a black and white school uniform with a crown crest on the jacket, and his tie is tugged almost completely off like he was nervously pulling it the entire drive to the house.

I don't even realize Mr. McCree is off the phone until he clears his throat and says, "Ambrose, meet Mary-Belle, or Belle for short."

Ambrose's eyes narrow as he licks his full lips and leans against the counter. "Well, that's just perfect, isn't it?"

Oh okay, so he is an asshole.

Good to know.

His dad points his cell at Ambrose. "No attitude."

"Oh, I'm sorry I thought that at least in my own home, I didn't have to worry about cameras." He shoves away from the white countertop and makes his way toward me. "Better strap in, Belle, because as of right now, you're not allowed to have feelings out in public and apparently not even in here."

"Ambrose!" He gets close to him. A muscle ticks in Ambrose's sculpted jaw. "I'll tell you what," Mr. McCree's smile is conniving as he crosses his arms. "I'll let you drive her to school in the Aston Martin—in fact, consider it yours."

"Drive her to school," he repeats. "To my school?"

"Yeah." His dad grins. "Who else is gonna show her the ropes? Your mom's on the phone enrolling her as we speak, which reminds me, the house is big, she needs a tour."

I open my mouth to say no when Ambrose holds out his hand to me and winks. "How's it feel to know you're worth a three hundred and fifty thousand dollar car?"

My cheeks heat.

I don't reach for his hand, but I do stand. Shame fills

me as I reach for my black trash bag, and my hands squeeze tight around it. I don't need to look down to know that I only have a few personal things in the bag, including one pair of brand-new white converse that my old guardian had just gotten me.

We were supposed to go shopping the day she died in the car crash, but when I first came to her house, she had a cute sundress and shoes waiting for me as a surprise.

I didn't mean to, but I burst into tears which then encouraged her that we needed a shopping spree right away.

And just like that, one of my shields sort of dropped, only to come straight back up again as Ambrose stared me down.

"Come on." Ambrose jerks the bag out of my hand and starts stomping away.

I have no choice but to follow him down the ginormous hallways of the first floor. It's like something a celebrity would live in. I don't even want to know how much this place costs, but I'm beginning to wonder if it's more than even an A-list actor could afford.

Elon Musk? Of course.

Tom Hanks? Maybe not so much.

Ambrose charges ahead of me and starts pointing his free hand from left to right. "Guest rooms, primary suites, game room, theater room." He moves swiftly up the stairs, my bag swinging next to his thick legs.

He's clearly an athlete.

"Bathroom, second bathroom..." He stops at the top of the stairs, and I nearly ram into him. "There's ten, just in case you get bored. Oh, and they're themed because why not? Mom gets bored." He smirks and then keeps walking.

"My room is on the second floor with another theater room." He turns a hard right. "Work out room is in the basement, which, since I see absolutely zero muscle on your scrawny body, I'm assuming you don't care to see." Another evil smirk. "My parents' primary suite is the entire third floor, definitely don't go up there unless you want to be scarred for life." He shudders. "Pool house and guest house are outside, there's an indoor sauna near the workout room, and an outdoor bar along with an indoor one on every single floor, if you want to raid it, it's not locked, my dad fully believes in the whole drinking at home if you're going to drink which I actually stand by since the last thing I need is to get caught partying and get kicked off the team." He sighs and shoves a hand in his pocket. "The drugs are, however, under lock and key, especially the mushrooms."

I let out a shocked gasp.

He bursts out laughing. "That was almost too easy. Do you really think my dad would do drugs, let alone have them in the house? Though I do hear microdosing is huge now." He keeps walking. "My room's to the left, more guest rooms down the hall, and…" He pulls out his phone and fires off a text.

I wait, feeling awkward as I stare at myself in one of the large mirrors in the hall next to some weird-looking statue that I'm sure cost more than my entire life.

"Fuck." Ambrose puts his phone back in his pocket. "And apparently, because my dad enjoys torturing me, your room is right over here, across the hall."

"Should we draw a line in chalk or something?" I joke.

He looks ready to laugh, then shrugs. "Or make a pillow fort, might be more appropriate. God knows my mom has enough throw pillows to smother everyone in Boise to death—no chalk though, fresh out of that."

"And here I thought you'd still be playing with it. My bad." I joke, trying to get a jab in.

He stills and locks eyes with me. "Are you going to be an annoying little problem, Belle?"

"That depends." I take a brave step forward. "Are you going to be a rich asshole?"

"A truce then." He holds out his hand. "Stay out of my way, I'll stay out of yours, smile when you're in public, don't make the family look bad, and remember we aren't friends at school. I already have those, don't need one more." He eyes me up and down. "And we really need to do something about your wardrobe."

I hug my chest. "Kind of hard when you've been bouncing from house to house."

He sighs and looks heavenward like he's about to make a choice he can't come back from, then drops my bag in the middle of the floor and drags me into his bedroom.

Panic seizes my chest until he releases my hand and walks over to a huge indoor closet that is bigger than my first room I shared with multiple foster siblings after my mom's death.

"What size are you?" he yells, then, "Nevermind."

He comes walking out with shopping bags—two Prada bags, one from Louis Vuitton, another from Gucci, and a box of Yeezy's.

I'm sure my jaw drops to the floor in elegant fashion when he shoves them into my hands, putting the box on top. "W-what is all of this?"

Is he giving me his clothes?

"Had a girlfriend with expensive taste; the day before

Valentine's Day, found out she cheated on me with Xander—who I would definitely stay away from since he's the worst—and decided not to give her any of her presents, never had a girl yell at me so much. She looks to be about your size, then again, I only slept with her twice and haven't even seen you out of this giant t-shirt and loose ripped jeans, but for now, they'll do."

I'm still standing there when he holds up a hand and walks away again.

What is with this guy?

I both love and hate him a bit.

So confusing.

Is this how all rich kids are?

He walks into a large bathroom that has a jacuzzi tub I want to sleep in or would sleep in, to be honest, then comes out with a Sephora bag. "Forgot that I grabbed her some makeup and her favorite weird skincare stuff."

He adds that on top of the box of shoes and then slowly ushers me out of his room across the hall and into mine. He grabs the bag from the floor and drops it inside the guest room.

Tears fill my eyes when I look around.

The bed is a King.

It looks so fluffy I want to nap.

I have my own bathroom, the only time I've had my own bathroom—ever. I almost drop everything in my hands when Ambrose very carefully takes them from me, sets them on the bed, and then starts to leave.

"Wait!" I lick my lips nervously. "T-thank you."

He stares at my mouth for a minute before looking away. "It's nothing, really."

"It is to me," I say quietly.

Tension swirls between us.

I've never had a guy look at me the way he is, and I don't know what to do with it.

"Anyway…" He knocks on my wall. "Dinner's at seven, don't be late, wear one of the dresses."

"Why a dress?" I take a step forward.

"Because it's a Tuesday, Belle, and on Tuesdays and every other day that ends in the word day… it's formal, just in case someone important stops by and wants to snap a shot of the perfects."

"The perfects?" I ask.

"What people call us." His face falls. "See you at seven."

CHAPTER THREE

Ambrose

She's really pretty.

Like the kind of pretty that has me almost uncomfortable during family dinner that I'm almost embarrassed about it. I feel like shit too, because I know that while I'm angry, I'm reacting to her in a weirdly physical way—it feels wrong. She came with a trash bag.

A trash bag.

I really am an asshole.

She put on some makeup.

Her hair has soft waves touching past her shoulders in a near-perfect fit, kissing them more like it. The black Prada dress has material wrapped around her right shoulder; the rest is strapless, leather, and she looks like a goddess.

Her eyes are wide as she stares down at the table at all the food as it gets served to us. Protein heavy for me, vegan for Mom, and both for Dad.

One of our maids pours some red wine into everyone's glasses, half for the underagers.

And so, the awkward small talk begins while I try not to look at her.

And try not to lust like some awkward loser while she takes a sip of her water and stares at the roll in front of her.

Her hands shake when she grabs it, and slowly, effortlessly, she puts butter on it, and I wonder when the last time any of the girls in my school ever put butter on bread—purposefully.

I smile at her and hope it doesn't look mocking.

My dad starts talking about work, Mom gets her second glass of wine, and we eat in somewhat weird silence as they ask Belle questions about her life before she went into the system.

I am truly not prepared to hear her story and almost want to tune it out when she starts talking about her mom's death years ago.

A single mom.

A never-present dad.

And then I look around the table and wonder if I really haven't been a total shit when it comes to my life just because I hate faking it for the media.

I sigh, my appetite suddenly gone.

"You should eat more," Dad says. "Don't you have that big scrimmage against Capital next week?"

"Yeah." I painfully chew the steak on my plate and then take a sip of wine to wash it down. "Should be a rough one."

"What do you play?" Belle asks as if she's interested, and I can even tell in her tone she kind of is.

"Lacrosse," I say.

"Captain," Mom adds. "Of the entire team."

"I'm not surprised." Belle reaches for another roll, then pulls her hand back like she's not allowed to eat, and something in my chest cracks in half as I scoot the plate closer to her and nod.

Tears shimmer in her eyes, and I hate myself all over again for having a shit attitude and not being the nicest to her at first because I was all up in my own head, not hers.

She had a fucking trash bag for her belongings.

That was it.

Fuck.

"Eat," I say. "There's a lot of food, and you don't want it to go to waste."

She gulps and then grabs another roll, and nods her head at me.

It's cute, the way her cheeks turn a slight pink color.

I suddenly want to eat something very different, and I wonder if my appetite would be sated or just set on fire by the taste.

I clear my throat. "May we be excused?"

Dad tosses his napkin. "Any homework?"

"Not that I know of. Got pulled out of school right after lunch, but I'll check online and try to get Belle updated on what classes she'll be taking if her name and registration number is there."

"Good man." Dad winks. "Thanks."

"Well, you did give me a car…" I joke.

He laughs with me, and even Belle and Mom smile.

I suddenly walk away from dinner feeling a bit more light-hearted than I did this morning and this afternoon.

Maybe I should be trying harder and not trying to make everything about me.

Belle follows me up the stairs and into the theater room; still in the dress, I can't stop staring at it, wondering how the hell Hailey would have ever looked even a quarter as good in it.

Maybe I bought it for the right person all along—maybe it was just bad timing.

I quickly turn on something random and realize it's the last Star Trek movie I'd been watching on repeat. I can't remember the name of it, but clearly, Belle does because she does a little gasp and then admits. "My only dream is to go to comic con."

She covers her mouth and shakes her head.

I actually laugh out loud. "Ah, closet nerd. Nice."

"Yeah, hanging out with the lacrosse captain… nice."

"Deserved that." I admit hanging my head.

"Yup." She leans against the leather couch, and I fight not to stare down the front of her dress like a creeper. "So, what kind of fresh hell am I going to be put through tomorrow?"

"Oh, well…" I walk over to the mini bar. "That's gonna take a quick drink."

"Underage drinking post wine at dinner, how very rebellious of you."

"Yes, I'm so rebellious. I wear a tie to school every day, joined every club in existence, including fencing, and have to be the student body president my Senior year while everyone else is out living their lives… soooo rebellious, one shot of whiskey."

I quickly make her one and clink our glasses together.

We both take it.

And then it's quiet, the movie is in the background, and

for the first time in my life, I don't want to burn down my school or my house. I want to drive her tomorrow in that car. I want to show her off. I want her to smile more and more and more. Maybe it's a penance from my own guilty conscience.

"So classes…" I grab my phone and then frown. "You're basically in all of mine, so no problem."

"How do you know?" She frowns. "You don't know my last name or—"

I show her my phone. "Mom already sent it to us, or did you forget you had a phone?"

She blushes. "Didn't really have any pockets in this dress."

"Mmmm." I nod. "I can see that."

Her eyes flash up at me.

I back off instantly. "We should go to bed." Her eyes widen. "No, no, no, no, not like no, not like that, we should separately go to sleep; school starts at 7:45."

"Why so early?" She whines.

"Because sports are equally important as well as extracurricular, so they want us out of class by 2:40."

She makes a face.

"Yeah." I sigh. "Believe me, I know. Now set that fancy new phone to get you up on time to put on a new uniform one of the maids is probably already ironing, and get some rest."

"And if I can't sleep?" she asks.

I gulp. "There's always the workout room."

She elbows me.

I laugh and stumble against her as we walk down the hall and part as we go to our rooms.

I try not to stare too hard as she slowly closes her door.

I'm awake for another two hours before I can finally close my eyes.

And when I do.

I see a black dress.

And her eating a roll.

CHAPTER FOUR

Mary-Belle

I have a hard time sleeping.

I keep thinking about him and then feeling dumb because I've known him for less than twenty-four hours.

When I finally do go to sleep, I dream about school uniforms and this weird new foster brother situation.

And mainly.

I dream of Ambrose.

I dream of him.

When my alarm on my phone wakes me up, it takes me a minute to actually realize where I'm at and what I'm supposed to do.

Go to a brand-new prep school with a hot guy I'm not supposed to even find hot, who weirdly made me think he's not the worst person on the planet, last minute.

I yawn, finally get out of bed, and walk to the closest bathroom I can find, my eyes still blurry from sleep.

I open the door to the bathroom and stumble into the heat, wait, why is it hot? I frown and turn around. The door was and still is from the hallway. Huh?

I'm still confused when Ambrose walks out of the shower, looking like a Greek god.

He's completely naked.

His eyebrows raise, so do his hands, and good lord so does something else—something huge. "Uhmmmm."

I cover my face with my hands. "I'm so sorry; I just walked to the closest bathroom."

"Like the one connected to my room?" His voice is deep and sexy. What the hell am I getting into here?

"Yeah." I gulp, needing to turn around and leave but afraid to uncover my eyes.

"I'm covered now," he whispers. I can almost taste his toothpaste as he grabs my hands and pulls them down.

I must be seeing things because he's looking at me like he needs my mouth for breakfast, not eggs.

I have a brief scenario in my head where he shoves me against the counter, and then I think I'm losing my mind.

With a bright smile, he says, "You okay?"

"Yeah, great, so great, awesome, totally perfect, you?" Too many words, damn it.

"Good, I just have one question." His abs are perfection. His towel isn't tight enough around his lean waist.

"What?" I try to sound normal, but my breath comes out raspy.

His smile broadens. "How much will you hate me if I make this morning a bit better?"

"How would you do that?" I ask.

He smirks, and I notice a small dimple on his right cheek. "Such a dangerous question, Belle."

He lifts me up onto the bathroom counter before I can say anything, and then his eyes ask it all—is this okay. His hands don't grab me, they pull back.

"I don't know," I finally say, still processing the fact that this guy is in front of me, slightly wet, looking like a hot snack I want to devour.

We barely know each other!

And maybe that's part of the appeal.

I lick my lips.

He stares at my mouth. "I'm probably going to steal that lick now."

"And if I say yes?"

His smile is so sexy I want to clench my legs. "I might say yes."

"You a virgin?" he asks.

I shake my head.

He leans in until his mouth presses against mine. "Good."

And then I'm lost.

I'm lost in the heat of his kiss, the heat of his body, and the way his towel seems to also be too much as his body presses into me. "You dirty?"

"What?"

He sounds like he's almost growling as he pushes me into the shower and runs the hot water down my body. I gasp as his mouth tries to capture each drop.

His hips move against mine.

"What are we doing?" I ask.

He shakes his head. "We're not being perfect, that's for sure."

I smile because I feel free for the first time in a while. I feel free with this rich prick, and even if he's using me—I'm going to use him right back. I grab him by his long hair and pull him down to my mouth.

He groans against my lips, then lifts me, pressing me against the shower as his cock presses between my thighs. "I could be the best thing that ever happened to you, and I really think…" He smiles against me. "…you could be the best thing that ever fucking happened to me."

I pull away. "What about being perfect?"

"Fuck it." He jerks away the rest of my clothes, tossing them roughly on the floor, followed by his towel, then grips me by the face with both hands. He looks the way I feel, desperate, afraid, uncertain, and full of lust that should be wrong but feels so right. He hesitates briefly.

I give him a small nod. It's all he needs as he thrusts inside me. "Right? Perfection is so overrated."

I've never felt so full.

So good.

So final.

My head falls back as he keeps thrusting into me. My hands dig into his muscular shoulders, and I know I'm doing something that can't be undone. I mean, we were supposed to be roommates for how long? Months? Days?

And now we're literally having sex in his shower.

And I'm no longer afraid.

I'm owning it.

And I'm loving it as his thick cock shoves deeper, harder.

I slump against him in a wet mess of satisfaction, and I can't even think straight.

Ambrose's breathing is heavy as he pulls out of me, sets me slowly on my feet, and then lowers to his knees.

"We're going to be late," I whisper.

"So let us be late." He winks from his knees. "Let me be the best boyfriend…"

"But you're not—"

"—Watch your mouth, princess… My cock may not fit inside it, by the way, but that's to try for another day. You're at my house. My school. In my life. And I'm not letting you go, so let me let you go."

My eyes widen.

And then his mouth is on me again, his tongue inside me.

Is this for real?

His hands dig into my ass.

And I'm there for him in so many ways I don't even know how to process until I'm orgasming against a tongue that should be illegal and a boy that shouldn't know all the ways to get arrested.

I laugh.

He stands. "Ladies first…"

I get out of the shower and think, best I've ever had, shower and… him.

Ambrose.

I'm in deep shit.

CHAPTER FIVE

Ambrose

can't believe I did that.

Literally, the entire dialogue in my head as we drive to school.

I reach for her hand.

She reaches back.

My phone's been blowing up like I'm some celebrity and at this point, after being with her this morning, I kind of want to swing my cock around like a total dick.

Because I have her.

I need her.

I want her.

She's mine.

Fucking mine.

I feel defensive. I feel territorial, and I wonder why I've never felt this way until now, and then I glance over at her… it's not just her beauty, it's her ability to fight me back, her openness.

Fuck, ladies first, I'd go to my knees for days for this girl.

And I barely know her, which makes me seem like I've lost it—but fuck let me lose it in her first.

Please.

I'm nervous for no reason.

I haven't responded to any of my friends' text threads and kind of feel like kind of an asshole for not saying anything, but is it wrong to want to keep this to myself? To keep her?

I pull into my usual parking spot and kill the engine.

Today, for the first time in forever, I don't want to burn the school down. I just want her to have a good day.

I want to have a good day too.

Then I want to end it with her in my bed.

I sigh. "Welcome to Hell."

She nods. "Aren't all High Schools hell?"

"Good point." I love the way she bites her lower lip before opening her door and getting out. Never have I ever... a game I've played several times, seen a girl look so fucking hot in a schoolgirl uniform.

Seriously though.

I quickly lock the car and follow her, my hand on the small of her back as we weave our way through the crowds. Girls are staring, guys are staring, faculty is staring.

We need Captain America's shield or something.

She ducks her head, and then she leans into me, and I'm letting her because I want to make a point. Nobody messes with what's mine.

And even though it's new.

It's still a thing.

I pull her closer as we open the doors to the main

hallway, and it's like time stops as my friends' jaws nearly come unhinged.

I haven't dated anyone since my ex Hailey, it's been at least a year, if not more, and the minute we pass her, I almost want to salute her with my middle finger; she looks so jealous.

Belle isn't just gorgeous; she has this purity about her that Hailey lacks—that most girls lack. It's in the way she laughs, she smiles, and she's not afraid to be herself, even if that means having a jackass like me next to her or kissing the hell out of her in the shower.

We make it to her locker without anyone saying anything, and then Hailey walks up and gives her a little shove, enough that I feel it and want to fight. "You new, yeah?"

Belle looks over her shoulder. "What gave it away?"

I snort at her sarcasm.

Hailey rolls her eyes. "Look, you can't just come strolling in here—"

"—Gonna stop you right there." I intervene. "She's with me, so if you have an issue with her, then you can talk to me about it. If not, run back to small dick Xander, then come back when he can actually make you orgasm, which will most likely be mmmmm…" I pretend to think about it. "Never, am I right?"

"You're such a—"

"—back off, Barbie!" Belle shoves Hailey so hard that her books fall to the ground. "He's mine, not yours, mine, so walk back to your castle and appreciate the fact that I haven't kicked your soft ass!"

"My ass isn't soft!"

Belle snorts. "Could have fooled me."

Hailey lunges.

I pull Belle away laughing.

And then I see my friends on the sidelines getting basically everything on their cameras, smirks firmly in place.

"Gentlemen." I wave.

They all give me a thumbs up as if to say, totally cool you didn't respond; we get it, we really get it.

The bell rings just when I'm ready to approach my friends, so I grab Belle and make a run for our first class.

The rest of the day passes by in a blur. Word spreads that a new hot girl is living in my house along with me; somehow I'm fucking my foster sister and a whole lot of other shit I don't want to get into.

Memes are made.

Tweets.

And yet, even though I'm livid that people can be so cruel, I'm smiling the entire ride back to the house.

People are strange… I mean, yeah it happened, but who just randomly makes that sort of shit up?

Belle moans. "That was torture."

"Correction," I say. "It was torture before you were there; now it's almost like a reward seeing you by my side."

"Huh?"

"I used to stare at the birds," I admit.

She sits up. "Wait, what?"

"Outside."

"Duh, because they live outside. What do you mean, though?"

I pull into my driveway and put the car in park. "I used to be jealous that they were outside, and I wasn't."

She frowns, her cute eyebrows causing a crease to form. "And now? Now, what are you jealous of?"

"The air," I whisper. "It's touching you." I lean in. "I'm not."

"I can't decide if that's cheesy or just really romantic."

"And I can't decide…" I tuck her hair behind her ear. "If I'm a lunatic for wanting to fuck you again or just really, really in love at first sight."

"You think that's possible?" she asks. "Love at first sight?"

"Do you?" I counter.

Her eyes dart from right to left and then land on my mouth. "I think that if it was, it would be proven already, don't you think? From this morning?"

"Oh, that was stalking at first sight, but I can see how you'd be confused."

She punches me in the shoulder. "I was tired and looking for a bathroom."

"Like what you find, though?" I tease.

Her smile goes wide. "I did. I do."

"Then the theory is proven, right?"

"Right." She throws her head back in a laugh. "How can you be both such an asshole and such a gentleman? I don't get it."

"The world's a confusing place, princess." I reach for my door and open it. "Just as long as I'm both to you—I'm okay with the weirdness."

"Both," she repeats, getting out of the car and following me into the house like it's normal that we live together and like it's not tense as hell once we're in the kitchen making snacks.

"So." She finally breaks the ice. "When do your parents get home."

I almost laugh before I point to the fridge. "They always leave a note."

She reads it out loud. "Don't wait up. Out for dinner tonight, order pizza."

They don't leave a twenty; they leave a hundred dollar bill as if we're going to feed the town or at least more than two people.

Belle grabs it and waves it in front of my face. "Pizza, huh?"

I lift her onto the kitchen counter and kiss her mouth. "Can I have you first? Rewards." I press a tender kiss to her lips. "Remember?"

She laughs. "Just how bored were you in school that you bird watched, and now you're kissing me?"

When she says it like that, I sound like a complete loser, but she's just… imperfect and doesn't know my past.

Most don't.

It's like a fresh start.

One I needed.

One that will help me forget. Which is selfish as hell, but she has a light that was lost to me when I was a freshman, so it just feels like, finally, things are going right.

The family will always look perfect despite the fractures in the foundation; she doesn't have to know the dirty details.

So yeah, maybe I want something just for me.

Is that so wrong?

"How are you so convincing?" she asks, giving me a little shove.

I laugh. "I was trained from a young age. They do that for rich kids, you know."

"Oh, they do?"

"It's a very elaborate training process; they even give you a silver spoon and shove it in your mouth when you're done."

She slaps me on the shoulder. "How difficult that must have been."

"They made us eat peas."

"I hate peas."

"Same."

"So pizza?" she asks, her mind seems to be constantly on food.

I nip her lips again. "Sure, sorry, I just saw something better, and they never teach self-control at rich kid school."

"Shocker."

"It's downright criminal."

"You know, you're not totally hateful."

"I can tell that came from deep down in your soul. Is this just because I gave you an orgasm or—"

She cups a hand over my mouth like someone's going to hear us, then wraps her arms around my neck. "This is strange, isn't it?"

"There is nothing strange about hugging in a kitchen before eating pizza."

"I mean everything else. Us."

"A day at a time."

"Ah, more rich kid training?" She laughs.

I shake my head. "Nah, that's just life stuff."

She nods. "A day at a time then."

"Just one, and then another, and another. Sound good?"

She nods, and I wonder how I got so lucky to get her dropped into our house. One that's felt so lonely that I never even wanted to admit it. Dinners were for photo ops, and now, I'm eating pizza with a beautiful girl that I can even call a friend.

I wonder what this feeling is in my chest and suddenly realize it's happiness.

CHAPTER SIX

Mary-Belle

His tongue could change the world—literally, all I can think of when it's inside me. In the back of my head, I realize that this probably isn't the smartest thing, but... I've been so lonely, and he's suddenly everything I see.

Is it insane that we're doing this right now? Again?

Yes.

Do I care?

No.

Because I've lived my life in the dark, afraid, constantly putting my shields up, constantly waiting to crack or fall.

Right now, I want to live. I want to make a choice for myself, not some social worker telling me where I'm going to sleep at night or some creepy stranger telling me how pretty I am.

I feel alive in his arms.

My head lolls back as he spreads my thighs wider and

starts to undo his pants, but he's going too slow, so I tug at the belt and buttons, shove them down with my feet, and then lay back on the expensive countertop waiting for more.

The incredible pizza is long forgotten.

His first thrust hits me so deep I cry out, and then he's pumping into me like a madman, and I'm screaming his name because I don't want him to stop.

His hips roll, and mine follow, matching him hit for hit as we both start to sweat across the granite.

I remember staring at it and thinking about how expensive it was, and now I want him and me all over it.

I want him in the stupid pool house.

The game room.

Every single bathroom.

I want him everywhere.

And with the way he's gripping my legs and kissing my mouth—I know he feels this inexplicable thing too.

He pulls out of me just when I'm ready to release.

"What the hell?" I whimper.

"C'mon." He pulls me to a sitting position, then picks me up and tosses me over his shoulder. "You deserve a bed."

"My ass is literally hanging out."

He slaps it. "Yes, princess, it is."

"Stop that."

He just slaps it again until I start hitting his with my fists. It's hard as steel, and so is he as his cock strains toward my stomach and thighs.

We finally make it to his room, and he throws me across his bed and then hovers over me. "I don't think I've ever been so thankful that I live in a perfect world until now."

"No more bird watching," I whisper, cupping his face.

"No." His mouth meets mine, and then he's inside me again, filling me, moving with me, clenching my hands in his, and whispering my name across my lips. "Now, I'll just watch you."

"I'm not free like the birds."

"You make me free," he says, tongue tangling with mine before he sends me soaring, just like his birds.

And I realize he's totally right.

We're two days in.

Things always change.

People die.

People live.

But right now—I choose to be free with my asshole bully turned lover and friend.

Or so I thought…

CHAPTER SEVEN

Mary-Belle

Good story, right?

I mean, that's what you're obviously thinking.

We drove off into the sunset, after you know, having amazing sex, living like perfect rich people, living our lives, and having it easy.

But you have no idea. You think that's where our story starts?

That's where our love ended.

Where the pain began.

This is our story.

This is The Perfects.

Strap in because we're just getting started…

CHAPTER EIGHT

Ambrose

One week earlier…

I can't stop.

I want her.

I stare at her door and know I shouldn't go in. Both parents are home, my dad would flip, I'd be grounded for centuries, probably lose the car, but it's like a siren's call, one I can't ignore and, let's be honest—won't.

I stare at my own door and, without even willing my body to do it, get up and walk over; my hand hovers over the handle. "Fuck it."

I grab it, and then I'm staring at her door like a total freak.

It's slightly cracked. Is that an invitation?

What does that mean?

Why the hell am I even analyzing shit right now at three in the morning when I have a game tomorrow night?

I have so many more things I need to worry about; instead, I'm staring at a damn door like it's going to eat me alive.

Focus.

You're the captain of the lacrosse team, and you can't even open a door or attempt to have balls of steel in an effort to have sex with the girl you like?

The girl that's in your house.

That the media has pegged her as my new *stepsister* rather than my foster sister yeah, that's the clincher, isn't it?

But we aren't even related.

And yet I know my dad would have a fucking heart attack if he knew, or if he caught us, it would be bad, but it's more than just sex, and talking about my feelings with my dad is about on the same level as getting seven root canals and both balls chopped off.

I hold my hand up to knock; I mean, what if she's naked? Not that I haven't seen her naked or held her naked—God, she's beautiful naked.

I'm still stuck in my thoughts when the door opens, and she's sleepily standing there in a pair of tiny black shorts and a pink crop top.

Her eyes widen. "Are you okay?"

"Huh? Yes. Why? Do I not look okay?"

She laughs, her smile always makes my day, my nights, my everything better. "You look distraught."

"I was thinking deep thoughts," I answer.

She leans against the door and crosses her arms. "Oh yeah? What kind of deep thoughts, silver spoon?"

I roll my eyes, then I look down. "About nakedness."

"Me or you?"

"Both."

"You're a relative scholar now, aren't you?" She teases, then grabs me by the hand and pulls me into her room.

My mouth is on hers before she can say another word, my hands tangle in her messy hair while she reaches for my shirt and, in a brief moment of us breaking apart, pulls it over my head.

I seriously can't with this girl.

She's perfect.

More perfect than this family.

We've been going at it more than we should, and I know that we could easily get caught, but I can't stop, and while I know I'm a horny asshole, it's more than the sex—it's the connection.

It's the fact that I can hug her.

I'll take it to my grave, but sometimes I just want to hold her, and I want her so badly to hold me back and tell me everything's going to be okay when it feels like my life's going to be something that's planned out and laminated for me, like an itinerary I want to burn but have to keep by my side and follow if I want to survive.

This completeness with her, this fullness… I've never felt it, not even with what people would perceive was the best of the best families.

Her thighs are hot as they wrap around me. We fall onto the bed in a clumsy, kiss-fueled fury of lust, want, desire, and need. Had I said that out loud, I would have slapped myself in the face.

But I'm living it, experiencing it.

"Needed you," I say between kisses. Her mouth is hot, her tongue so smooth as it slides against mine like she's testing how deep she can go and wants to devour me but is taking it easy on me when really, I just want it rough and hard, and now.

Belle flips off her shirt, tosses it onto the ground, then reaches for my head, pulling me down again for another heated kiss.

I pull away. "Knew it was a good idea to cross that hall."

"Knew it was a good idea to open my door." She laughs.

I'm completely wrapped up in her, in the moment, so I don't hear the creak of the stairway; I forget that her door is still open, and we aren't being quiet.

I forget everything but the taste of her mouth and the way she feels pressed up against me.

And then I hear a throat clear, followed by, "What the hell are you two doing?"

Belle jerks away from me, her eyes wide with fear.

I slowly turn and see my dad standing there, face pale, eyes barely containing his fury.

"Ambrose. Downstairs. Now." He shakes his head at Mary-Belle like he's disappointed, which I know is going to break her heart, and then gives me a light tug toward the door and down the stairs.

"I'll be right back," I whisper.

"No," Dad says. "He won't."

Tears fill her eyes as I look at her one last time before my dad shuts her door and points to the stairway as if I'm eight.

I thought they were sleeping. Don't most adults go to bed at like eight? Even mine are in bed early. Plus, with my practice, I just assumed he wouldn't still be up.

The walk feels slow, and embarrassing, and daunting. We make it to his lavish office that overlooks the backyard and pool. Torches are still lit around the pond, and my dad has whiskey in a short crystal glass—his favorite and the only glass he'll drink whiskey out of.

Paperwork is spread across his modern metal desk, along with folders. His laptop is open, showing the reflection of the windows behind him, and he looks tired.

Very tired.

"I don't know what to say." Dad finally breaks the silence and turns away from me. "Do you understand how important everything you do is for your future? People's perception is everything! On top of that, it's in the early morning, and you have a practice and a scholarship at risk, and you're..." He pauses like he almost can't say it. "You're in your foster sister's room taking her clothes off?"

I flinch. "We were just kissing."

He turns around so fast that I take a step back. "Do you think I'm an idiot?"

"No, sir."

"Clearly, you do!" He pounds his fists onto the desk, papers go flying, and then he shoves more off before sitting in his chair and holding his head in his hands. "Son, I created an empire, for you, for our family. The press is all over this situation with Mary-Belle. What's going to happen when your friends say something? Or when you get caught like you just did? I know you're not related, but it's not right. You need to be focused on you, on our family, on sports, on taking over the dynasty one day—"

"—What if I don't want that?" I press my palms onto his desk, onto all the other papers that make me feel sick to my stomach. "Whoever asked me if I wanted this perfect fucking legacy? You? Mom?"

He glares. "Don't for one second think you're untouchable because you're rich!" His voice shouts louder, making me take a step back. "I did this for you, and you do nothing but mouth off, nothing but make mistake after mistake, nothing but do the exact opposite of what I ask!"

I smirk at him, angry that he's making sense but also angry that he doesn't see me or care about my feelings or wants. "Maybe you should have told me to screw her first, then I probably wouldn't have."

He comes barreling around the corner of his desk, hand flying across my right cheek before I can move.

I'm so pissed he slapped me that I don't even know what to do or what to say. Eyes watering, I shake my head and press a hand to my cheek. "Really? That's what it's come to?"

Dad grabs the hand touching my cheek. Dark circles frame his blue eyes. What the hell has him so stressed out?

Everything's always perfect.

So why isn't he right now?

"Why do you even care?" I ask. "You're never home. And we live a fucking lie. Everything is perfect and has to be, or you lose your shit. Who cares if I'm kissing the girl you took in all because you wanted people to look at you like some sort of savior!" I'm raising my voice and can't help it. "Look, just leave me alone. I'll be the perfect son, even when I'm home, but I'm not touching your legacy. Because you never really did it for us. You did it for yourself. Everything is for you, and I'm sick of it. I'm sick of pretending. Do you even realize the only time you played catch with me was when the cameras stopped by for a photo op?"

Dad pales. "You never asked.

"I asked all the time!" I shout. "I begged you to give me

five minutes, and you told me that your five minutes cost at least five grand, so I finally stopped asking!"

Dad stumbles back. "I was trying to take care of you the only way I knew how!"

"Wow." I toss up my hands. "Good job. When all your son wanted was time. Not money. Fantastic job. I hope you enjoy your expensive whiskey and lonely office." I sneer. "I'm done here."

For once, he doesn't yell at me to stay or demand I apologize.

So I walk off and stomp my way up the stairs directly into Mary-Belle's room. She's sitting in her bed, staring down at her hands, breathing slowly like she's trying to calm herself. Hands shaking, she slowly looks up, tears streaming down her face.

I rush to her, jump onto her bed, and then pull her into my arms. She rests her cheek against my chest. "You should go."

"Not going anywhere, sorry." I rasp back.

"No, really." She looks up at me. "Your dad was right."

"He was wrong." She shivers next to me. "Besides, what's the worst that can happen at this point? He finds us cuddling. You know he slapped me? I'm so pissed at him, so fucking pissed—"

"—go find him, talk it out. You at least have a dad, Ambrose. I don't condone hitting your kid, obviously, but he loves you."

I roll my eyes. "Perfect, now you too?"

"I'm serious." She grips me by the shoulders. "Go back downstairs and make it right."

"You know I came in here to comfort you, and now you want me to leave?"

"Ambrose, I just think—"

"—you're all the same! All of you! Everyone trying to think for me, decide for me, tell me what to do. I'm so over it!" I jump out of the bed, knowing I probably messed up again but so pissed and exhausted that I grab one of my team sweatshirts, run down the stairs, grab my tennis shoes, and go for a nearly four am run.

I blame them.

Both of them.

Why can't I just live my life?

Why does everything have to be so complicated?

I'd left my phone in my room, so I don't go far. About twenty minutes later, after laps around the neighborhood a mile over. I run back.

Only to find an ambulance and cop cars at the house.

What the hell?

Panic washes over me as I run up, all sweaty. "What's going on?"

"Sir, this is a private matter we're going to—" It's like the cop suddenly realizes who I am. "I think it's best to talk with your mom."

"Is she okay?" Oh God, what if my mom fell? Got in an accident? She hasn't been feeling well lately.

I run my hands through my hair just as Mary-Belle comes out of the house covered in a blanket, her eyes haunted.

"Mary-Belle!" I yell her name, but it's like she doesn't see me as she stumbles to the ground and sits. "Mary-Belle."

"I tried," she whispers. "I tried to fix it."

"Fix what?" I'm wrapping the blanket tighter around her when my mom walks up to me, tears streaming down her face. "Fix what?"

"You!" Mom screams at Mary-Belle.

"Mom!" I yell. "Stop it! Can't you see she's scared?"

"Scared? Scared?" Mom's voice raises. "She killed him!"

"I was trying to fix it," Mary-Belle whispers again and again. "Fix it to make Ambrose and his dad happy. When I walked in, he was already on the ground, so I tried to fix it, to save him."

"You." Mom shoves Mary-Belle back against the cold grass. "You didn't fix it. You killed him!"

CHAPTER NINE

Mary-Belle

"Sir?" I yell and run toward him. "Sir?" He's on the floor, his salt and pepper hair—normally slicked back—off to the side. His mouth is open, his eyes too. I rush over to him, put him on his back, and start CPR right away.

I can barely remember how to do compressions but know it's important. He looks up at me, and his mouth moves.

I'm haunted by it.

I stare as I continue compressions, then scramble for the new phone he gave me that I've somehow dropped next to him.

When did I drop it?

I shakily dial nine one one, put it on speaker, and continue compressions as he stares up at the ceiling like he knows.

He knows.

"Stay with me!" I scream.

Another scream sounds—it's Ambrose's mom.

"You whore!" she yells. "So this was the big secret, huh? She's sleeping with you?"

I'm so confused and disoriented that all I can do is keep pushing down on his chest and hope that it does something like keep his heart beating while she's continuing to break it over and over again with her words.

Tears stream down my face as she yells, my arms burn, my palms, my fingers—while I don't know Ambrose super well, I know this will devastate him.

It's his father.

And as much as he didn't want the dynasty—he wants the father.

She starts shouting, then grabs a glass sniffer of whiskey and throws it onto the ground. I think she's drunk, but I have no time to even ask as I continue pressing into his chest.

He sucks in a breath, his eyes roll back, and I pray this isn't the end as Ambrose's mom continues throwing things around the room like he isn't just dying in front of us.

"Stay with me," I whisper.

"Oh, you'd like that, bitch!" she yells.

Hot tears stream down my cheeks, falling onto his limp body as he stares up at me; his blue eyes don't look away, almost like he needs to tell me something. It's a pensive yet holy moment. His wife stomps away in her expensive sweats and equally expensive tennis shoes.

"…Yes! Hurry the hell up! He's not responsive!" she yells into the phone. I didn't even realize she still had it in her hand. Finally, she falls into a chair. "They're on their way!"

Good. Good.

I continue to press into his chest like my life depends on it while she sits and watches. Out of the corner of my eye, I see her flinch when he moans, and I wonder if she actually wants him to die, to punch him.

I look back toward him.

A tear slides down his left cheek and lands on the expensive carpet.

And then, just like the tear, in all its effort to escape his eye—he's gone, the life removed from him as his eyes go dead.

I don't even realize he's gripping my wrist until it's too late.

Until the police arrive minutes later and have to pry his fingers from me.

Until his wife screams that I killed him.

Until I realize that even though I'm innocent—I'm guilty.

I'm just a foster kid taken in by the perfect family.

The Perfects.

I sit in the middle of the floor while I'm questioned and realize I will never be a part of Ambrose's life or love again.

All because I tried to right a wrong.

"What did you do!" Ambrose shouts, bringing me back to the present. "Mary-Belle, what did you do!"

I killed him.

I somehow killed him.

I stare down at my shaking hands, then back up at him; his mom is bent over sobbing.

How does a dream shatter so quickly?

How does a life just suddenly—disappear?

"M'am…" An officer walks up to me and slowly crouches down. He has a black mustache and is wearing a bulletproof vest. He's almost blurry because of my tears. "We're going to need to ask you a few questions, but because you're a minor, we'll need your guardian present."

Ambrose's mom cries harder.

I can't swallow.

My tongue feels thick in my mouth.

And as he asks a few questions and writes them down on his little notepad, I turn and look at Ambrose, my eyes searching for the nice boy that told me I was his.

But when he locks eyes with me.

All I see is hatred.

And all I feel is pain.

PART TWO
SPRING SEMESTER

CHAPTER TEN

Ambrose

Six Months Later

I hate being rich.

I hate school.

I even hate lacrosse now because it reminds me of that night, not that I even have a break from that since she lives in my stupid house, eats my food, and drinks my fucking water.

Lives in my fucking world.

That was a lot of fucks—but it hurts.

Burns from the inside out, like someone took a hot coal and shoved it down my throat, then told me that every time I swallowed, I would both think of her and feel that same burning, raging pain.

It's been six months.

We have thirty days left until school's out. She's eighteen but has to get her diploma, but my mom's promised me that she'll be gone after that, on the streets. Who the hell cares?

She keeps to herself.

Eats at her own table in the cafeteria.

Her hair's longer now, a bit darker, more natural.

She's still beautiful, but beauty can be deceiving. After all, she did kill my dad, even if the experts say he had a heart attack... she was the one with him, the one who stressed him out, could have saved him, and now we have nothing.

Now we're in two lawsuits.

Now things are brought to light.

All because she was there.

I can't stand her. I can't.

It takes everything in me to look away from her so I don't rush up to her and do something that can't be forgiven. Do I sometimes dream of her lips? Of the way she tastes?

Yes.

And it pisses me off even more.

Because everything was perfect.

Until it wasn't.

Until I was standing there staring at a body bag.

At my mom bawling her eyes out.

At Mary-Belle saying it was her fault, on her grass-stained knees, a day after I was inside her, thinking this was it, she was mine, I was hers, and this was forever.

I slam my locker door twice before it finally closes and grab my bag, tightening it on my shoulder, my grip so strong my fingers turn numb.

I wish the rest of me would be numb instead of all these feelings. I wish so many things. I wish I would have listened more to my dad and that I would have been more of a man than the punk kid I was.

But now, I'm forced into a world I never wanted to be a part of.

And again, it's her fault.

The foster girl with her black trash bag and hole-filled shoes.

I turn.

She's there, right in front of me, with the fancy bag my mom gave her, it's a Prada backpack, black, she has whatever else my family gave her in it, like her shiny new cell phone and credit cards since my mom felt guilty she had nothing.

And she's holding a book.

History.

Ironic, isn't it?

Her hair's cut to her shoulders, dirty blonde, and her eyes lock on mine. Her uniform is pristine like she's just ironed it up. Her black thigh highs dip into red combat boots, and her lips have a shiny gloss that would entice any guy, gay or straight.

Her brown eyes search mine for something I'm not willing to give, so I look away. I can't take it.

It's hard enough living with her.

Even worse, going to school with her.

Even worse than that? The fact that the entire school, regardless of what she does, seems to think she's suddenly the second coming.

She volunteers for everything.

She's a straight-A student.

She's just nice to everyone no matter how they treat her, which is irritating in and of itself—and she's done all of this in the span of a semester. Sometimes I think she does it on purpose just to make up for her sins.

I wish, for once in my fucking life, that she would be cruel the way I know her to be cruel to destroy something so perfect.

Instead, she continues her Mother Teresa act like its normal when I know she's a killer.

Am I being extreme? Yes. Emotional? Yes. But get back at me when your dad dies at the hand of someone you trusted who refuses to tell the cops what actually happened.

That's the kicker.

She said it was an accident, but no details were given, no matter what, and since she's a minor, they let it go, since my mom probably paid them off, they let it go, so it was ruled as a freak heart attack.

The autopsy proved it, but what the hell caused it? He was fine, he seemed fine, and a little meeting with her is enough to set him off?

Besides, she was the only one there.

The. Only. One.

Did she kill him? Maybe. But why?

And how did he really die from a small foster girl walking into his office?

I shake my head in disgust.

My mom thinks we keep our enemies closer, but is it so horrible to want to push them off a cliff, no matter how pretty and enticing?

"Ambrose," MB, which is what I call her now because I can't use the energy to use her full name as it makes me want to commit homicide, says. "Do you have a minute?"

"Ten seconds." I turn around. "One, two, three—"

"—-if you count, I'll panic. I just wanted to let you know—"

"—Four, five…" I roll my eyes. "…six, seven—"

"—That—"

"—Eight—"

"—I'm sorry, okay. I can't… I just can't. You don't trust me, but you need to. One day… One day it's going to make sense. I care about you—"

"Nine." I lean in, voice hoarse. "Ten. Wow, new princess, time's up; if that's all you had to say, it's pathetic. Try harder next time. Lie better." I smirk. "You're a horrible excuse for a human being. Maybe I'll meet you in Hell one day. Oh, look…" I laugh. "…we're already there!" I pat her on the shoulder. "Have you gained weight?"

She jerks away from me as tears fill her eyes. Good. "Why? Why are you so cruel? You know me, you were… with me."

"I was inside you. I knew your body, not your dark heart. Know the difference, princess. You're not mine. You don't even belong to yourself. I mean, how could a liar even know themselves? They can't. Go to class. Leave me alone."

I shove past her and wish I could feel better.

Instead, my heart hurts.

My body aches.

And I wonder if things will ever be the same again.

I used to hate being rich.

Now I just want a reset.

Where things were perfect.

Where I hated it.

Anything would be better than this nightmare.

"Miss you," I whisper. "Dad."

I should have told him.

I should have listened.

And now, I'm the legacy.

I sit in calculus as people try not to make eye contact with me, and I wish I had the tears to cry.

Instead, I open my textbook and focus.

All our dynasty has left is me.

And I intend to make sure it lasts.

CHAPTER ELEVEN

Mary-Belle

I'm numb.

Not in a good way.

I smile, get good grades, and try to cook for the family that took me in as much as possible, even though they bring in a chef every weekend.

And I'm miserable.

I miss his kisses, I miss his kindness, I miss his laugh, all he sees when he looks at me is blood, and I don't blame him, but I can't go back. How does he not see that? How does he not see my own trauma and how I can't go back?

I take three deep breaths and go into the lunchroom; as always, everyone looks away while I take my tray to one of the empty tables. They know I sit by myself and do homework or listen to a random podcast but really, it's just because I'm exhausted trying to be perfect all the time at school, at the house I'm afraid to eat in front of everyone.

I'm the interloper, the person everyone blames, and even doing all the things I do at school is only so that I'm not at the house as often. So I don't see his door or watch him walk in and out and sneer at me... the memories cut deep. It was a short moment or amount of time, but it fed years of loneliness.

And now I'm back at square one.

On a happy note, I've figured out a way to keep my hands from shaking while I carry the white tray. You see, I clench it so tight that it keeps it stable. It's the same thing I do with my teeth. I clench them until my jaw hurts, then I take a step every two seconds.

It works.

I appear confident.

Cool.

Ready for anything.

I even time the way I eat.

For example, if I have carrots, I chew at least ten times before calmly swallowing and taking a drink of water. If we have something messy, I use a fork and count to three, even though I'm starving, to cut another bite. If they have milk, I attempt to keep myself from putting an extra in my bag just in case I get kicked out.

I'm ashamed to say that I've done that a few times; I even saved my carrots once when I was scared Ambrose's mom would kick me out. I had no money, and I was worried about food since I had already turned eighteen.

Thankfully, even though I never see her, there's always food at the house, then there's Ambrose, with his perfect friends, always leering behind me, ready to kick me when I'm down.

I know he's angry.

But he has no idea.

He has no clue I'm doing what's best for him.

And I'll take it to my grave.

Because regardless of what I'm going through, it's the right thing to do, and I can't go past that, there are a lot of lines I've obviously crossed, but this is one that needs to stay firm.

For him.

I mean, maybe, I won't have the perfect life, maybe I'll end up dead—he has the best chance at doing something great, and I believe in him, so I'll take the hits again and again.

Until I'm bloody, bruised, dying because isn't that what this world needs? More heroes?

Mine will be sacrifice.

His will be acceptance.

I chew on a carrot and look down at my tray.

I tell myself that tears are useless; what purpose have they ever served in my life other than to tell my body that I'm sad?

I keep them in, though I struggle, then take another bite, then another. Someone comes and sits next to me. I don't acknowledge them. What good is it to make friends when nobody cares? Nobody's loyal?

"Hey," a male voice sounds. "You're either high or really hate carrots; never seen someone eat them so slowly. You good?"

I look up.

It's Quinn. We have Math together. He's really smart, nerd hot with black-rimmed glasses, dark hair, dimples, and super tall yet weirdly built like he has a home gym but is embarrassed to tell anyone.

65

I look down at my tray—I'm used to that by now, looking down, hiding my face with my hair as much as possible considering how short it is now.

Being invisible. "Sorry, just hate carrots."

"Why?" He laughs, popping one into his mouth and crunching.

"They're hard."

"Life's hard," he answers back right away, running his hands through his glossy black hair. "Isn't there like this whole boomer saying about life's hard get a helmet."

I try not to smile and fail.

The guy's even got dad jokes.

"Ah, I got you! Wow, I just won Monday. Do I get a high five now, or are those allowed? I mean, I don't want to make you look less cool while you suck on carrots and stare into the oblivion that is high school."

I shake my head and offer him a side glance, my hair still covering part of my face. "Why are you sitting here?"

"Got bored. I'm too smart for the smart kids' table; they get super competitive when we play frisbee golf. I got kicked off the team yesterday for a foul I will still say and take to my grave was miscalled. Plus, I mean, at least take in the wind, right? So yeah, I saw you sitting here looking all depressed, chomping on carrots like your world depended on it, and thought, damn, she's clearly having a worse day than I am, and sat. So… how's it going?"

I don't even know what to say. I gape at him. "You talk a lot."

"You talk too little."

I smile, maybe for the first time that day. "It's going okay. I have carrots, meaning I have food. Whenever you have food when you haven't had food, your perspective changes."

He's quiet, then leans back. "Deep for an eighteen-year-old."

I scoff. "Eighteen going on thirty."

"Ohhhh, you're one of those? Good to know. Also, I'm Quinn; just in case you forgot, captain of the Mathletes—we have jackets just like in Mean Girls. I'll give you a minute to catch your breath, so you don't pass out from the sheer awesomeness of our popularity. Last year we did a car wash to raise money. Made bank…"

I laugh. "Did you, though?"

He pauses. "No, but to be fair, Arnold's still coming into himself; he'll get there." He points over at a kid who looks like he's still in middle school and reading a book upside down. "He'll come into his own, I have a feeling."

"Oh yeah." I nod. "I can see it; he'll be great."

"Hey, don't mock Arnold." He points a finger at me and leans in. "Sooooo, now that I've told you all my dirty, dirty gossip, you ready to tell me yours?"

"I don't know you."

"Ohhh, I'm sorry, I'll explain… this is how friendship works. I'm here, you're here, conversation happens, carrots are eaten, I tell you about my amazing math skills, and you tell me why Ambrose won't even look at you anymore despite the fact that you're living with him."

I instantly freeze, I grip my tray like I always do and stand, but my hands won't stop shaking. Why can't they stop shaking?

I stumble backward, then trip over my own feet and fall onto the ground. I swear you can hear the crash around the loud cafeteria as carrots and ketchup fall all over my body, covering part of my face and uniform.

Quinn's eyes widen.

And then just silence.

I'm brought back to the time when I first went to Ambrose's house and felt like a freak. This is that same feeling, maybe worse because the entire school's watching.

Slowly, I get to my feet.

Quinn holds out his hand and helps me to my feet while people murmur around us. I try to act normal as he hands me a napkin, and then I hear footsteps behind me. They're loud.

Purposeful.

I take a deep breath.

I don't turn around.

I don't have to.

I know that walk.

I feel that sigh.

It's part of me now.

He's part of me.

Quinn grabs my hand and pulls me close to him just as a finger taps my shoulder.

Quinn's eyes are wide.

I'm sure mine and everyone else's mirror his… after all, Ambrose went from popular guy to god of this school. He bows to no one. He's not just popular, not just perfect; he has the money, the looks, and the personality, to back it up.

And he's the heir to everything.

He's basically sitting on the Iron Throne while the rest of us rest in the dungeon, just waiting to get eaten by dragons.

Slowly, I turn.

He looks the same as always. I've tried to forget how beautiful his face is, just like I've tried to forget the taste of his mouth, but the problem with tasting perfection?

Nothing will ever compare.

I steel my expression.

"Foster Girl," he says. It's what he calls me now as if to draw a line in the sand that we aren't siblings. I'm no longer family. I'm just this random interloper he never had or wanted, annoying the hell out of him.

Tears burn the back of my eyes as I whisper with trembling lips, "Random stranger I live with."

He shoves past me and laughs. "Might need a clean uniform tomorrow after all that ketchup... never saw you as one who'd slum it with someone like Quinn, good work with that stellar reputation."

Quinn stiffens; I can feel him.

I grab his hand.

And it's at the same time that Ambrose turns and sees. His eyes light up with fury before he grabs my arm. "Be more careful."

Quinn smirks. "Maybe be more polite."

"What the fuck did you just say?" Ambrose asks.

The bell rings.

It saves us.

I jerk away and stumble into Quinn's arms while Ambrose watches, angry, vindictive.

I wonder if it's the worst move I could have accidentally made.

A challenge.

A wave of the red flag.

Because I've never seen Ambrose so angry.

And I've never felt so safe.

In Quinn's arms.

CHAPTER TWELVE

Ambrose

I hear her come into the house a few hours later. She's trying to be quiet, and I refuse to feel bad about it even though my heart pounds in my chest. She's always so afraid of making noise, and it makes me wonder, no matter how much I despise her now.

What caused that?

Why is noise bad?

Who hurt her?

I have so many questions.

I have zero answers.

I lay in my bed, and despite my hatred of what happened of what went down and her inability to be honest.

I wait.

I wait more.

Click. Her door opens.

Click. It closes.

Ten minutes later, it opens again.

She must be going downstairs to grab a snack like she always does because she was too nervous to eat dinner with us, or according to her, doing homework and taking a nap because she didn't feel well, but I know the truth, she knows she isn't wanted so she waits with her excuses every night. I jump out of bed and run down the stairs. Sure enough, she's in the kitchen making a peanut butter and jelly sandwich— her favorite.

I hate that I know that.

I watch her eat it like she hasn't eaten in days, and the guilt comes back full force even though it shouldn't.

She moans and takes another bite like our peanut butter just saved her life or something.

She finishes it off with a glass of water, then leans against the counter.

That's new.

She usually just runs back upstairs. I stay and watch as she grips it, her nails nearly digging in.

She shakes her head. "I can't, I can't. It wouldn't even help. I can't. I love him."

Who the hell does she love?

What can't she do?

I stay and watch her longer than I should, and then the front door alarm makes a beeping noise as my mom strolls in.

MB swipes tears on her face, walks right past me, makes zero eye contact, and walks up the stairs.

I follow.

My mom sees nothing but the wine on the counter that she's been waiting to chug; that's how it's been since my dad's death. And I still only see MB and hate her for it. Mom isn't even paying attention to us; she goes to the counter and stares at her phone while I'm chasing MB up the stairs.

"Stop," I say as she grabs the knob to her door. "Why are you upset?"

She glances over her shoulder, her expression frozen, emotion completely gone. "No reason." Her smile is forced, just like mine is.

The Perfects.

The Perfect smile.

She flashes it so well, so fucking well, I almost feel sick as she closes the door to her room.

I'm shut out.

And I have only myself to blame.

And yet, I still blame her.

CHAPTER THIRTEEN

Mary-Belle

You'd think it would be easy to ignore such an asshole.

Maybe it's because he smells so good or because I remember his warmth, his smile. He's fully immersed himself in the last month of high school as one of the guys every girl wants to sleep with.

Been there, done that, wish I would have at least kept the t-shirt.

And the guy that every other "bruh" wants to be best friends with, dumbest word ever. If he was popular before, then he's a god now, and I wish I was joking about that, but he's basically going to go down as some sort of legend, I'm convinced of it.

I literally saw a girl faint when he winked at her the other day. I wonder what she'd say if she knew that his mouth spent hard time between my thighs.

Inappropriate, but sometimes I just want to scream it.

To scream that at one point in my life, everything was perfect.

I clutch my designer bag in my hand and grab my books from my locker in a vain attempt not to get noticed, but who am I kidding?

I'm officially Ambrose's technical family.

Everyone notices me.

I could be in full disguise, and I'd still get stopped and asked, "So what is he really like?"

I change my answers depending on my mood, but I always say that he's nice when he's anything but nice.

This morning I woke up to find my toothbrush in the toilet with a little sticky note on the seat that said. "Oops."

He's hurting.

Lashing out.

He's being the boy you always read about in books that you know has a heart of gold but refuses to acknowledge it because to acknowledge it means you have to acknowledge the rest of it... the dirty, the ugly, the pain.

Acknowledging his soft side would mean coming to terms with his father's death and their relationship, and I wonder if that wouldn't just fracture him so much that he breaks.

I can hurt enough for both of us.

I can take it.

I've lived my entire life this way, and he hasn't, so if that means I'm taking one for the team so that he smiles again— what else can I possibly do? I know I owe him nothing, and yet it feels like I do.

Because for the first time in my life.

Ambrose made me feel safe.

So I do owe him, I really do. The moments were fleeting, I shut my locker, and I tell myself that they were enough. That the one week we had was enough to remind me that the world wasn't all bad.

All because he treated me like a human and made me love myself more than I hated myself.

"Your skin's so soft," Ambrose mumbles against my neck. "I hope it doesn't sound creepy that I want to lick my way down your neck just to feel your heated skin against my tongue."

I laugh.

"Saying it out loud was so much worse than in my head," He chuckles against my neck. "But no takebacks."

"Promise?" I ask.

"Forever," he responds as if it's simple, as if forever is something he can promise, and I believed him.

I fell asleep in his arms that night for the last time.

I shake my head and suck in the tears and nearly run into another locker; the door shuts quickly.

"Hey, stranger." Quinn winks at me. "Were you looking for a super-hot nerd with a Star Wars fantasy? Because if so, I'm your guy." He's wearing an Obi-Won vintage black and white shirt like the ones I've seen in the guy section of expensive department stores, and his hair's pulled into a man bun that has him looking weirdly sexy.

He smells good too.

I sidestep him; I don't want anyone to see the tears. "I'm sorry, I wasn't paying attention."

I swallow slowly and move to the right.

He follows.

I swerve to the left.

Same.

"Wait." Quinn reaches for me.

It's the first time someone's touched me since the accident, I mean, really touched me in a way where you know they're concerned.

Tears burn the back of my eyes.

I almost forgot what it felt like, the warmth from someone's hand on my skin. It's unfair, but I tell myself it's okay, that I don't need it.

I've only ever needed me, right? Who else can a person depend on anyway?

I slowly pull away, only to have him grab my wrist this time, then my hand. "Are you okay?"

It's the absolute worst thing you can ask someone who's just gone through trauma or, in my case, a lifetime of it.

My lips part; I've rehearsed this answer perfectly; I get asked dumb questions a lot. Nothing comes out right away. I try, I try so hard my throat hurts, but I have nothing but air coming into my lungs.

In and out.

It's okay. Just breathe.

"Hey." He pulls me closer to him until all I can smell is his vanilla scented cologne; he presses my face against his chest.

I exhale.

Once. Twice.

"There you go," he whispers in that deep voice of his. "It's not okay right now, obviously, but it will be because what other option do we have but to breathe, and take it all in, even when things need to come out—which they always do. You still have to breathe, Mary-Belle."

A solitary tear slides down my cheek.

I don't know if he can feel it on his arm.

I don't ask.

And I'm so afraid to relax against him, to trust a relative stranger with a Star Wars fantasy who's suddenly in my universe when I've done everything in my power to make sure it's a one-person show since the incident.

"Your tears," Quinn whispers into my ear. "It's not a waste to shed them."

I jerk away immediately.

That was close.

He's too close.

And I'm too close to making another mistake. In one short month, I'll be on my own, most likely paid off to live my life elsewhere and only make appearances at Christmas or Easter, so we keep up the perfect facade.

I tell myself that the money isn't stained with blood and sacrifice.

I tell myself I won't ever believe the lie.

"I um, should get to class."

"Yes." A low voice says behind me. "You should."

Ambrose.

Goosebumps erupt all over my body as I slowly lower my head and start to walk past Quinn. He grabs my hand and twirls me back around. It hurts to look into Ambrose's eyes, and it feels like Quinn's punishing me for making me do it. I try to avert my own, but it's like Ambrose has magical powers.

Slowly I lift my chin, people stop walking past us and stand. They stare at us like we're a reality show dream when we're in a nightmare.

Ambrose's uniform is pristine, just like that sharp

jawline. His smile is friendly, but I know it can be just as cruel. "What would Mom say?"

"What?" I ask.

"Mom, she wouldn't want our ward to fall behind just because she's flirting with the dipshit in the hallway?"

Quinn stiffens and then bursts out laughing. "Wow."

"Glad you're impressed." Ambrose rolls his eyes. "All I'm saying is, get to class, get your work done, we all know how easily—" he glares at Quinn "—distracted girls like you can get."

Girls like me.

Girls like me.

Girls. Like. Me.

I start shaking.

Embarrassed and angry at myself for just standing there and not fighting back, hating myself for hoping that one shred of decency would come back and restore a little bit of what we had.

But his eyes hold nothing but pain.

And he refuses to stop inflicting it onto me.

I nod my head. "I'll study extra hard then today. The last thing I want to do is let the family down."

Ambrose scowls. "Too late for that, don't you think?"

He starts walking past me, then stops and whispers over his shoulder, "Iron your uniform next time. You look like the trash you brought the first time you came to our house. Weren't you carrying a bag?"

"Enough, Ambrose." Quinn clips. "Fucking. Enough."

Ambrose glares at him. "Are you her savior now?"

Quinn smirks. "What would make you think this girl right here ever needed saving? She can do it on her own;

maybe you've just been too blind to see it this whole time. You need her more than she will ever fucking need you."

I'm at a loss for words as Quinn grabs my arm and pulls me down the hallway. I feel like my body's floating through a heated swarm of moisture and sunlight. I'm partially aware that I'm walking, but my brain can only focus on what Quinn said.

What Ambrose said.

What people heard.

"You okay?" Quinn asks.

I feel the tears well again as we stop at my next class. I grip my bag so tight my fingertips start to tingle. "I'm good."

"I um…" His eyes won't meet mine. "I can't do that again."

"I'm sorry?"

"I'm just…" He starts backing away. "I'm probably the worst person to be defending you at this point, especially against him, all things considered. I just wanted you to know it's not you, it's—"

"—me." I finish for him. "I've lived through a million apologies in my lifetime Quinn; what could possibly make you think that this one would be any different?"

He reaches for me.

I back away and shake my head once. I have no idea why he's suddenly acting like he's bailing on me, and I don't need to know his reasons.

People fail you.

People leave.

"I don't need a savior, remember?" I don't say anything more and walk into my classroom with my head held high.

I listen to the teacher talk about numbers.

I grab my school planner and cross off the date.
Twenty-nine more days to go.
But I'll never be free.

CHAPTER FOURTEEN

Ambrose

Every time I see her, I want to fight, but how do you fight someone who's so fucking pure looking?

I slam my hand against my desk, then reach for my phone.

"Heard you and Quinn had it out earlier." Hudson sits down and laughs. "I knew it would happen one day."

I roll my eyes. "Not this again."

"Bro, you went to comic con every year together until the tenth grade—of course, this conversation is going to happen. I mean, that was the biggest falling out of friendship I think the world has seen, and I watch Euphoria."

"For all the sex and dick, good for you."

He shoves me away and grabs his earbuds from his pocket. We both know he's not going to be listening to any chemistry for the next hour, and because of how rich he is and how good his grades are, nobody really cares.

The guy scored a near-perfect score on his SATs and ACTs.

I hate him.

I mean, I did well, but still, he didn't even do test prep, asshole.

He pulls his black lacrosse hoody over his head and slinks back into his chair, still watching me with that stupid smirk on his face like he knows things.

I try to focus on the textbook in front of me as people file into the classroom, and then I stare at my phone and see a picture of my family and want to throw it at his face.

"You haven't talked to Quinn in two years." He just has to point out.

"He was in my way." I lie.

I saw him holding her, and I just snapped. I don't even remember everything that I said, but I do know it was hurtful.

"Look," Hudson's about to give me advice, perfect, just what I want on a Tuesday morning while suffering in agony over my father's death, the pressure, the person at fault, and why she was being held by my nemesis. "It's not like he stole your girlfriend on purpose... Tessa always liked him. She kissed him first, blah, blah, blah, they dated, she..." He clears his throat. "Clearly moved on just like him, I mean, of course, only after the whole we may have a kid now thing, which got real intense at fourteen, but he's a different guy now; she's happily already at college, living her life..."

It's like he thinks he knows what really went down between the three of us. There was always speculation on how close we were.

But nobody really has it right.

Nobody has any clue.

I couldn't tell my parents or my friends.

The only person who knows is Quinn and the one girl that destroyed our friendship without even batting an eyelash.

"It's not even about Tessa," I finally say. "That bitch can rot in hell. It never even was."

Our teacher walks into the classroom.

Hudson is silent. "You know you can talk about it, I mean, I have a theory, but it's pretty deranged even for you."

"It's probably tame compared to what really happened, Hudson. There's a reason we don't talk about it. She almost ruined our lives."

"Don't they say history often repeats itself?" Hudson asks before putting his pods in his ears and closing his eyes like he didn't just give me a stomach ulcer and near heart attack at the same time.

Quinn would never.

He's a lot of things.

But he wouldn't go there again, not after the last time.

Right?

I warned him away enough, and the last thing either of us need is attention or gossip after last time, and this close to graduation. Both of us have companies to take over, families to run, and adult shit to do.

He wouldn't.

I look to my right and stare as he leans back in his desk. He's good-looking enough, all the girls think he's the sweetest nerd on the planet.

But I know his darkness.

Maybe it's time they did too.

CHAPTER FIFTEEN

Mary-Belle

Something's off when I get home later that day—at least I'm making progress and calling it home, right? It's all I have, and while I'm pretty sure Ambrose's mom, Susan, plots my death every night while she chugs her wine—she's at least given me a space where I have a bed, clothes, a toothbrush that isn't losing its bristles and actual food I'm allowed to eat.

We don't talk to each other; in fact, the few times I've even seen her, she's been sleeping on the couch with the TV on. She doesn't get out much, stopped getting her nails and hair done. She's spiraling, and I know Ambrose notices it, but there's nothing either of us can do.

A therapist visited the other day, but Susan just stared into the blank space of nothingness and continued to drink.

Life is not perfect. It's a lie. Ambrose's life is a lie. And weirdly enough, he got exactly what he said he always wanted.

Brokenness.

The lawsuits are ongoing against the family company—talk of cover-ups is never a good look for any business, but I can't imagine anyone speaking a word against the dynasty after the death of its CEO.

It's bad to speak ill of the dead, but I think about him in those last minutes, the look of fear in his eyes as he reached for me with the same hands he used on his own son.

I hope he forgave himself for acting out of anger.

I've been slapped enough to know that it's not just painful but demeaning as if you're nothing but a thing, and he made his son feel that way. There is never an excuse to touch someone unless it's in self-defense, least of all your son.

I got none of those words out when he was lying there; all I could think about was what would happen to Ambrose.

I gently put my bag on the tall white leather barstool and walk around the breakfast bar to grab a bottle of water and maybe a granola bar, it still feels weird to grab food from their pantry, but I'd starve if I didn't.

It feels even weirder when I see cash on the counter with a sticky note, my name on it, as if to say, use our money, buy whatever you want.

I don't know what's going to happen in twenty-nine days though, so I keep the money in a jar under my bed—hoard it, really. So far, I have three grand. I'm hoping it's enough to at least get me started away from this place just in case they don't take care of me.

I mean, they owe me nothing.

And now that I'm eighteen and have had a full stomach from food, the thought actually makes me want to puke—not having food.

I remember getting free breakfast and lunch at my

other schools and bringing ziplock bags so I could store the leftovers for later. The amount of cold tater tots I ate at night was astronomical. I'm still tempted to do it during lunch out of sheer habit, especially when they let me grab more than one burger.

It's embarrassing but necessary.

I sigh and reach into the fridge. There's no bottled water which is weird because the fridge is stocked on a weekly basis. I grab a diet coke instead and go to the pantry.

It too has a limited amount of food.

Something's wrong.

I look around the house and notice that it's super pristine—clean, just like the first time I was there.

Again, something's off as I make my way toward the main living room. Susan isn't there like she normally is. The blankets are all folded.

I walk further down the hallway and check the garage; maybe she left?

One of the sports cars is gone.

And it's not Ambrose's.

Frowning, I walk back into the house and the kitchen.

Ambrose is there, he's leaning over the white granite, and he has a letter in his hands.

Maybe it's from a family member?

I stop walking when he looks up at me, tears in his eyes.

Did we get sued again?

Did someone else die?

Is this family cursed?

He takes a deep breath and surprises me when his next words are. "Well, I guess now I know what it's like to be an orphan."

"What?" I ask, panic seizing my chest as he goes over to one of the many liquor cabinets, grabs a bottle of expensive-looking booze, and just sits on the marble floor in the kitchen. "What do you mean?"

"I hate you," he says. "I hate me too."

I don't know how to answer that.

He pops the cap off and takes a swig. "Read it."

I'm afraid to grab the piece of paper, but I do anyway. I pick it up and look at the fancy cursive.

I can't do this anymore. There are too many memories. I moved to the penthouse in LA. You're eighteen now anyway; you'll be fine. Your father's secretary will be in touch with the next steps. You look like him. I love you. but you look like him. I'm sorry. I just can't be the mom you need right now. You have your uncle close by. And Mary-Belle can keep you company. I thought of buying you a cat or something. I know this comes across as a shock and harsh. but you've always been more of an adult than a teenager. Take care of yourself. I'll be in touch when I'm ready.

— Mom

"What?" I drop the piece of paper. "What is this? What do you mean she just left? Does she think this is easy for you? And now she's gone?"

"Defending me even when I hate you?" Ambrose takes another swig. "Look who's perfect now?" He chuckles.

"It's not funny!" I yell. "This is child abandonment!"

"Look around you, B; we aren't children. We're both eighteen, living alone in a giant mansion with an unlimited amount of money…" He tilts his head. "Really, we should celebrate."

He's hurting. I know he is.

He's masking it.

But he's lost everything.

I know the feeling. The feeling of just wanting someone to tell you they love you and mean it and being disappointed every single time they don't.

"Ambrose…" I lean down, ready to rest my hand on his shoulder. He bats it away instantly. "We can come up with a plan. I can cook more. I'm good at cleaning—"

He snorts out a laugh. "Okay, Cinderella, you ready to be my fucking maid?"

I swallow my pride. "If that's what it takes, then yes, I'll be your maid."

"Unbelievable."

Why is he angry? "I understand if you want me to leave, I can probably find a place tomorrow if I need to—"

"—Stay, it will be entertaining for me to see you cleaning bathrooms, but B, we have plenty of maids who come in and out."

I swallow. "I should at least help out somehow."

His eyes darken. "I think you've helped enough; just

stay out of my way and keep eating your peanut butter and jelly sandwiches in the dark." He grabs his phone and starts furiously texting with one hand. "Until then, I'm inviting some friends over."

"Like, Hudson?" I ask lamely.

"Like…" He sends the text. "…the entire Senior class." He eyes me up and down. "I'd change if you ever hope to get any guy to look at you twice. This girl, thinking she can clean my house when she can't even iron."

"I fell asleep in my uniform," I blurt. "I was studying."

He grins up at me. "Aw, how cute, hoping to become something someday? Well, look where that gets you; not near drunk enough on the kitchen floor talking to a foster kid. Good luck, princess."

I bite back my response and stand, pissed that he's lashing out at me while I'm trying to do the right thing, trying to protect him. I get that he's hurt, but he's going beyond trying to break me.

I almost smile.

After all, I don't need a savior.

I'm my own hero.

I'm alive.

I have food.

A bed.

And while I don't have friends, since I keep to myself, I have me.

Me is all I need.

It's all I've had until he tempted me with more.

He wants me to change?

Okay. I'll change my clothes.

I jerk the bottle from his hands, take a giant gross swallow, and hand it back. "Thank you."

"For the drink?"

"Oh no, for the reminder." I glare. "That your taste really wasn't as good as I remember."

His nostrils flare. He jumps to his feet, we're chest pressed against chest; his look is a challenge.

One I accept as I stand up on my tiptoes. I run my tongue along his lower lip; he doesn't push me away; he barely breathes. "See? Nothing."

I don't wait for his response.

I simply turn around and walk up the stairs leaving him alone in the kitchen, wallowing in his anger.

One day he'll know that I was protecting him. One day he'll feel like shit for being so cruel.

But today?

Today I'm going to remind him who I belong to.

Me.

CHAPTER SIXTEEN

Ambrose

I'm already feeling better, could have been that half a bottle of whiskey that I drank earlier, but at least I don't see MB, and my friends are all at my house partying, something that my parents always said I couldn't do.

If I hosted a party, it was more like, oh look, we catered and bought sparkling cider and some soda! Wanna watch Avengers again?

I went to other parties and prayed not to get caught, then left early so that I wouldn't smell like weed and alcohol. The last time I left was when Quinn and I fought freshman year.

Shit, I don't want to even go there or think about It.

Stupid Hudson, he really can't let it go; then again, most can't since nobody talked, but duh, that's what money does.

I grab another bottle of something and toss it back as music pounds through the house. I have the pool open, the cabanas have several couples desecrating them, and I just ordered nothing but a shit ton of junk food, then took out all of my dad's old mixers and liquor bottles and set them up.

Honestly, it looks planned.

My mom would flip.

And I hate that my heart flops a bit and then teases me, saying, if I'm no longer perfect, she'll come back.

I mean anything to save her reputation, right?

Or does she not even care anymore?

Why did we work so hard to have this image when she just abandons her son? Why did I spend years in agony? Why did I let my parents cover everything up when nothing ever even mattered?

As if on cue, Quinn walks by me—of course, he'd be here.

He holds my stare.

I hold his.

I still remember that moment even though I try like hell to forget it. The way it felt, the manipulation from Tessa, and the jealousy between us.

The betrayal.

The confessions.

He licks his lips and looks away from me.

People would lose their shit if they knew the truth about our fallout, why Tessa had to leave, and what she put us through. That woman deserves a special spot in Hell, that's for sure.

Then again, she is at community college despite the payouts from both of our families, so I find some triumph in the fact that her Ivy League school refused her after my dad let them know what she was into, what she did, what sins she committed and forced us to partake in. If it was just the sex, I'd be like whatever, but it was so much more, so much more less "perfect" than anyone could possibly imagine.

I can't think about it anymore.

It ruins my drunken mood. Quinn approaches me. I want to punch him in the dick; instead, I just sidestep him and then get ready for a confrontation when his jaw drops.

He's looking at the stairway.

The party kind of stops a bit which is weird.

I look where he's looking.

And I nearly drop the bottle in my hand.

Instead, I grip it, clench my teeth, and tell myself to breathe.

MB walks down the stairs in what could only be described as half a dress. It's like this tight white number that wraps around her neck, exposes her sides down to her ass, and has a tiny slit up her thigh. I do not remember giving her that dress; I don't remember my own address right now either, though, so… maybe that's on me.

She's wearing a pair of expensive black and white Jordans that weirdly don't look bad with the hot as fuck dress.

And she has makeup on.

Actual makeup.

It's just enough to bring out her pout, her high cheekbones, her eyes, just her everything.

Her dark hair's pulled up into a high ponytail like she did it in a hurry, and pieces are already falling out, kissing her shoulders. She looks like an upgraded Greek goddess.

"Damn," Quinn says under his breath.

I almost shove him.

Even though I agree.

She smiles and holds her head high, a huge change from the last few months with her looking away.

Well, apparently, Cinderella came out to play.

And two can easily play this game of charades.

We are *The Perfects*, after all, right?

I stroll up to her and offer her my arm.

She glares and then takes it, whispering under her breath. "I changed."

"I have eyes."

"Too bad you don't have a heart."

I almost stumble. Is it horrible that I'm turned on by her confidence? "Ah, you noticed; I was afraid you only focused on my dick."

"Only because I had such a hard time finding it."

I snort out a laugh. "Princess came to play? You drunk? High? Should I be worried?"

"Just following orders," she says through a frozen fake smile as we walk past an irritated-looking Quinn and go outside.

People are swimming and dancing, a few look over, and one dude trips. I almost want to say yes, solidarity; I get it, she's hot look away before I drown you.

I have no right to be jealous or upset; it's all I can do to own her in this moment and show her who has the true power.

Me.

CHAPTER SEVENTEEN

Mary-Belle

Maybe this was a bad idea. I'm walking with Ambrose around the pool; everything looks so perfect, and isn't that just the keyword here?

Perfect.

It's all so perfect.

My smile feels frozen. I might throw up. His grip is tight, strong like he's afraid I'm going to bolt any minute as people leer at us. Guys and girls alike.

The attention, it feels weird, it feels like I'm on display, but I did this to myself while convincing myself I could play this game with him when I'm already in over my head. I may as well be in that pool, drowning.

He may as well be the person holding me down as we walk around and around, looking every bit the perfect family with no parents.

Funny how it started, no parents.

How it ended.

Ambrose.

And no parents.

Apparently, money can't buy you everything, and while I walk, I lift my chin, and wonder if money can really truly buy you anything at all because we're both broke, aren't we?

Living in this huge empty house by this ginormous pool, loads of cash, and what really did that ever get either of us other than heartache in different ways?

I want to hate him, but right now, I actually pity him more than I pity myself.

"Look at them stare," Ambrose whispers. "They want what you have."

"And yet," I say, "they have no clue it's nothing. That they'd come up empty if they even knew."

"That's the facade. It always has been."

"It shouldn't be."

"Life." He grips my arm tighter. "Takes no prisoners." He stops walking and stares down at me. "If I didn't hate you so much, I'd say you're pretty."

"If I didn't want to drown you in the pool, I'd say thank you," I retort back.

Ambrose smiles. "Needed that, thanks."

"The threat?"

"The reminder," he quips. "That you're dangerous, a bad idea, that I blame you for everything, and yet here you are reaping all the reward."

I snort. "This is a reward? A slutty dress and walking with a slutty glorified foster brother around the pool? Wow, sign me up."

He turns me toward him and tilts my chin with his pinky

finger. "Careful, people might hear or even get confused about why we're so close right now."

He purposefully pulls me into his arms and lowers his head like he's going to kiss me, then whispers in my ear, "Want a drink?"

"Or a bottle," I mutter, my nerves on edge; every part of my body comes alive as I feel his breath against my neck. It's hateful to want him the way I do when he's the worst, when he's blamed me for everything when I'm the one who tried to help.

Both my brain and heart are misfiring, and I have no way of stopping them as he grips my hand and leads me to one of the tables where at least forty bottles of alcohol are placed.

He doesn't ask what I want. He just makes some random thing and hands it to me in a small red cup, then I swear, looks around at his kingdom with a smug grin as if to say, I own this. I own you.

I take a sip and nearly choke. "No mixers?"

"You're tough enough, right, Cinderella?" He grins. "You don't need it."

He makes a drink next and tosses it back.

Things aren't going to end well if he keeps drinking.

Is he smoking too?

High?

He has nobody looking after him. He only has me, the girl who can't remember if the eyes dilate or not when you're on weed. The last thing I need is for him to pass out and fall into the pool, drown, then get accused of murder.

Twice.

Wouldn't that be a great Lifetime movie?

I grab him by the arm. He jerks away instantly and then,

as if realizing that people are watching, takes my hand in his and holds it, like everything…

Perfect.

We stare at one another, and I suddenly don't know what to do. Do I say something cheeky? Does he caress my cheek? Do we pass it off as something that's normal? He leans into me.

I don't back down,

I'm done doing that.

He looks up at me, and I know this is the moment that will define us.

Is he brave enough?

Am I?

I step up on my tiptoes and press a slow kiss to his mouth, waiting for him to respond, and he does right away. He pulls me into his arms, and then we're falling, falling into the pool in what feels like slow motion, our lips still touching, our arms embracing.

A splash sounds.

Cheers.

And I know I will never come back from this.

Neither will he.

And I'm okay with it.

I'm okay.

Even if I hate him while I kiss him.

Even if he resents me while he kisses me back.

We're in this.

Friends.

Roommates.

Lovers.

Haters.

Us.

CHAPTER EIGHTEEN

Ambrose

wonder what would happen if I never woke up. If the last moments of my life were spent kissing her and falling into my own pool. I wonder, I wonder so much, what would transpire in those last few minutes, seconds... I remember watching my life pass me by, the window, the birds, going, what does freedom actually feel like? And then I fell into a pool with her.

The crash.

The sound of the splash is deafening, our lips are still connected, and I suck. I pull, I drink. I devour.

We fall.

Deeper.

Deeper.

And deeper.

Of course, I'll blame it on being drunk. Of course, she'll say she pulled me in because I pissed her off, and of course, half the party won't even remember at this point anyway.

So easy, isn't it? To justify reasons for doing something bad, something you really, truly know you shouldn't do. So why does it feel so good every damn time?

Her dirty blonde hair spreads out as we hit the bottom of the pool, as our eyes both open, as we finally stare at each other and go this, this is it, what do we do?

And she clings to me.

I cling right back.

There will be rumors.

There will be whispers.

I don't know what to do. I need my dad to tell me, but he's not here.

Mom's gone.

I have her.

All I have is a foster girl clinging to me the way I've always wanted, so what the hell do I do?

I cling right back.

We swim to the top. I breathe in the air, and she does as well, and we both turn and look at each other.

And then stupid Quinn jumps in the pool like some fucking lifeguard from Baywatch and swims over to us.

"Holy shit! You guys okay?" He grabs her first. Expected, then pulls her out of my arms and to the side of the pool. Weirdly enough, nobody seems all that fazed as more people start jumping in and drunkenly shouting. Wow, I do one bad thing in front of everyone, and so far, no repercussions if you don't count Quinn. "I thought you hit your head. How many fingers am I holding up, just in case you have a concussion from getting shoved into the pool?" He holds up two fingers.

I wish to God she would answer six as I swim over toward the side as well. Instead, MB goes. "Two."

"Okay, take your time." He has her fully pulled up against him as if she can't swim and needs a hero when she's fully able to save herself.

I want to kill him.

I want to kiss him at the same time for grabbing her, which is a whole different scenario.

He grabbed her the minute she swam to the surface— and I just treaded water like an idiot, staring around at the party, wondering if I just ruined my own life by kissing her, by teasing and tempting her.

Him.

Did it really have to be him though?

"She's just tired," I say quickly and attempt to pull her away. Quinn's eyes lock onto mine with an intensity I'm extremely familiar with and won't ever be able to forget.

I know that look.

I stare him down.

"Does she though?" His dark smirk says it all. It's like every secret between us is dangling, waiting to be plucked from the air and exposed to everyone. He pulls her closer against his body while she looks over at me.

I'll kill him.

It's like deja vu.

"You're not scared, are you?" Tessa taunts, standing between us. My eye is already swelling up, and his lip is bloody from my punch. We're both running on way too much anger and adrenaline.

"Come on." Tessa kisses him right in front of me on the

mouth; his eyes burn into mine, and then she turns around and winks at me. "See? Sharing is easy, Ambrose. Didn't you ever learn that in school? More is better…"

I think that's when I started to hate her.

I don't even think she realized at that moment that she was pushing herself away and starting something way more dangerous than she could ever realize.

Something that would include cover-ups.

Payouts.

Secrets.

Lies.

"I'm good." MB finally pipes up and looks between the two of us, then frowns at me. "Did you hit your head?"

She doesn't reach for me, but I imagine she mentally does, that she's concerned where Quinn probably wishes death on my soul. Then again, I have been in an epic staring contest with the guy I used to call a friend.

Splashes from people jumping in hit all of us in the face, and her sexy dress is plastered to her body.

"You're nipping out." Yes, this is what I choose to say as I get out of the pool and pretend not to care.

Quinn swears under his breath.

The moment between the three of us completely forgotten. The look he gave me was another thing from the past that I'll tuck into that box my mom told me to bury and never mention again.

MB shakily gets out of the pool and stands, dripping wet. I look over my shoulder to make sure she really is okay and then want to vomit when Quinn stops Hudson and mimics for him to take off his shirt.

Hudson loves every opportunity to show off his abs, so he immediately strips while Quinn puts it over B's head. It dwarfs her, coming down to her knees, reminding me of what she used to look like stumbling out of my bed wearing my clothes.

I feel like I can't breathe as she wrings out her now darker hair and thanks both Hudson and Quinn. Quinn gives her a high five and then messes with her hair.

Bastard.

I stumble toward the drink table, suddenly realizing how drunk I really am, then lean over it. I can hear MB's laughter, I can hear Quinn's stupid voice.

I know he saw us kiss.

I know he cares.

I blink away the blurred vision and see Hailey standing over by the cups swaying to the loud music; she's wearing a red crop top that barely covers her underboob and a pair of loose jeans that are falling off her flat ass.

Whatever.

I don't care.

"C'mere." I motion toward her knowing she will. She may have hooked up with Xander, but she's too drunk to care about who kisses her right now.

Her eyes widen a bit, or maybe mine do, so I can see better. I jerk her against my body and plant a sloppy drunken kiss on her mouth; she responds with way too much enthusiasm and tastes like cigarettes.

I hate every minute of it, and if she shoves her tongue down my throat any further, I'm going to puke whiskey all over her.

I shove her away and laugh. She stumbles back and nearly lands on the drink table, grabs a pack of old-school cigarettes, attempts to grab one, and lights it with a blue lighter.

I think in her head, she thinks she looks cool; instead, she's struggling to even get a flame.

I ignore her, wipe my mouth and turn.

MB's right there.

"Oh, didn't see you." Quinn's close behind her watching us. The hurt on her face makes me feel a bit more sober as she sidesteps me. "Where you going?"

"To change," she says in a clipped voice. "Apparently, I'm nipping out after my foster brother thought it would be funny to kiss me and then push me into the pool."

"You forget you kissed me back." I look around her. "Right, Quinn?"

"Isn't that incest?" He frowns. "Asking for a friend."

I roll my eyes.

MB shoves past me and goes into the house.

I glare at Quinn, then turn and follow her inside. I'm chasing after her, then curse when she nearly takes off my nose after slamming her bedroom door in my face.

I open it despite her anger.

She's standing there with that t-shirt covering her, hair still wet, lips full.

She's beautiful.

I hate her.

I scowl. "You forget this is my house now."

"You're the one that said to change earlier, which I did, and you're the one who was just disgusted that I was wet."

I smirk. "I'm never disgusted when you're wet, only if it's me—"

"—Do not finish that sentence." She warns, crossing her arms.

I approach, taking one step, two, and then we're facing off yet again.

"It's like you're begging me to choke you." She hisses.

"It's like you want a little violence with your…" I tug at her hair. "Dampness." I look down her body. "Or should we say wetness?"

I know I'm being mean. I know I'm hitting close to home here, but I can't stop the words coming out of my mouth… even if I wanted to.

She bats my hand away. "I'm not yours, Ambrose."

"Yeah." I step back. "You'll always be mine, and you know it." I look over at her closet. "Wear something that covers up your ass and tits this time."

"And if I don't?"

"Then I'll assume it's an invitation, and so will every other prick at this party. You wouldn't really want that sort of rumor spreading, right? Kisses foster brother, moves onto Quinn, displays her best assets because that's all she really has going for her?"

"I hate you!" Her lower lip trembles.

And I break her down more and more because it feels like vengeance. It feels like love when it's the opposite. It feels real and raw.

And then I realize it's because I'm actually feeling, and I haven't felt since the night my dad died.

I'll keep pushing her as long as she pushes back.

Maybe one day I'll be the one that gets pushed so far I go off the cliff.

Maybe she'll be the one to end my misery and loneliness with her hate.

Cheers.

CHAPTER NINETEEN

Mary-Belle

don't want to go back to the party, but I want to piss Ambrose off even more, and I can't be found guilty of his murder if he does something stupid or, as I said before, drowns in a pool of his own vomit with only me as a witness.

I put on a pair of short designer jean shorts, a white crop top and add some slides, I was tempted to actually put on another dress, but I'm too tired. I pull my wet hair back in a scrunchy, make my way down the stairs, and nearly collide with Xander once I'm in the kitchen.

It's just us; everyone else is either swimming or outside drunkenly dancing.

Xander has really blue eyes and looks off—like he is clearly high on something. His blonde hair is tucked under a black Supreme beanie.

"Oh, sorry." I smile and sidestep him so I can go outside.

He grabs me by the elbow and jerks me against his massive

body. He's easily like six foot three. "Don't be. Maybe I want you to run into my dick."

"Huh?" I pry myself away only to have his hands come to my hips. I stumble against him. Gross. I don't want to be drunkenly groped in my own home. I wonder when I even started thinking about it as my home.

Maybe when I had no choice.

Or maybe when Ambrose said it was.

"Knew it," Xander says. He's beautiful in an I probably got into Harvard already way. But I don't like him; I don't want him kissing me or touching me, and I'm suddenly transported back to all the foster homes.

Getting grabbed.

Touched without permission.

Without consent.

My breathing slows and then speeds up hard and fast as I start to struggle against him. "Xander, stop, please, stop, you're drunk and—"

"—You want this; I know you do. What, you can't kiss me, but you can joke and kiss Ambrose? Why don't we just pass you around, create a new party game." He leans in; he smells like pot. "Nah, I think I'll keep the trophy for myself."

"Hands off." Comes Ambrose's voice. "Before I kick your ass and tell your dad you were getting high again."

Xander freezes.

"Pretty sure that means you'd lose your lacrosse scholarship," Ambrose says. "The one that meant so much to dear old Mom and Dad, I forget, was it in the paper?"

Xander curses and shoves me away, but hard enough that I nearly fall.

Ambrose catches me. The familiar smell of his hateful

cologne washes over my body, but in that moment, I'm thankful.

I don't realize I'm shaking until he grabs my hands and stills them with his own warm hands, then keeps them there as if to ground me.

"Party's over for you, bro." Ambrose continues to hold me tight. I lean into him more than I should and fight the memories of his touch like my own personal demons. "Don't worry, I won't say anything. Just don't forget your joints, I may not be going to an Ivy League school, but I'm pretty sure weed is still illegal here, wouldn't want to get caught red-handed or anything." Even though we both know parents no longer exist in this house. "Need me to call you an Uber, or are you able to actually stare at your phone long enough to order one without passing out?"

"Fuck you, Ambrose!" he shouts. "If you tell anyone, I'll kill you!"

"Cool, I'll pencil you in after her. She gets dibs." I think I'm the *her* he's referring to. "I'd rather stare at her pretty mouth than a dickface before I die anyway."

"You're a dick!"

"Um, thank you?" Ambrose laughs. "We'll just be outside while you stare at your phone and try to figure out how to use it."

Ambrose tugs me with him.

I walk numbly behind him.

I expect him to say something cruel.

Instead, he turns me around and pulls me in for a hug. "Nobody's looking. Are you okay?" His voice is low, it's hypnotic and deep, and regardless of what he's done—it's safe.

"Do you care?" I whisper against his chest, my mouth almost tasting his shirt.

"Does it matter?" He counters. "Do you want me to?"

We both fall silent.

And then I relax a bit, I let my guard down more than I should, and I whisper, "Maybe."

He stiffens.

His arms brace me even harder, like he's afraid to let go. "I don't know what to do anymore."

Clearly, he's super drunk if he's confessing to me.

"That makes two of us," I say, my arms slowly wrapping around his body. "I still hate you... for hating me, but this is nice..."

"I'm not nice."

He doesn't get it. He'll never see himself the way I see him. "Ambrose, you're a lot of things, but you have the potential to be nice; it's just a matter of making that choice rather than wrapping yourself in your hate."

"The therapist is back, yay..."

I pat him on the back, then turn and elbow him in the gut. "You're welcome."

He laughs. "Really?"

"How drunk are you? Should I be worried?"

"Should I get drunker so you worry more?" he asks.

I roll my eyes, typical Ambrose response. He'd probably crack a rib if he wasn't being sarcastic and flirty all the time, even with people he hates.

Even with me.

"Don't find out. I mean it." I point my finger at him and then jab him in the chest. "Go drink some water."

"Yes, Mom." He winks.

"Wow, you really are wasted."

"I see feelings." His drunken answer.

"Not possible."

He reaches up, grabs something out of the air, and then blows it to me. I feel it, and weirdly enough, it makes me smile. He smiles back, which again confirms how drunk he really is since he's been a giant asshole to me recently. I so desperately want to be like, ask me, ask me what happened, don't just blame me, ask me!

Instead, he just stares at me with a sloppy grin and then holds a hand to his mouth.

"You're going to puke, aren't you?" And who gets to babysit? The therapist.

I want to announce that the party's over, but Ambrose is currently puking his guts out in the bushes, over and over and over again.

I would laugh if I didn't actually care about the jerkface. I pat him on the back and look around, only to see Quinn walking toward me.

His expression is concerned, and then he frowns. "Everything okay?"

"Oh yeah, just puking up his stomach, no big." I rub Ambrose's back again. "Think you could get everyone out of here so I can sober him up?"

"Sure." Quinn nods, then frowns. "When is his mom getting back tonight?"

I don't know what to say, so I just shake my head and keep rubbing Ambrose's back.

Quinn's eyes narrow, and he looks between us. "Do you have an ETA on when that will happen?"

"Never!" Ambrose says, wiping his mouth with his hand.

"She's not coming back. Apparently, this perfect life was too much for her. It's just a foster kid and an orphan; how fucking perfect!" He pukes again.

I flinch.

Quinn looks like he doesn't know what to do, then finally, he nods his head and turns around. "COPS!"

"What?" I screech.

People start running.

He crosses his arms. "Works every time."

"Expert at killing the vibe, yeah?" I tease.

Ambrose pukes again. "I think I'm done."

He makes a noise.

Quinn scrunches up his nose. "I think you just started."

"Son of a bitch!" Ambrose yells. "I can't stop."

"Should have never started," I add.

"Do you guys think you could be a bit more helpful while I barf out my internal organs all at once?"

Quinn actually smiles at Ambrose even though he can't see him from the desecrated bushes. People continue to run, and suddenly, gone, done, we have no more underage drinkers and weed users at the house, but we do have a hell of a mess.

Gee thanks, bro.

"Hey." I grab his hand. "You done?"

"Never," he rasps. "Maybe. Who knows? Might come back... it's like I got food poisoning."

Quinn snorts. "More like almost alcohol poisoning."

"Not now." Ambrose raises a middle finger. "Argue with me when I'm not staring at the bushes of vomit with the girl I fell in love with behind me, comforting me, when I don't deserve it, when she killed everything, when I died, don't, not now, everything's gone, everyone's left."

Quinn is silent, then says. "Weird because I still see two people standing here with you, man."

Ambrose lowers his head, bracing his hands on his thighs before standing up and then stumbling to the left.

"Fuck, it's like that now." Quinn catches him and then wraps an arm around him, helping him walk toward the house. "I'll be back to help, Mary-Belle; let me just get him to bed, not our first rodeo."

It's weird how they hate each other yet have this connection I can't quite understand. Ambrose doesn't even fight Quinn.

And earlier, it seemed like Quinn was almost afraid of him, but now he's taking care of him. I'm so confused but also exhausted, so I do the only thing one does after a party's ended.

I grab a black trash bag, and I wonder how I went from carrying everything I owned in one to cleaning up a party at the mansion I now live in with my foster brother.

And no guardians.

I shake my head and start picking up random cups and beer bottles. The pool's a mess of red cups just left there, and let's be honest, most likely puke and other things I don't want to think about.

I'm out there for about ten minutes when Quinn finally comes back, his expression blank.

"He okay?" I ask as he starts picking up trash. I can't read his face at all; he looks like he's closed off to the world, which what little I know about him, isn't normal.

He nods. "Yeah, Ambrose isn't dying in his own vomit, and he's in bed, mouthwash has been distributed, and I gave him some Advil with two bottles of water. He's gonna be feeling it later though."

"Thanks." I hold out the trash bag.

Quinn smile. "Don't mention it. I might actually just crash here tonight if that's okay with you? I shouldn't drive, and I want to keep an eye on him later… he's going to be a complete bear when he wakes up, and you don't need that on you."

I shrug. "Kind of used to his bear-like antics."

"He slept with you, didn't he." Quinn just drops the bomb like it's no big deal.

I freeze. I can't even drop the cup into the trash bag and stand there like an idiot.

"You don't have to tell me. I just figured you're sexy as hell, like the perfect temptation for someone like Ambrose, and he clearly likes you."

"He hates me."

"He hates the things he likes." Comes Quinn's fast response. "Trust me on this."

I pick up another cup. "Trust you, hmm? Then tell me why you guys hate each other—he like you?"

Quinn smirks. "Oh no, he has both hate and hate for me, at one point, maybe, yeah…" He looks back at the massive house from the yard. "Some choices you make, you never come back from, like a wound that never heals, you see that person, and it's just blood and gore all over the place again. I'm like that to him. He's like that to me. Trauma," He grabs another cup. "Sometimes, has no place to go, so it just continues to exist until you acknowledge it, but what do you do when you can't? When you can't even talk about it? It just lingers, so yeah, he truly hates me."

I shrug. "Didn't seem like it tonight."

"He was wasted. Trust me when I say all will go back to rights in the morning when he sees me."

I frown. "Are you guys, were you guys like…" I don't even really know how to ask it or say it, but it's a suspicious thought I can't let go of.

Quinn throws his head back and laughs. "Ah, wouldn't that be the best situation? A horrible breakup between the best friend I fell in love with and me. Nah, I mean, yeah, no, I'm not gonna talk about it anymore. Some secrets die with you, but there has never been a moment in that guy's life where he's ever seen me as anything but his best friend or enemy. Trust me on that."

"And what about you?" I ask, kicking a cup, then picking it up.

Quinn freezes; his hand hovers over the red solo cup before he picks it up and tosses it in the trash bag. "Hmm, jury's still out on that, never really did the whole let me explore my sexuality thing in an intense way, but I will agree that it's important to see people as people. I haven't thought about it in two years."

"Did you ever…" I swallow. "You know, like, experiment—"

"—Ah, story time is officially over. Thanks for coming. You can see your way out." Quinn tosses a cup at my face; it's empty, it makes me laugh. "You're really pretty, by the way, just in case you don't get told that enough. I felt like you should know.

My breath hitches. I don't know what to say. Quinn raises his hand, it's trembling, and then it's pushing my hair away.

He looks pretty in the moonlight.

His hand drops. "Do you sometimes think that history repeats itself? Over and over again until you solve what went wrong?"

I swallow, lick my lips, and then have nothing to give him, no answer because I've wondered the same thing for so long. Are we just in a constant repeat motion? Will I always want Ambrose? Will I always fall for him even though I know better?

I shake my head. "I wish I knew."

Quinn nods then. "Same. Same."

"We should, uh…" I look away. "…go inside."

"Did you though?" he asks as I start walking away. "With him?"

I don't answer.

But it's answer enough.

CHAPTER TWENTY

Ambrose

"Kill me," I moan. "Kill me now. Put me out of my misery. Make it end. Whyyyyyyyyyyyy." I can barely move as I reach for the bottle of water on my nightstand and the Advil.

It feels like someone took a sledgehammer to my skull on both sides, both temples, and refuses to stop jamming it in.

I'm such an idiot.

Oh God, I puked in the bushes.

I vaguely remember Quinn taking me to my room and telling me to sober up and stop being an asshole, typical Quinn, but that's it.

Is Mary-Belle okay?

Did people just leave?

There was running. I definitely remember running.

"Fuck!" I jolt up, my head pounding. Didn't someone yell cops? Am I getting arrested? Shit! I'm dead, so dead if cops came to my house and I'm passed out, am I able to say someone just like, drugged me, and I didn't know what was happening.

I moan into my hands.

"Sleeping Beauty." Quinn's raspy voice just randomly appears out of nowhere.

I look around my room—it's still dark, so clearly not fully time to wake up yet, time to be sleeping and suffering in silence from being the drunk dumbass.

"Down here," he says.

He's lying on my floor, not in a guest room, wearing no shirt; he's on his side. "You."

"Me." He goes to his back and puts his hands behind his head. "Honestly, I was going to gloat but felt like it was too soon. At any rate, everything's cleaned up, Mary-Belle crashed a few hours ago, I've been here sleeping slash listening to you moan while thrashing around your bed like you were going to puke again, and I left the trash can just in case. Nobody wants to wake up to someone puking on them because they can't make it in time. Also, bonus, super embarrassing, and my phone's fully charged, so I would take a picture of that shit and post it, not even gonna be sly about it."

"Fuck." It's all I can say as I lay there. "How is this? You know what, I'm in too much pain to even ask—but she's okay?"

"She's okay."

"Did you guys… hang out?"

"Seriously?" He sits up. "That's what you ask me? If we hung out? What do you want to know if we held hands, if I kissed her, if I fucked her in your backyard? Damn, bro, just take a break. I'm not trying to do anything other than be a non-shitty human being. Is she pretty?" I gulp and wait for his answer. "Yes." He sighs and lays back down. "Do I want to kiss her?" He's silent for a few seconds. "Every time I see her." His voice lowers. "Would I go there again? Knowing what I know now? No. I wouldn't. I wouldn't dare, so tuck your dick back into your pants and get some sleep."

I don't really know what to say, so I just kind of stare at him. So much hangs between us, so many lies, secrets, so many things, and I don't even know how to acknowledge it or even talk about it.

Talking means it's out.

Like the universe knows and will punish you for it.

So I lay back down and stare up at the ceiling. "Did you mean it? That day?"

Seconds go by, then a full minute. He probably fell asleep, right? I turn toward the wall.

"Yeah," he whispers. "For what it's worth, I did mean it back then. And I won't take it back because it was my truth, and you can't make that a lie once it's said out loud. You have to just accept it, own it, and know that in that moment, you were the most honest you've ever been, and it ended up breaking you."

I squeeze my eyes shut, suddenly feeling emotional and not angry for the first time in two years. "I was never mad at you. I was mad at what she made us into."

"I think we can at least both agree she's the devil."

"I pray for her death. Is that horrible?"

"She's not even that pretty."

"THAT'S WHAT I'M SAYING!" I nearly shout. "Like what the hell, man?"

Quinn bursts out laughing, then sits up. I look over my shoulder and smile. "More truth?"

I gulp. "Sure."

"Good." He lays back down. "I miss my best friend."

That's how we end it.

Maybe I'm still drunk.

I know we should have talked years ago, but both of our parents made it impossible. He wasn't allowed here, and I wasn't allowed there. In the hallways, news would somehow get back to my dad if we chatted or even looked at each other, and then the resentment between both of us burned. It was a catastrophic firestorm that left nothing in its wake.

And left us both empty.

Very imperfect. Very used. Very alone.

I close my eyes and finally let out the words I should have said a long time ago. "I missed you too."

I think he's asleep when he answers back. "You totally slept with your foster sister."

Weirdly enough, I laugh.

He laughs.

And then I fall asleep, thinking, it must have been a really good dream, having him in my room again and knowing that when I wake up, he'll still be there telling me that we'll be ride or die, dicks before chicks, but knowing that he won't be.

He won't.

Because when I needed Quinn the most, when he needed me the most—we both bailed.

CHAPTER TWENTY-ONE

Mary-Belle

I wake up to the smell of bacon. Then I truly jolt up from my bed and look around my room, thinking I'm hallucinating. Is his mom back? Is she cooking us actual breakfast?

It's Saturday.

He said his dad used to cook breakfast on Saturdays. My chest hurts a bit as I try not to think about that night. I grab a black Nike sweatshirt—the first thing I can find—then put on a pair of loose gray sweats that I'm pretty sure Ambrose gave me but can't remember since I'm still sleepy and my stomach's growling. I pull my hair into a messy bun and leave my room in search of food. The stairway is long and winding, with its stark white marble stairs as my bare feet slap against each step until I make my way into the main entryway. A thirty-foot ceiling with a huge chandelier greets me as if to say, hey guess what? We're still perfect; everything's fine—how could it not be when you walk into this house? A family picture sets on the wall, and I almost stop to stare at it.

Ambrose's smile is fake.

So is his dad's.

His mom's, however, in that trapped moment, seems real, and it hurts my heart even more that she's gone because I think she tried, she really did, but how does anyone stand this sort of pressure?

Ambrose will grow up to be just like that, constantly picking at lint on his jacket and looking over his shoulder.

I know he was drunk last night, but he at least deserves to go a bit crazy once in his life before the heaviness of his family name comes crashing down on him.

I follow the large pristine hallway into the kitchen with its white walls, black accents, and ginormous stainless steel freezer and wolf appliances. I nearly choke on my tongue and trip over my own feet.

Quinn's completely shirtless, in nothing but a low pair of gray sweats that are literally hanging off his ass, cooking. I had no clue he looked that good without a shirt, his hair actually touches his neck, messy and still nerd hot, and he's humming the Home Alone theme song, which is even weirder. Then again, from what I know about Quinn probably more normal than anything.

"Whyyyyyy?" Ambrose bangs his head against the table once, twice, then jerks his head up and glares at Quinn. "You know it's going to stick in my head now! And don't mess up my eggs; I like them completely cooked." I don't think I've ever seen him point at someone so aggressively, like it's life or death, and death is coming.

Quinn starts humming the Darth Vader theme.

I cover my mouth to keep from laughing. How have I missed all this? And are they both drunk right now? How are they not fighting?

I stand there. Is Quinn the maid now? What is happening?

Quinn looks over his shoulder with a smirk. "You had soupy eggs one time, over easy, shall I say? And said it tasted like piss, get over it, bruh."

"Do. Not. Bruh. Me. It triggers my anxiety."

Quinn laughs. "Remember that one time that shitface from freshman year was all bruh, what's your damage bruh, and you punched him in the face?"

Ambrose groans. "Got grounded and my phone taken away for a week."

"Worth it; I laughed so damn hard." Quinn keeps humming.

Ambrose groans again.

"Get over it, Bruhhhhhh," Quinn says. "Drink your Bloody Mary."

"You get over it." Ambrose bangs his head again. "This isn't helping." He groans and grabs his Bloody Mary again, chomping down on his celery. "It's supposed to make it better."

"Bonus," Quinn adds, turning off the stove. "You stopped puking, yay…"

No fights have broken out, yet, I'm almost concerned as I stand there and watch their interaction.

"Ummmm," I point between the two of them. Quinn glances over his shoulder. "What's this?"

"Breakfast," Ambrose says in a raspy voice. "He cooks better than me, and I may have begged."

"Not on his hands and knees though." Quinn jokes.

I frown. "Um, is the whole we hate each other and might end up in prison thing over then?"

"No," they say in unison.

"But it's bacon." Quinn salutes me with the spatula.

"Bacon." Ambrose nods. "It's like waving a temporary white flag after battle."

"...battled hard last night, man," Quinn adds.

"So hard." Ambrose looks ready to puke again. "I never want to drink whiskey again. Why did nobody stop me?"

I snort out a laugh and pull out a stool. "Yeah, because that always works super well for the person trying to get on you about anything."

"Get on me any day," he says under his breath.

I flick him on the chin with my fingers.

"WHY?" he shouts.

"Because you're a dick!" I shout right back.

Quinn just laughs. "That he is."

Ambrose curses. "Can someone just be on my side for once? I'm so fucking hungover I want to cry, and I never cry; tears are for pussies."

I glare.

He glares back, then finally flicks his fingers at me like I shouldn't be offended. "You know what I mean."

"Do I though?" I ask, leaning forward. Quinn turns off the stove and brings over the bacon, dropping it onto a white paper towel while Ambrose chugs his drink. It's super hard not to stare at Quinn's six-pack or the fact that he's sporting his typical black-rimmed glasses.

Clark Kent is literally in my kitchen.

Superman is sitting next to me.

My life is no longer normal.

Ambrose smiles over at me, it's sloppy but sexy, and it's hard not to remember what that mouth has done to me. "Don't get offended just because I talked about my favorite—"

I grab a hot piece of bacon and shove it into his mouth.

"WHY!" He spits it out. It falls onto the table and bounces toward his hand. "It's hot as hell!"

"Oops." I throw up my hands while Quinn laughs. I like his laugh; it's easy, not like he's forcing it.

Quinn tosses another piece of bacon toward Ambrose. Grease gets on the white counter, but I don't really care, and neither do they. "Don't be a baby; get some protein in there."

"You get protein in there." Ambrose grumbles, then grabs the bacon and tears a piece off with his teeth.

"He's weird when he's hungover," I comment after staring at him for a few seconds. Truly though, it's like he has no filter, and I love it.

"Normal." Quinn nods. "It's like watching an animal go savage in Zootopia."

We both look to Quinn.

He shrugs. "What?"

"That's the example you come up with?" I laugh. "Zootopia?" Ambrose tears into another piece of bacon. "I'm not savage, you piece of shit. I'm just… damn, so tired, so so so tired."

Quinn grins and grabs another bite of bacon. "He's like the sweet little otter that loses his way from a night howler, and why are you both looking at me like I've lost it?"

Ambrose crosses his arms. "It's not like I bit you, jackass."

"Yet you wanted to."

The room tenses.

Ambrose shoves back his barstool.

I imagine a fight breaking out.

He leans over the counter until he's inches from Quinn's comically stunned face. "Why don't I just bite her?"

"Bet she'd like it." Quinn doesn't even flinch.

"Bet she'd kill you." I grab a piece of bacon.

"Didn't kill me last time." Ambrose winks over at me.

I throw my bacon at him. "Not funny."

"No, it wasn't." He's serious.

Quinn takes a deep breath and then exhales, and looks away. "So it's like this now, is it? God's clearly punishing us."

"I think of it as a reward." Ambrose tosses a piece of bacon on the table in front of me. "Want more scraps?"

I jump to my feet. "Want me to strangle you?"

He licks his lips, then bites his bottom. "Yes. Please."

Quinn curses under his breath.

And because I eat boys like these guys for every meal or in my head think so, I lean in and shove a piece of bacon in Ambrose's mouth, then tear the last part away from his mouth and chew.

His eyes widen.

Quinn dies laughing.

I keep chewing and then whisper in his ear. "I'll find some rope."

CHAPTER TWENTY-TWO

Ambrose

I gulp and look away, all thoughts of bacon completely gone, while Quinn's smart smirk calls me out; the guy doesn't even need words.

I have to fix the tension.

Fix the situation.

Fix the knot in my gut and the pressure in my chest as my brain tells my body we're all the three of us completely alone.

And it's the weekend, so really there are so many options, aren't there? Unfortunately.

Luckily, it's Quinn that speaks up first. "Well, on that note, I think I'll leave each of you in capable hands." He nods. "Then again, you don't really have adult supervision, so make sure you don't get the cops called on you or burn the house down or whatever; I don't even know why I'm saying all this." He stares me down. "It's you."

"It's me." I agree.

He shakes his head. "The perfect super responsible…" He takes a step toward me. "…Ambrose."

My breath legit catches in my chest as he looks me up and down, then over at B. "Have fun, kids. Find someone else for bail money; I'm gonna be out this afternoon fixing my Jeep."

"Wait." I grab his arm. "What happened to He-Man?"

"He-man?" MB repeats. "What the hell is a He-Man?"

"Childhood dream." Quinn points his key fob at her. "Back off, I wanted to be a badass superhero, so I named my car after the best one of all time."

B snorts out a laugh and crosses her arm. "Are you forgetting Iron Man? Mr. Fantastic? Captain America? How can you even call yourself a fan of comics if you don't at least mention Charles Xavier!"

I do a double take, she's literally pissed about this, and it's probably one of the sexiest things I've ever seen. Hell, she mentioned Xavier.

I'm so dead.

I love X-men.

Fucking got drunk one time and yelled, "I'm Wolverine, bitches." And proceeded to grab straws and hold them between my fingers like I had claws.

In hindsight, I'm lucky I still had friends after that.

Quinn thought it was hilarious, then again, he did burst into tears about how Wolverine lost Jane, and it was like a whole moment.

Thank God nobody got it on camera.

Quinn reaches out and pats B on the head. "I think we'll keep you. Anyone who doesn't forget that the X-men are actually part of the marvel universe can sit at this table. Am I right, Ambrose?"

"That would be correct."

Quinn winks at her and then looks over at me. "Give my regards to Wolverine."

"Yeah okay, Jane." I roll my eyes, refusing to be embarrassed. I mean, at least I was Wolverine. He was my crush, yeah as I even say that in my head, doesn't work, doesn't bring back good memories.

He bursts out laughing and, still shirtless, just walks away from us without a care in the world. The sound of the front door slamming is pretty damning as I look over at MB, and she looks up at me, her pretty brown eyes full of questions.

"So…" She reaches around me for another piece of bacon and chomps it down. "Wolverine, hmm? There a story there?"

I lean closer toward her. "Wouldn't you love to know?"

She shrugs and walks past me. "Meh, I'm good."

Okay, so now I want to tell her.

Women! So manipulative!

"Where you going?" I follow her as she weaves her way around the pristine living room; they really did clean up great for me, huh. She opens the back door and walks out into the backyard. I almost bump into her and barely stop myself.

She eats the rest of the bacon and then stares out at the pool. "Wanna swim?"

"You sure I won't drown you?"

She lets out a laugh and turns to give me a light shove. "You're like a baby giraffe right now; you can barely stand up, let alone hold me under."

"Wanna bet on it?" Are these words actually coming from my mouth? I want to smack myself. Instead, I just wait for her response, thinking she's going to shove me harder, get offended, or just pissed… instead she pulls the shirt over her head and drops it onto the ground.

My mouth goes completely dry.

She's in nothing but a white Nike sports bra and small gray underwear that, after kicking off her sweatpants, yup, I lick my lips, barely cover her ass cheeks as she sways away from me, her long legs giving me visions of a lot of very naughty things for my future.

Shit.

I'm supposed to hate her.

Foster sister.

Foster sister.

Responsible for my dad's murder, or was actually there when he died, blood covering her hands, figuratively, not literally.

And yet I can't stop my feet from moving after her; step by step, I finally make it to the edge of the pool. Her splash hits me in the face, and I swear I can smell her in the water droplets as they slide down my face.

She comes up from the water and smiles. "So what do you say, Wolverine? Cease-fire for one day, pretend we don't have a past, know we won't have a future. Maybe, today we just relax, swim, and try not to burn the house down."

"Twenty-four hours." I can't get my voice to stop shaking. "Why now? Why twenty-four hours?"

She swims toward me and leans her arms on the side of the pool, I never noticed, but her nails are a pretty shade of blue. When did she paint them? When did she buy nail polish?

Stupid questions that I literally can't stop fixating on as I lean down and put my feet in the pool next to her. "So?"

She tugs my ankle. "I'm tired, Ambrose. I'm so tired." Her eyes fill with tears. "I just want a break. Haven't you ever just needed a break? I have no idea what's going to happen after we graduate. I have no clue where I'm going, I have nothing, nobody, and I'm so, so sick of worrying about the same thing over and over again. So yeah, I want a cease-fire. I want to swim and feel free. I don't want to fight with you. I just need—"

"—Freedom," I answer in a harsh whisper. "Where you don't feel like the victim even if you aren't."

Her eyes narrow. "Yeah."

"All right." I don't know what the hell I'm doing as I peel my shirt over my head and toss it onto the concrete. "If we're going to do this, we're going to do this right."

Or wrong.

Let's be honest; all of this is wrong, even if it feels right, but who am I to say no.

Not when she's right there.

Not when I'm right here.

Damn.

I feel like an addict waiting for my next hit while still trying to push away the one thing that will destroy me.

We have no other option but destruction.

And yet, I give in.

I fold.

Maybe I always will.

She swims back with a small smile, pieces of hair are sticking to her cheeks. I want to touch them.

I'm tempted to lick the water from her face like a psycho, but damn I feel dehydrated suddenly.

I'm cold, yet the flame feels like it's getting higher and higher; it rises the closer I get to her, telling me we're about to get burned, telling me I'm repeating a past mistake, like we'll both be burned this time, again and, again, and yet I pull off the rest of my clothes and jump into the water, splashing her, I'm swimming toward her.

It hits me, the idea that maybe I can't quit this girl—no matter what I feel or what I think, she just exists in my universe, and my universe is part of hers.

She swims toward me; I try so hard not to look at her long legs, but I fail, and then she's right in front of me, panting, out of breath, asking for that cease-fire, asking me for twenty-four hours of normalcy that I want nothing more to give her.

Because I need it too.

I need her more than I ever want to admit.

"You nervous?" I ask with more bravado than I feel.

She just shrugs and brushes that hair from her cheeks and grins. "Are you?"

"Yes." I swallow slowly. "I've never spent twenty-four hours with an enemy."

"Funny, I've never spent twenty-four hours with someone I would call a friend."

I soften, I shouldn't, but I freaking do. "Are we though?"

"Were we not?"

I have so many things I can say; instead, I just swim off and say, "Race you."

"What do I get if I win?" She laughs after me, so free, more free than I've ever felt in my life. "Pizza? Ice cream?"

"You only ever think about food?"

She sighs loudly, she's not splashing anymore. "When

you haven't had a lot of food in a while, you tend to fixate on it. I mean, don't get me wrong." She swims toward me. "Not all of my foster parents were horrible, but food… food feels like gold to me, so yeah… I sometimes fixate too much… on food."

My chest hurts so much it hurts to breathe. "I promise, right now, if you beat me in this race, you'll always have food."

She laughs, her head goes back, and her laugh is pure and beautiful and everything I've always wanted to experience but never had the chance to.

It's just pure, and I love it.

"Okay." She swims toward me, both of us are at the edge. "So we race from one end to the next, and if I beat you, I get unlimited chicken nuggets… I mean, at the very least?"

"For sure." I nod. "At the very least."

"Deal."

I hold out my hand. "Deal."

She shakes it, and I want to pull her toward me; instead, I let her go, and she goes to her side of the pool. I stay at mine.

"Ready." She grins at me. Is it weird I want to keep that smile?

"Yeah."

"Set." I nod again.

"Go." She laughs.

I follow her. Both of us are fighting to get to the other end, and then I just stop and watch her go. And go. And go.

"Yes!" she shouts. "Triumphant!"

"Totally." I tread water. "Chicken nuggets for life, dude."

"We're so fancy."

I laugh. "So fancy."

"Should we eat?" She winks and swims over to me.

I want to eat.

I want to eat so bad.

I want something other than chicken nuggets. I also don't want to scare her.

I want though.

Damn, I want.

"Yeah," I nod again. "Let's eat some food, but also, don't ever, ever fucking worry about not having food. I'm your food. I'm your friend. I'm your person, even if you hate me in the morning and love me in the evening. Even if for the rest of your life you want to murder me. You will always, always have someone or something. And that's me."

Her eyes well with tears.

I don't know what to do. I'm not prepared for any of this.

She nods her head, then just drops it against my chest and sobs. "It's hard."

"I know."

"I don't know what's going to happen."

"Twenty-four hours," I say. "That's what's going to happen. Us. For twenty-four hours. The perfect family. Alone. Eating chicken nuggets."

She looks up at me, tears in her eyes, and I think it's going to get worse, but she just says. "Can we get fries too?"

I burst out laughing. "Yeah, girl, we can get fries."

"But the greasy ones."

"Yup."

"And Mountain Dew."

I laugh harder. Of course, she wants Mountain Dew. "Done. Anything else?"

She pauses, and then those big brown eyes blink up at me. "I'd really like to spend those times eating with my foster brother."

"He'll be there." Forever. Even if he shouldn't be. "Of course, who else is gonna keep you in check?"

"Only you.

I laugh but sober and say, "Only me."

CHAPTER TWENTY-THREE

Mary-Belle

I'm so full." I groan and lay face down on the couch in the theater room. It's the only one they have, a giant red leather-looking behemoth of a thing in the very back of the theater room. The rest of the area is covered with black recliners in four rows leading all the way to a screen that covers the entire wall.

Honesty, it's better than most movie theaters I've ever been to back in the day when—usually on my birthday—I was able to spend two dollars to go to the really crappy old theater that played movies that had been out for nearly a year.

It was a highlight.

Just like chicken nuggets.

I look around and smile to myself… how things can change so fast is remarkable. And how I could be given a respite with my, ahem, foster brother, is even better. I don't have to stress about anything for the next day, my stomach's full, and I'm in a theater room with air conditioning.

Ambrose left to go grab something, and I'm drinking my body weight in Mountain Dew which, even though I know it's horrible for me, I've never been able to drink a lot because of my situation, so it's something I always seem to crave, maybe because when I was like seven I asked for some at the gas station and my foster mom at the time let me have it, and it was years before I tasted it again.

This is my third time drinking it since then, and it still tastes the same—it holds the same happy memories of thinking I was going to have a forever home only to have my foster mom's husband say no to my adoption. She later found out he was cheating. He left a week later, and so did the rest of us foster kids.

I still wonder about her sometimes.

She was nice. She was one of the good ones we always pray to be placed with.

She was good, just like this Mountain Dew.

I tip back the can, then crush it and sit up. I'm in a random white t-shirt that I'm pretty sure at one point I stole from Ambrose's clean laundry—and a pair of black sleep shorts that you can barely see, thanks to the t-shirt.

I stare down at my bare feet and then lean back on the couch further. Maybe I should paint my toenails? I wonder if Ambrose's mom left behind any polish?

"You alive?" Ambrose's voice sounds, and then he's shoving my legs off the couch so he can sit.

I roll my eyes. "Do you have a death wish?"

"Does death include you in the afterlife?" He winks. "If so, maybe."

I stare a little too long before answering. "Stop being too nice. It's weird."

"Hmmm…" He pulls a black sharpie out of his pocket and taps it against his chin. "I can't be nice, and I can't be mean, is that it?"

"Normal." I scrunch up my nose. "Just try normal."

He reaches into his pocket, his smile wide, and pulls out a piece of notebook paper. "Normal's hard for someone so perfect."

"Wowwwww." I kick him with my foot.

He laughs. "What about the whole twenty-four-hour cease-fire?"

"It slipped." I cross my arms and sit up. "Are we doing homework now or what?"

"Yes, because I'm always known for doing homework on the weekends when a hot girl's sitting next to me."

I gasp.

He shrugs and leans forward; I swear I can taste his lips and confusion in the air. "What? It slipped."

I feel my cheeks heat and look away. "Seriously though…"

"We fight," he says clearly. "And we're sometimes better at fighting than anything, so I figured I'd write some house rules for the next twenty-four hours, and if we can actually make it through without shoving each other off the roof, we can maybe discuss making it permanent."

I'm suspicious by nature, but I'm also curious. "Make what permanent?"

"This." He spreads his arms wide. "The living situation, the way I see it, if we can make it for twenty-four hours and take a few slow steps toward progress, then maybe when

143

you graduate, you don't have to grab another black trash bag and dump your shit into it. Maybe instead, you can live with an abandoned perfect kid in his giant house with all his memories and no parents."

"Very depressing sentence," I say.

My throat nearly closes as he asks, "The trash bag?"

"The no parents," I whisper, then tuck my feet under my body and scoot toward him. "What sort of rules would we put on here anyway?"

Subject change. I need a subject change.

He grins down at the piece of paper then bites off the cap of the sharpie, not really giving me an answer as he writes down a number one. He spits out the lid and looks over at me. His amber hair is still damp, sticking to his forehead, and his strong jaw seems almost more pronounced for some reason. Maybe the lighting, maybe I'm going crazy, maybe it's the way he smiles at me like he means it, like I'm important to him when I know I'm not. How could I be?

"No talking at school," he says as he writes it down. "That way, nobody will talk about us, the only communication…" He puts a little dash underneath it. "…will be strictly stuff about homework, saying hi, and bye."

I nod. It actually does make sense, self-preservation and all that. "That works, and it's not like it's hard since that's how the last six months have been."

Something flickers in his eyes before he clears his throat and looks back down. "Number two, we don't tell anyone mom's gone."

"Agreed." I nod. "That's a bad look, after all."

"Can't be perfect without the perfect family," he grumbles, then writes a number three.

I grab the marker from him and then lean in so I can write on the paper.

"Number three, the house is off-limits, rules don't exist, only us." I'm proud of the freedom I created until he stills and looks over at me.

"Are we sure that's a good idea?"

"Are you sure it's a bad one?" I counter quickly.

His eyes move to my mouth before he looks back down at the paper. "I guess it's just a test anyway, right? We still have to survive the next twenty-four-hour disaster before we put this bad boy on the fridge."

I smile so hard I think I freak him out.

"Why are you so happy about me putting rules on the fridge with a magnet from my mom's yoga studio? It literally says namaste, not in a fun color, but what they call cucumber cool green. It's supposed to be more relaxing, you see."

"I'm more worried; how you know that?"

"Mom asked." He laughs. "Only esthetically pleasing things near the food."

My jaw drops. "You're just joking, right?"

He shrugs. "It upsets the freshly squeezed juice, don't even get me started on the milk..." He crooks his finger toward me, then whispers, "It spoils."

I nearly shove him off the couch. "Now I know you're full of shit."

He throws his hands into the air laughing. "I shit you not. We had a family meeting about only saying positive things when we opened the fridge, something about how negativity makes the food go bad—it has feelings."

I lift my Mountain Dew to my face and whisper, "I love you."

This time Ambrose does fall off the couch onto the ground; he's laughing so hard he looks like he might start crying. "Holy shit, I meant food, not Mountain Dew. That shit is dead; it's fucking formaldehyde!"

"TAKE IT BACK!" I yell, throwing a pillow with my free hand. "YOU HURT ITS FEELINGS!"

"DID NOT!"

"DID TOO!"

"WHY ARE YOU YELLING!"

"MOUNTAIN DEW MAKES ME UNREASONABLY AGGRESSIVE!"

He stills and then puts his hands behind his head. "Oh? Is that so?"

"Not. One. More. Word. Especially with that suck-my-dick look on your face!"

His jaw drops. "That's an extremely inappropriate thing to say to your foster brother." Ambrose puts a hand on his chest. "I'm almost horrified."

"First off…" I chuck him with the pillow again. "…that's what every boy does when he wants bad things—"

"—That's not a bad thing."

I snort. "Second, I know that look, so stop looking with that look." I almost stutter. "And third. No."

"Can I talk now?"

"Do we need a talking stick?"

He bites down on his lower lip. "You stepped right into that one, girl, can't help you there." He looks down at his dick, then back up at me. "But if you insist."

"I hate you."

He grabs my foot and gently pulls me to the ground across from him. "No, you don't."

"Sometimes."

"That's better." He pulls my other foot until I'm somewhat straddling his body from the side, then he looks down at my feet. "You need to paint your toenails."

"Yeah okay, mind reader." I roll my eyes. "I don't have any polish."

"I do."

"You do?"

He shrugs. "I went through a phase. Besides, who says guys can't wear nail polish? Fuck, guys from eighties hair bands to KPOP idols wear nail polish, and why are you giving me that look right now?"

I wipe a fake tear. "You know pop culture!"

"Hey, I'm not all perfectly tied ties and charity dinners."

He gets up off the floor and holds out his hand. "Come on, let's go."

"Where?" I ask.

He frowns. "To my room, where I keep my polish, in a secret stash under lock and key by my condoms."

That...we probably should have used the first time. Thank God I had the shot.

"You lock up your condoms?"

He licks his lips and squats back down next to me. "You know I don't."

All I know is I don't know anything. This cease-fire is dangerous to my soul.

He's hot and cold.

He's sexy and friendly, then cruel and hateful.

He's everything all at once and impossible to contain, and it drives me wild.

I think this boy is the first person in my life that makes

147

me want something—so desperately I can taste it when I lick my lips, just like I still taste him. It's not a feeling, it's a need, it's not a want, it's survival.

How can one single person do this to me? How can they turn it on and off so effortlessly while I'm dying inside?

With shaky legs, I let him help me to my feet.

"But first…" He grabs the marker and adds in a few more numbers. "Just in case we think of anything else, we'll add it here." He turns me toward the door. "Onward, to the fridge, just remember to whisper happy things."

"Okay, creature of habit."

He moans. "Damn fridge, you're so cold right now; bet all those veggies crunch so hard when you bite into them."

"I'm annoyed that sounded somewhat sexy."

"I'll be the peanut butter to your celery all day…" And he just doesn't stop as we walk down the hall and into the kitchen.

"Wanna see my Hummus? Think you could season my steak? Oh, what's that? Oh God, you've got sharp cheddar in your drawer and wanna show me?" He looks ready to collapse to the ground and start humping it in anticipation of food.

I'm shaking with laughter by the time we make it in front of the actual fridge.

He gives it a little pat and does indeed grab the yoga magnet and put our twenty-four-hour cease-fire on the front of the stainless-steel door.

He flicks it with his thumb and forefinger. "Done. Easy."

Not really. Not easy.

"Now…" he jerks his head toward the stairway. "Your nail appointment awaits."

"W-what do I do for you?"

"What?" He runs into my back and then helps stabilize me. "What do you mean?"

"You're letting me use your nail polish. Do I need, like…" How do I even say this? "I mean, nothing's free. I'm using it, and if you want to use it some time and I used it all up, I guess I can pay you from what your mom gave me the last few weeks for food… Yeah, I'll do that. The cash is in my room; I'll just grab it now and—"

"—Stop." The word is low… it kills the mood.

I have to make it better. "No, No, I mean, this is good. I shouldn't have to owe you any—"

"—fucking stop, B!" He grips me by the shoulders. "It's nail polish. Nail. Polish. I don't even want it anymore. I don't think I can bear to even look at it if it's causing you that much stress. Just take it, use it, and don't think of it as a favor for…" It's like he can't even think of the words. "Is that how I made you feel?"

I can't breathe. "What?"

He pulls me against him, then tilts my chin with his hand. I suddenly realize he's shaking. "Is that how I made you feel? When you came here? When we… in the bathroom, is that how I made you fucking feel?"

"I liked you." Is the only way I can answer. It didn't necessarily feel cheap, but it was expected. Hormones, high school seniors, new situation. But no matter how much I justify it, I realize the sad reality.

I felt like I wanted something for me, and maybe a small part of me felt like—it would be easier to get it over with.

My silence is answer enough at first, and then I shake my head. "I wanted it, I wanted you, but I'm used to… I'm used to it, maybe, I guess, I don't know, you're you, I'm me, I was being selfish, maybe using you as much as you were using me. When I look back, I don't think I was thinking at all." Tears well in my eyes. "I was scared. I was sad. And you made me feel safe."

By the look in his eyes, you'd think I just stabbed him in the heart. He quickly glances down at the floor. Down at my toes. His shoulders slump, all bravado gone, all teasing about vegetables and cheese dead, just like the feelings he used to have for me. Just like his dad.

Gone just like his mom.

After a few seconds of silence, he breathes out a curse and still doesn't make eye contact as he breezes past me. "Let's go paint your toenails."

I follow him and wonder if the cease-fire just ended itself.

CHAPTER TWENTY-FOUR

Ambrose

I. Am. A. Piece. Of. Shit.

Like, I was aware I was a dick, but this is so much worse, I can't even look at her—which should be normal since I've been purposefully ignoring the anger and hatred. Today for whatever reason, it felt easier, but now that it's been a few hours and confessions have been made, I just feel like the biggest douche on the planet.

How could I even begin to understand the life she lived if I never asked? Is that how it was? Did she honestly think she had to use her body to gain my approval? I'm a horny guy, so yeah, I was angry I was attracted to her, the situation presented itself, she was into it, and it happened. I just never thought…

I didn't think.

I just made a choice she felt like she partially couldn't say no to.

All, what? Because she's hot and I had morning wood?

The house is eerily quiet as we make it into my room. It's clean, thanks to the maid that comes every week. The only thing out is my PlayStation center in the corner with the flat screen hanging across my bed.

I go into the adjoining master bathroom and grab a bottle of black fingernail polish and a towel.

She's standing in the middle of my room as if she's never been naked in it before.

Rather than sit on the bed, I just collapse to the middle of the floor and lay down the towel. "Sit."

The last thing I need to see is her on my bedspread with all the memories of her breathy moans and candied eager kisses.

She puts her hands out in front of her almost like a shield, which kills a part of me, though I pretend it doesn't faze me. "Oh, no, no, I can do it."

I manage to smile despite the turmoil in my head. "One thing you've never heard, a secret I'll take to my grave... I'm a really good artist. I could paint your toenails in my sleep and ace it. Sit."

Slowly, MB moves to the floor. She's already barefoot and in shorts long enough to cover up her perfect ass—just barely, she slumps forward with both legs facing me.

It would be like painting her toes backward, so I move her a bit and slowly pull one leg onto my lap.

She lets out a tiny gasp.

I smirk down at her toes. "It's not like I'm planning on chopping off your foot or sucking your toes, you know."

"That's a very specific fetish."

"Mmm..." I open up the nail polish. "Pretty sure people do that on OnlyFans—not that I would know."

"Surrreeee." She actually laughs. "You're probably into all that weird stuff, paying people ten dollars just to reach up and change a lightbulb."

"Pay you fifty to climb a ladder." I joke.

A giggle escapes past her lips, making her leg move a bit, and along with it, her toes, they curl just slightly, and it's just one more reminder.

She has adorable toes.

I'm losing my mind here.

I clear my throat at least twice before moving to her big toe. "Okay, you're going to have to sit still."

"Thought you were a super good artist?"

I snort. "No artist can create a masterpiece with movement unless they're finger-painting, which can be arranged if you keep bouncing your foot."

"Sorry," she mumbles.

The minute I start painting, goosebumps break out across the silky skin on her legs. I pretend not to notice the room's gone completely silent like our past ghosts are watching, and the moment is too intense for words to fill the space between us.

I clear my throat and then need to clear it again as I move down to her second toe, then the third.

The goosebumps on her legs are more pronounced as I make my way from one foot to the other. "Do you, um, want a second layer?"

"Sure." Her voice is so quiet, I swear it's like she's afraid to speak too.

I nod and don't even look at her as I start to paint and then finally decide to just put it out there. "I'm sorry."

"For?"

I can't look at her, plus I find focusing on her feet is soothing. Damn, maybe I do have a toe fetish—just her toes, only her pretty toes. "For that morning, for taking advantage, for being an ass and not even knowing you long enough to have a one-morning stand."

"Cute, since it wasn't night?"

"Naturally."

Her foot bounces a bit. I turn and glare.

She winces, then tugs her bottom lip with her teeth. "Sorry, I forgot."

"I'm right here."

"I know."

I just sigh. "It, it…" Wow, good job Ambrose; you said the same word twice. "All I'm saying is it won't happen again."

I hate myself.

I would commit murder for it to happen again. I bite my tongue and wait for her to say something as I finish the second coat and start blowing on her feet.

"Because it's only a short cease-fire," she says. "Right?"

I stop and look up at her. "No, not because of the cease-fire, but because I was wrong, and it wasn't fair, and you should feel safe without sex."

Her smile grows, it's so damn pretty. I go dizzy with this need to lean over and kiss her. Great, a full minute after I promise not to get carried away.

I clench my teeth so hard my jaw hurts. I've always been able to control myself—especially because I always had people watching me, so why am I losing my grasp on that control?

She looks down at her toes. "Pretty."

"Um, yeah, see, told you, artist." I hold up the bottle, make sure it's sealed shut, and then toss it onto my bed.

"That's exactly the sort of thing that makes girls fall for boys that are bad for them." She finally says.

"That I'm an artist?"

"No. That you should feel safe without sex."

My lips curl into a smile. "Yeah well, I've been practicing not being a jackass in front of the mirror. How am I doing?"

"Meh." She holds up her hand and waves it back and forth. "You moved from negative five to at least a three today after the cease-fire, fridge incident, and painting my toenails."

"Does the apology at least bring me to a five?" I ask rather than beg.

"Kiss me." She challenges.

"Shit, don't do this to me." I groan into my hands. "You're testing me, aren't you?"

She shrugs one shoulder and leans back on her hands.

"And you wonder why I hate you," I say in a grumpy voice. "No. I'm not going to kiss you."

She holds up her hand to me. All five fingers. "Congrats, you're now at a five."

I high five her, then fall back against the carpet with a laugh. "Life goal made!"

She falls back on the carpet too, and we both stare up at my ceiling. "You do realize you still have those cheesy stars up on your ceiling."

I put my hands behind my head. "Yup."

"Don't you want to take them down?"

"Nah." I shake my head even though she's looking up. "I used to look up at them and make wishes."

"What sort of wishes?"

I realize it's getting late, and we both have school in the morning, but I like being in her universe, and I like her asking me about mine.

Way too much.

I swallow the lump in my throat as I think about the first star I put up. When it didn't work like Sesame Street said it would, I put up another, and another, until I had this giant ass constellation up there, surely that would be enough wishes to give me what I wanted.

"You're going to laugh." I finally find my voice.

She turns on her side and looks at me. "Try me."

I glance over at her, and our eyes lock; I never realized how pretty brown eyes were until this moment, until her. "I wanted a sister."

She frowns, and then it's like she can read my mind as she whispers, "So you wouldn't always have to be perfect."

"So I wouldn't always have to be perfect."

She stares deep into my soul. I swear she knows me more than my friends, more than my mom, when she nods and, with a small smile, says, "I guess your wish was finally granted."

I groan into my hands. "Not what I had in mind, and I mean that in the best way possible."

"Not to make it weird," She licks her lips. "But at least your wish was semi-granted."

"You're here now."

"Yup."

"But call yourself my foster sister one more time, and I'm jumping from the roof, okay?"

She bursts out laughing and stares me up and down.

"Yeah, definitely not blood-related."

"It got weird."

"So weird."

"My fault."

"Can we go have ice cream?"

I laugh and jump to my feet. "What's with you and junk food?"

"What's with you and not eating it?" I counter. "Food is meant to be eaten!"

I laugh and then pull her to her feet and swing her easily across my back, giving her a piggyback ride. "Your carriage awaits."

"Thank you, good sir."

"Milady." I laugh and carry her all the way down the stairs while simultaneously cursing the stars on my ceiling.

Wish granted?

Except she's not my sister.

She's my roommate.

And I think I can fall in love with her if I let myself—and that's more dangerous than being a teenager left alone with unlimited amounts of money and her across the hall from me.

Sex, I can do.

Love? It isn't perfect, which is the biggest temptation at all. It's messy, chaotic, it hurts, and it makes you bleed over and over again.

It's the perfect sort of torture you never want to let slip through your fingers.

The universe granted me two things.

And I have no choice but to pick the one without any residual damage.

Friends.

Family.

And nothing more.

"Kiss me," she'd whispered.

Jokes on her because the minute she asked, I replayed every single one of them in my head—and for a few seconds.

I was free.

CHAPTER TWENTY-FIVE

Mary-Belle

I don't remember falling asleep on the couch in the living room, but I do remember wishing I could reach for his hand. My throat is scratchy from all the talking we did the night before and probably from the severe amount of junk food that made it past my lips.

For whatever reason, I was starving again at two in the morning. It's almost like I had food now, and my body was telling me it was going to go away, so I wanted to just keep eating and eating and eating.

I tried sneaking past a sleeping Ambrose only to have him jolt awake in a panic that we were getting robbed. I think he'd been dreaming. "Why????"

"Starving." My grumbly answer.

"Shit girl, you put it away like an MMA fighter trying to bulk up, then look like a wrestler who just dropped weight."

"Huh?"

"Nothing, never mind, I had a dream about The Rock."

"That a nightly occurrence or…"

He opened one eye, then the other. "Yes, yes, it is. Every night I pray I dream of Dwayne Johnson. No, we just fell asleep to Jungle Cruise!"

"Oh, righttttt." I stepped past him and went into the kitchen, then heard rustling. Soon he was behind me, opening the fridge and pulling out a whole bunch of food. "What's all this?"

"Quesadillas, you can't eat fruit snacks at two in the morning, MB, that's a crime, and we're perfect, remember?" He grinned. "You want shredded chicken or pork? I have both."

I rolled my eyes. "Of course you do. You have a taco truck in the back too? A Starbucks?"

He paused. "Should we get them? I'm not even sure my mom would notice it on the credit card."

I laughed, then. "Well, the taco truck isn't the worst idea you've ever had."

"I want a taco bus."

"I would drive that bus to school." I nodded.

"Nah, that's my job." Was all he said as he started making the quesadillas.

I ate three.

He ate four.

And then I fell asleep with a smile on my face—and my stomach full.

sit up and yawn; the blanket falls down by my feet, wrapped around me, I hear a noise and look over my shoulder. My jaw drops as Ambrose walks around the corner in nothing but a white towel and all the abs on display.

His hair's still wet.

He reaches into the fridge, grabs the orange juice carton, and tilts it back, his mouth on it like he has ownership of the juice.

"Germs," I call out.

He chokes and then wipes his mouth, and looks over at me. "Don't you think it's a bit too late to be worried about germs?"

My face instantly heats.

Don't think about it.

Do not.

Do not go there.

Foster brother.

Roommate.

Semi-friends at home.

Enemies at school.

I try to stand, then realize that I'm tangled up too late, crashing to the floor with a giant thud.

"You all right?" He laughs.

I hold up a thumbs up. "Not so much my pride, but my body broke the fall into the coffee table, then the floor."

"Good to know." He laughs harder. "We have school in a few. I'd shower and do something with that hair before I have to step in and braid it for you."

I jerk up and look at him from the floor. "You braid? Who are you?"

He frowns. "Um, a super smart guy who likes to impress

girls and watched youtube for three straight hours just in case the moment arose? Why?"

I rub my eyes. "Why does that make sense?"

"Exactly." He nods and then winks and looks over at the stove. "PS, the cease-fire ends soon."

"I know."

We share a look, then both of our attention is on the fridge, on the stupid yoga magnet, on our pact.

He flicks it again, then hangs his head and runs his hands through his hair. "Remember our rules."

"How could I forget?"

Silence falls between us before he clears his throat. "We gotta leave in thirty, I'd hurry."

"Crap." I untangle the blanket and jump to my feet. It takes me around fifteen minutes to put on some lip gloss and mascara before pulling my hair into a messy bun and dressing.

I snatch two protein bars and a cold brew from the fridge. By the time I have my designer bag, Ambrose is already out front in the car waiting for me, looking every inch like one of those Tik Tok guys you see in uniforms looking way too hot to actually attend school.

He's wearing aviators and leaning against the car texting someone, and I'm instantly jealous.

Not sure if it's of the phone or the way he smiles while texting.

"Ready," I announce.

He looks up, his bored yet annoyed expression back, and part of my soul feels crushed.

My reality isn't the same as it once was over the last day, and it feels like loss all over again.

The loss of him.

The loss of understanding.

The loss of peace.

My smile feels all kinds of wrong as I get into the expensive car and put on my seatbelt. He blasts the music on the way to school, and without even realizing how lost in my lots I am, we're in the parking lot, and he's killing the engine.

I feel like crying. I feel so stupidly weak that I hate myself a bit as I exhale and reach for my seatbelt.

Just as I'm about to hit the button to unbuckle it, Ambrose's large hand grips mine right on the buckle. He's still looking straight ahead, jaw clenched, watching all the students walk by, point at his car, and gape. The hero worship is real.

I don't know what to say, so I say what's on my heart, regardless if it hurts. "I'm here now."

"Steps for life," he finally says.

"Sometimes stars work, even if it's not the way we expect." I take a deep breath. "I can be perfect too."

He snorts out a laugh. I'm instantly hurt until he whispers, "You already are."

He jerks his hand away and gets out of the car, slamming the door like he's pissed.

It takes my heart a few minutes to slow down as I unbuckle my seatbelt and follow behind him at a distance. Just another day with no friends, being terrified of bullying since I'm living with Ambrose. He might think it's perfect for me, but I get stares from girls, mean comments. And then, in front of his face, all they say is that I'm the absolute best. Only to get to him.

I can take it.

I've had worse.

I keep my head held high and breathe a sigh of relief as Quinn jogs over. "He seems to be in a mood today."

My smile's dopey, then I turn serious. "Yeah, he's got a lot on his mind post drunken night and sober breakfast."

Quinn just nods. "I bet he does."

I frown. "What's that supposed to mean?"

"Ohhhh, nothing." He elbows me lightly. We're almost at the front doors when Ambrose freezes.

He always struts through the doors like he owns the place. People are kind of gathered around, which isn't totally weird, but they're watching his expression, their eyes wide, and suddenly they're looking at us.

"That's weird." Quinn grabs my elbow, and we start walking a bit faster and that's when I see this gorgeous, shiny blonde-haired girl that can't be that much older than me. She's in a cute white dress, jean jacket, and what looks like expensive sandals; her makeup is perfect, and she's smiling at Ambrose like she knows every inch of him.

"Quinn, who is that---"

"—What the fuck are you doing here!" Quinn roars, jolting Ambrose out of his shock.

"Quinn." The girl grins. "Always good to see an old friend."

Quinn starts shaking next to me, then abandons me, grabs Ambrose by the arm, and shoves him away from the person and toward the door.

They just leave.

Ambrose hangs his head. Quinn's yelling down the hall. Then I hear Ambrose cursing.

I'm still frowning when the girl turns her eyes toward

me, cold, calculating, perfect, and now she's walking toward me. "Are you the replacement for those two? Didn't realize I'd have competition when I came back."

"Competition?" I ask.

She holds out her hand. "Hi, I'm Tessa. I'm in Elementary Education and working here for the last month of school and summer school to get my credits. And you are?"

I hold my head high, shake her hand and say in a clear voice. "Another perfect."

She frowns as I drop her hand. "What?"

"I'm Ambrose's foster sister. By the way, he doesn't look too happy to see you... again. I'd back off before you end up in the hospital instead of the school..." I flash her a huge grin. "Byyyyyeeee good luck with your teaching degree!"

And then I stomp off in search of the two boys, who are enemies, even more curious about what connection they have and what made them both so upset.

CHAPTER TWENTY-SIX

Ambrose

I can't breathe.

That's my first thought.

My second is complete rage.

The third is that MB is watching.

My hands are shaking before I make them into fists, and then I'm wondering how much trouble I'll get into for hitting a woman, which again sounds horrible, but people don't know our story, they don't know our damage, I don't think of her as anything but a monster, and monsters are villains, shouldn't they all be punished?

She got away with my dad's money.

Quinn's dad's money.

She took our pride.

She broke us then promised to fix us.

She lied.

So many thoughts run through my head, and then I

feel a hand in mine, one I recognize, the skin too easy to remember, the feel of it pressed against my palm, the smell of his cologne.

And I fucking hate that she's staring at both of us like she's about to feast at a Vegas buffet.

I want to vomit.

I want to jump onto Quinn and beg him to save me, and I'm not that sort of person. I've always told myself I'm strong enough to save me, that I don't need anyone, but when it counted, when it mattered, he did.

And I still hate myself for being so weak, so imperfect.

I don't realize I'm hyperventilating until he's rushing me into the school and down the hall, roughly jerking me into the men's bathroom and shoving me against a wall.

"Breathe!" he yells in my face.

I forget how demanding he is. His hand comes around my throat lightly as he taps my right cheek like I need to snap out of my stupor.

Am I really not breathing?

I see spots and squeeze my eyes shut, then open them again.

I stare into his blue eyes and almost want to hold my breath, so he yells again. I need the yelling. I need a fight. I wonder if he'll slap me too.

Punch me in the stomach.

A rough exhale follows my short intake of breath.

Quinn's eyes are wild. He shoves me harder against the cement wall next to the hand drier.

"Fucking. Breathe. Ambrose!"

I am. Right?

I don't even know anymore.

Is this what a nervous breakdown feels like? Because it's not fun, it's severe. It hurts. I hate everyone and everything.

The door opens behind him, and someone walks in, but he doesn't let me go.

A familiar scent of perfume washes over me, and then MB is standing next to him.

My people.

One who abandoned me, who I loathe.

One who I project everything onto because to take it on just might kill me.

Both of them shouldn't be here.

And yet they are.

In the men's restroom.

"Bro." Quinn's forehead crashes against mine, it's nearly painful, but it shocks me out of my own misery as my heart pounds against my chest. "You need to take one deep breath for me, okay? I'm gonna count to three, and you're going to take a deep breath and exhale for five seconds. Nod if you understand."

I nod.

I still feel numb, yet in so much pain that it's impossible to think beyond the fact that my forehead hurts from his.

"One," Quinn starts. "Two. Three."

I suck in a sharp breath, then count to five and release it. MB puts her hand on my shoulder.

He repeats the instructions.

I do it again.

And again.

I don't know how many times… I have lost count of the breaths I've taken of the grip MB has on my arm, or the way Quinn is looking at me, not with pity but understanding.

169

Has it really been that long since that night? Since his confession, since she did what she did?

Since we were caught.

Since she threatened us with everything.

It's like Quinn can read my mind. His eyes lock on like a vice, and I can't even blink as I stare into them, as memories wash over us. His hands cling to my shoulders in a familiar way that I refuse to forget.

MB's watching us with concern. I can feel her anxiety, see her standing next to him, her eyes searching me for the bleeding when it's all internal.

The pain, the blood, the trauma.

"She's a bitch," Quinn finally whispers. "And you didn't deserve that—I'm sorry." His voice cracks. "I'm so fucking sorry, Ambrose, I didn't—I was drunk—and she used our friendship. She just—"

I pull him in for a brief hug. Apparently, I just touch and kiss people when I want them to stop talking. And then, in an uncharacteristic move, that feels like coming home. I press my mouth against his neck and breathe.

He tenses and then relaxes against me, holding me as tight as I'm holding him.

Solidarity.

The things she forced on us.

The things we allowed.

The past.

Present.

Future.

And, of course, MB is standing right there, probably wondering what the hell silent conversation is going on, but I don't want to shock her, nor do I want to embarrass Quinn.

So I just hold him the way he holds me, not giving a shit who sees us.

What's the worst that could happen over what already has?

"You know…" Quinn sounds like he's smiling as we hug. "I really wish you were into dudes too."

I burst out laughing and shove him away. "You'd be the only prick for me."

He touches his chest with his hand. "Thanks, bro. I really felt that in here." He taps his chest and keeps laughing while MB looks between us like she's about ready to get a story about us.

Nope. Not the time.

The bell rings.

"Ah, back to hell." Quinn winks at MB. "Want me to take you to class, or do you need to stay and chat.

MB is silent, and then she looks from me to Quinn. "Are you into guys?"

In typical Quinn finesse, which makes me want to punch him in the throat, by the way, he grabs her and pulls her against him, his mouth inches from hers. "I'm into you."

"I'm killing you after class," I mutter. "Stop messing with her head."

"She likes to be messy, I think." He smirks over at me. "Be gentle."

"He's never gentle," MB says in my defense, holding her head high.

"Yeah." Quinn nods. "I'm aware."

Shit.

"Go." I roll my eyes as he releases her and leaves the men's bathroom. "And Quinn?"

He looks over his shoulder. "Yeah?"

"Thank you."

"Dicks forever, you bastard, not like I forgot."

"You're the dick." I point out.

"Sureeeee," he calls and then leaves us alone.

"We should, um…" I point toward the door. "Go to class."

MB's eyes narrow. "Will you tell me the story later? Promise?"

"What story?" I play dumb.

She glares. "You and your little dick club, will you tell me later?"

I sigh as the warning bell goes off. "It doesn't have a happy ending."

"I've never had one either. I think I can deal."

My heart instantly clenches. "Yeah, just go to class, and forget about it until we get back home, all right?"

She nods. "Are you really okay?"

"I will be." I start walking toward the door and open it. "Besides, I have a really cool roommate that likes to eat quesadillas late at night, so I think I'll make it because, you know, cheese."

"Solves everything." She hangs her head like she's almost sad this moment's over.

I pull her in for a quick hug. I want to kiss her so badly; instead, I just hold her for a brief few seconds and let her go, then, in a dumbass move, kiss the top of her head before bolting.

Her soft gasp says it all.

I want to turn and run toward her.

Instead, I run toward class as if she isn't important even

though we'll be in the same one; I want to protect her and to selfishly protect my past.

My secrets haunt me.

And it's funny, I've had this perfect life, hers has sucked, and I'm still one hundred percent sure that if she really knew, she'd stay away from me, from both me and Quinn.

Because history always has a way of repeating itself.

Why does he have to like her too?

I ask myself this all the way to my desk, then I see her sit across the room and shake my head, my answer obvious.

Because how could he not?

She's like sunshine despite being born in the darkness, and when you're still there, waiting for salvation, and the universe gives you this bright light—you'll do anything to take it.

She's my light.

And I think; unfortunately, she's his as well.

Shit.

CHAPTER TWENTY-SEVEN

Mary-Belle

I feel like I'm seeing things that aren't there. Then again, I'd like to think I'm more intuitive than most. It's a self-preservation thing when it comes to protecting myself and making sure I stay safe.

And something about Quinn and Ambrose's interaction has me wondering what went down between them and why that horrible girl set Ambrose off into a near nervous breakdown.

I think about it all day.

I'm in English class when I see her again. She's up front with my teacher. Mr. Decker.

The girl is smiling at everyone like she's just won prom queen or something. I glare.

I don't like her.

I don't respect her.

And I kind of want to stab her with my pencil. But

175

I keep my posture calm when all I want to do is storm toward her, pull her hair, and see how many clumps I can collect.

Maybe I'll make her a nice hair-filled necklace?

Wouldn't that be so sweet of me?

Like charity.

I clutch my pen in my hand and stare down at my English book in an attempt not to commit murder and go to prison before college.

Why am I so invested in this?

In Ambrose?

Even Quinn?

My brain says it's because Ambrose is all I have, but my heart says a whole bunch of different things that make me wish I had a best friend I could talk to.

Of course, Quinn chooses that moment to be late to class and drops down in the desk next to me with a plop. "Think they notice I'm tardy?"

I smile over at him. "You were loud enough."

"I can't help it." He winks. "I'm loud with everything and everyone."

Damn.

His eyes fall to my lips before he looks back up at me.

I clear my throat. "You doing okay then? Now? Today?"

"Eh, life is life, and I wouldn't do well in prison—I'm too sexy, I'd probably get fucked within an inch of my life by a guy named Butch. The wedding would include a naked cat, our two rescue dogs, and a cover band for Coldplay. It would be glorious."

I burst out laughing and cover my mouth with my hand, then say, "Thought this through, have you?"

"Daily." He laughs. "But maybe not Coldplay. I'm more of a BTS sort of guy, smooth like butter and all that."

I roll my eyes. "You're dangerous is what you are."

"To your heart." He deadpans. "Really, I'm touched." He makes a move to tap me with his pencil.

"Reach for my hand, and I'm stabbing you with my pencil."

"Damn it." He leans back into his seat, all relaxed and cool looking, which is even more annoying. "You're no fun."

"Oh, I'm loads of fun. I just can't get over that girl up there smiling like she didn't just somehow wreck you and Ambrose, and I too, wouldn't last in prison."

He pauses, and I can see the hesitation on his face before he recovers. "Right, but what would your wedding theme song be? I mean, that's what's the most important here…"

I think about it for a minute while Mr. Dekker keeps droning on and on about the new teacher's aid from Hell and finally say, "Wildest Dreams by Taylor Swift."

Quinn glances at Mr. Dekker to make sure I'm assuming he's not watching us in the back talking, then whispers, "Why that song?"

"Because…" I chew on the end of my pen and then pull it out of my mouth. "It's about her fantasy. Her fantasy with the perfect guy, only to have reality shatter the minute they're both back in the real world. I kind of imagine my life like that. Where you get your hopes up and you enjoy the moment as much as you can, and then suck it up when you realize it's not real."

Quinn's face falls. "What makes you think you can't have that as your reality?"

"What makes you think I can?"

"Do you own a mirror? Not to mention, even if I had to put a bag over your head every day so I could stare at you without vomiting, you have pretty much the best personality ever."

I shake my head. "You're an ass."

"But a nice one." He points out. "I'm all about personality, regardless of age, sex, gender…" He says the last part quietly.

I tilt my head toward him. "Ever kissed a guy?"

"Once," he says. "But, and I swore I would take this to my grave, he was super, super bad at it. I had to teach him not to shove his tongue down my mouth. Girls are much softer."

"Are we, now?"

"Very." He nods.

It's so strange. How different Ambrose and Quinn are, and yet, they have similar personalities, almost like Quinn's allowed to be himself and Ambrose isn't.

My body suddenly feels heavy.

I'm not surprised by his confession. Everyone experiments in high school, right? I remember going to a weird camp, and the first friends I had and I were so nervous about our first kiss that we all ended up practicing on each other by the campfire.

It wasn't weird at all.

So why make it weird now?

I got some good pointers.

I smile to myself.

"Something funny, Mary-Belle?" Mr. Dekker asks from up front.

My head jerks up. "No, no, sir."

He grunts, which he does so often I've started counting them over the past month. Last week he grunted seventeen times in forty minutes. I think it's his either nervous tick or annoying tick. He's completely bald, wears tiny glasses, and I swear the same suit every single day, or maybe he's the type to just buy ten of the same thing to keep things simple.

Either way, I think he hates his job.

"Now," Mr. Dekker grunts again. And that's number three. "Tessa Andrew, after completing her community college degree, went on to Ivy League, and her schedule cleared up so she'll be volunteering here for the last month of school, getting experience for her degree, and doing work for the school that's desperately needed. She'll also be one of the TAs during summer school, so if you're one of the unfortunate people who fail your senior year, you'll have her to look forward to."

Tessa giggles, then waves. "Hi guys, as you know, I used to go to school here. I finished my credits early and wanted to get in on my TA credits so I could graduate college even earlier. The school board was more than happy to let me back in, and I'm so thrilled to be back at my alma mater."

I almost roll my eyes. Isn't that what they call your old college? Or is it the same way with high school? Either way, I'm instantly annoyed.

Her red lipstick looks stained against her lips in that perfect way that makes her lips look dewy yet full. I would bet money that if I tried to wipe it off, it would stay.

Ugh.

See? Annoying.

And why am I letting this bother me? I don't know their drama or history; all I know is that something about her is off, and something truly went down that I know nothing about.

I randomly look over at Quinn.

His hand is gripping his pencil so hard his fingers are turning white, and his face looks relaxed, but I can tell something's not okay with him. As Tessa and Mr. Dekker talk, I slowly lean over until I'm in his personal space and whisper.

"You good?"

His jaw clenches tighter. "No."

"Do I need to pull the fire alarm?"

He actually smiles now, releasing a bit of the tension in his aristocratic-inspired face. "I don't think that would fix this."

He keeps holding the pencil, then starts tapping it against the desk over and over again like he's more than just agitated—almost like he's afraid.

"What would?" I ask, trying to distract him.

He glances from me to the front of the class and then back to me. "A reset. Got any time travel devices in your fancy bag over there?"

"Fresh out."

"Damn. And I was so optimistic."

"Seems to be the theme with you, optimism." I throw out, then smile. "You know, it's okay to feel things, but don't ever feel them because someone forces them on you. Choose to be sad, happy, choose to be angry, but don't allow another power to make that choice for you."

"Ah…" His smile is slow. "So she was a philosopher in another life?"

"She clearly was because she's brilliant." I wink.

He stops tapping his pencil and then looks up at me just in time for Tessa to walk between our desks. "Something interesting back here?"

Quinn grips the pencil again so hard I'm almost afraid he's going to stab her with it. He glances at me, then leans back and smiles like it's just another day. "Sorry, was flirting, she's super-hot, and I wore red today, so I was feeling myself. That a problem?"

Her nostrils flair. "Pay attention in class."

"Yes, Miss Tessa." His legs are bouncing a bit, and I can tell he's not just enraged, he's terrified. "I'll make sure to pay really close attention. After all, details are everything, wouldn't you agree?"

Her lips part open, and then she turns away from us. "Sure."

I'm ready to ask what just happened when Mr. Dekker starts talking about another pop quiz. When Tessa stops by my desk, she not only drops the paper onto it only for it to fly off but steps on my bag.

I hear a crunch and want to cry.

"Oh, sorry!" She's so fake I want to smack her as she picks up the bag and puts it on my chair. "Remember, bags go on the chairs, not on the floors. We wouldn't want anything to break."

It's probably a bag of chips or my sunglasses that I've had for the last five years, one of the only things I kept from my favorite foster mom when I saw them at Wal-Mart, and while it may sound dumb like they're not Louis Vuitton so who the hell cares. I care.

Because I treasure small things.

Small things are all I have.

And she took that away with one look and a footprint on my designer satchel. I think maybe, looking back, I'd laugh that I couldn't care less about the designer bag but the sunglasses that cost my foster mom maybe five dollars. They were my first pair.

Shaking, I reach for my bag after she passes my desk and

starts talking to other students or helping while Mr. Dekker lectures.

The bag is a cream leather, beautiful Prada. I reach into it and then down. I'm afraid to look in, so I just feel while attempting to pay attention. Quinn's watching me from the right like he's not sure what to say or how to react. He's dealing with his own demons.

My hands hit the potato chips first, they're good.

And then, they shakily reach for the black sunglasses.

The lenses are both completely gone from the glasses, but both sides are intact, so I could at least put them on if I wanted to.

No shield from the burning sun, not that it ever really mattered... I've been getting burned my entire life, what's two lenses? I tell myself this as I grab the glasses and clutch them in my hand.

Quinn snatches the bag out of my hands before I know what's even happening; he reaches in and pulls out the sunglasses like he knows. Gently, he sets the lenses down on the desk and starts trying to put them back in the glasses.

"It's fine," I say.

"You're shaking." His response.

I bite down on my lip to keep from crying. Seeing them on the desk feels so dumb, so stupid, so annoyingly childish, but I want to cry.

I miss my twenty-four hours with Ambrose.

I miss the peace.

I even miss my black trash bag with all of my belongings that nobody would ever care about.

It's my treasure.

Quinn meticulously starts adjusting the lenses and then

goes into his backpack and pulls out gorilla glue.

I frown. "Didn't see that on the class list for supplies."

"Because they're idiots." He glares up at Tessa. "Clearly."

I swallow my tears as he works like a surgeon, then puts the glasses gently back on my table.

They look normal.

No broken pieces. "She's a witch."

"She raped us," Quinn says under his breath like he's talking about the weather.

I still. "Did you just say—"

"—Mary-Belle, can you please stop distracting the class?" Mr. Dekker sighs again, but I literally have trouble inhaling air into my mouth.

Rape.

He was raped?

No. He said *us*.

I don't think I move for the next twenty minutes, and when the bell finally rings, Quinn strolls right past me like he didn't just drop a bomb.

I run after him, but he's faster, and I lose him in the crowd of everyone trying to make it to their next class.

Us.

He said *us*.

I finally stop chasing him and look up.

It's Ambrose, his face is still pale, and Tessa is standing right in front of him.

I don't even think. I just run toward him, press my mouth against his shoving her out of the way, and nearly collapse against him when he kisses me back, not with passion or sexual tension or even fury.

But relief.

CHAPTER TWENTY-EIGHT

Ambrose

"Been bulking up, I see." Tessa leans against my locker like she owns the space, and I'm finding it harder and harder to breathe—the worst part is she knows it. She knows how she affects me.

It gets her off, and I hate her for it. Sweat starts pooling at my temples all by itself; people are seeing this, seeing the perfect guy panic, seeing the strong one break.

And she wants to be the one to do the breaking.

It's what she likes.

Some might say it's her kink—broken pieces she can rearrange and keep for her own sick pleasure.

I tell myself it's going to be fine, the bell will ring, and I'll be off to my next class, leaving Satan behind me, but the seconds are going by so slowly that it feels like an eternity. She steps closer. She's wearing the same sweet perfume of my nightmares, the same perfume. I don't know the name of it, but I do know that the last time I was in the perfume section, I not only ran to the bathroom to puke but had a panic attack and then had to lie to my parents and say I had the flu.

Tessa reaches out; her innocent pink nails graze down my arm as she touches me.

I hate how scared I feel, how insecure, how stupid, but most of all, how ashamed I was when she showed me the video.

"Guys…" Tessa laughed. "Relax, it's not a big deal; I mean, it could end up being a big deal, I guess." She laughs harder while Quinn and I start to come around.

The room is a complete mess.

It smells like sex and sweat. My head's pounding, and my mouth is so dry I can barely lick my lips. I glance over and see Quinn naked on the floor, holding his head in his hands, most likely trying to make sure his head stays in place since it hurts as bad as mine does.

"What the hell?" I rasp. "What happened?"

"So much." Tessa looks like she just went for a run, she's in short shorts and a pink sports bra, and she has her phone out, showing me her screen. "Wanna see?"

"Huh?" I grab the phone.

I watch, Quinn gets up and looks over my shoulder, and when I can't take it anymore, when I can't take what I'm seeing, I run into the bathroom and puke up everything I've eaten and drank over the last twenty-four hours only to have Quinn follow me in there and do the same in the sink.

"Relax!" she calls out. "It's not like I'm gonna share it."

The sound of Quinn's puking makes me puke even harder,

and then I'm just sitting on the bathroom floor, tears running down my face.

My dad's going to kill me.

He's going to kill both of us.

I had a funny feeling about the party, but I never knew it would come to this or that she would go that far. And for what reason? Her own sick enjoyment?

"What do you want?" I finally ask as she makes her way into the bathroom and tosses a towel at my face.

Tessa leans down and grins. "Insurance."

I'm still frowning when she walks off. Quinn can't even look me in the eyes... I don't blame him, it's awkward as hell, and had I not seen what I'd seen, I would have never believed it even happened.

All I remember is being hot and horny.

That's it.

"Bro," I start out.

"Not now," he says quickly. "I can't even... I can't process it right now. Let's just go home, shower, and just figure out a way to delete the video from her phone by any means necessary."

"So..." Tessa pushes me closer to the locker, jarring me out of the painful memory. I don't know what to do, I swear I have PTSD from her. That one moment defined our relationship with her, or lack thereof, it eventually ruined our friendship, it eventually destroyed us, and now she's back, and I'm both petrified and full of rage. "You wanna hang out? Talk about old times?"

I'm on the verge of saying something like, I want to choke you when MB just comes in guns blazing and kisses the shit out of me. I don't even have time to react, and then

I do. I kiss her back so hard you'd think it was my life's work, my life's goal.

She's all over me, her tongue shoves so far into my mouth I have to open it wider to accept her. My hands are suddenly on her ass, and then it's all over. I know it's over because everyone saw.

And I'm living with her.

And this is an actual disaster, but I don't care because she didn't think about what people would say. She thought about me.

So when she pulls back, I pull her right back in and kiss her again and again until Tessa finally walks away, her heels slamming against the tile floor.

When we stop kissing, MB looks up at me with large eyes. "Whoops."

"You know, you're really bad at following orders and the rules on the fridge."

Her smile is wide when she responds. "Sorry, I was hungry."

"By all means…" I lean in. "…eat."

She kisses me again, and now it's like neither of us can stop, I'm sure people have phones up filming, and all I keep thinking is, well, if we're going to burn in Hell, destroy my family's reputation, and dine with Satan, may as well make it official.

I reach for her ass and grind against her, then throw her against the locker. We keep kissing until a teacher starts yelling at us.

And then, we both make eye contact and laugh.

CHAPTER TWENTY-NINE

Mary-Belle

The world didn't end. That's really the only thing I keep repeating in my head as Ambrose drives me home with Quinn in the backseat banging his head against the window like it's going to make everything better.

All it took was Quinn seeing the kiss, then watching Tessa walk off, for him to jump into action.

I mean, pulling the fire alarm was probably not the best idea in the world, but nobody caught him, and it caused much more drama around the school than a few people in the hall seeing us kiss.

Rumors haven't spread—yet.

I'm sure they will, but until then, we're safe, and I don't need to change my identity and move to a foreign country. Plus, people make out all the time in high school, it can mean nothing.

Right?

Ambrose had pulled away from the kiss and frowned down the hall, only to see Quinn flip him off and disappear.

Apparently, that was all the invitation he needed to invite Quinn over to make a plan of attack about Tessa.

I'm still confused about how two eighteen-year-old athletes with more muscles than she has in her pinky finger are intimidated by her, but I also know that manipulative women can be terrifying.

"Did you love her?" I break the silence.

Ambrose slams on the brakes at the red light. "Sorry."

Quinn's head bangs against the front seat. "Shit, a warning next time!"

"Sorry, I was just surprised."

Quinn starts rubbing the front of his forehead. "Damn, I'm gonna bruise."

"He bruises easily." Ambrose hits the gas again, throwing Quinn back against his seat. "How's the head?"

"Hate you," Quinn grumbles. "You aren't in NASCAR, bro."

"But I could be." Ambrose grins.

"You'd crash into a wall during the first lap and go boom, but sure, everyone needs a dream."

"Someone's cranky." Ambrose must find joy in it.

Quinn rolls his eyes. "Yeah, well Satan rose up from Hell and decided to join us in second Hell, and I didn't get to kiss a hot girl today, so forgive me for being cranky."

"Aw, you think I'm hot." I tease.

Ambrose growls. "Not the time."

"Possessive of your foster sister much?" Quinn grins at Ambrose through the rearview mirror.

Ambrose glares right back.

Quinn holds up his hands in surrender. "Wow, it's worse than I thought."

"What do you mean?" I ask.

Quinn's silent and then. "Oh nothing, just that I know Ambrose better than he knows himself, and we tend to have the same... appetite." I gulp nervously. "I mean, we both like pizza and yogurt. Stop panicking." He winks.

Liar. He meant me. I can see it in the way he looks me up and down like he'd pick me over pizza any day.

Ambrose reaches across the console like he's going to grab my hand, only he pulls it back and clenches his hand into a tight fist in his lap while he keeps the other on the steering wheel.

The tension is palpable in that expensive sports car. Finally, we reach the house and pull in.

It feels lonely even with two people. I think I'd prefer a shit apartment that felt like home instead of a mansion that felt like a museum.

The boys are quiet again as we grab our bags and walk into the house. Ambrose puts his on the floor next to the door like he has zero intention of doing homework today, and Quinn does the same like they've done this a million times in this house. I suddenly feel almost like I'm the third wheel, even though I know the tension between them is still super thick.

I can't get over what Quinn said earlier, and the fact that Ambrose won't speak about any of it makes me super uncomfortable, like how long can you keep that sort of heaviness inside your soul until you snap?

The words might make it real-but words disappear instantly once they're out into the world. The more you keep them in, the bigger they get.

At least, that's my experience.

Ambrose grabs a water from the fridge, slams it shut, pounds it, then tosses it to me. "Want some?"

I catch it mid-air, then toss it back. "I'm good, so um… should we talk about why everything was chaotic at school?"

"No." They both said in unison.

I drum my fingers across the white countertop. "So what you said after class, Quinn?"

"What?" Ambrose stands up straight rather than leaning against the countertop. "What did you say to her?"

"Leave it." Quinn grits his teeth at me.

"What the fuck did you say!" Ambrose yells.

Quinn kicks the barstool in front of him. "It just came out, okay!"

"The hell!" Ambrose chucks the water bottle at Quinn, who is smart enough to duck just in time, only to stand back up and charge Ambrose shoving him against the fridge.

"None of your damn business!" Quinn swings for Ambrose's face, but Ambrose blocks the punch.

Ambrose grabs Quinn by the shirt and punches him in the stomach. "What." Punch. "Did." Punch. "You." Punch. "Say!"

"THAT WE WERE RAPED!" Quinn yells. "Is that what you want me to admit? Should I yell it louder so the neighbors can hear us?"

Ambrose loses his footing and just crumples to the floor in a heap. He doesn't look up at me, and Quinn isn't looking at me either.

"I should go," Quinn says once Ambrose has his hands covering his head.

"No, stay." Ambrose gets up. "I'll go."

"No," I yell out. "Nobody is leaving this house until we talk about this."

"Well…" Ambrose starts walking away. "…good thing it's a big house."

Quinn's eyes squeeze shut for a brief moment. I walk over to him and put my hand on his as he braces himself against the countertop, his fingers white.

"Quinn?" I reach for him.

He abruptly pushes off the counter and turns to me, eyes blazing. "I'm swimming. Wanna join?"

"Are you planning on swimming with me or drowning me?"

"Depends, are you going to ask me about it again in front of Ambrose?"

I shake my head no.

"Then I'll most likely swim with you."

"Most likely?"

"Shit." He throws his hands in the air. "It's all I've got right now, all right?"

Not exactly comforting, but I still follow him out to the pool.

And when he just starts stripping and jumps in the pool without any clothes on, I hesitate.

Ambrose is right upstairs.

Their relationship is already on rocky ground, so I sit near the shallow end on the ledge and drop my feet into the water.

"Afraid of a bit of dick?" Quinn teases, swimming over to me.

"Me? Never. I just thought I should save your life."

He frowns.

I point back at the house. "You'd be the one getting drowned."

"Nakedness is natural." He swims up toward the stairs and then stands, fully erect, his eyes hone in on mine. "See? Nothing weird about being naked."

"Yes, but there is something weird about being turned on by that unicorn floaty behind you." I tease, mouth dry as I try to look anywhere but below his chest.

He's like a Greek god, and I've always hated that comparison, but really, where Ambrose is more bulky, Quinn's lean, has a runner's body, and isn't afraid to show it.

Why are all problematic boys running around with the perfect V?

Shit, I looked.

I lift my eyes again, hating that it's kind of making my stomach feel funny, my heart skips a few extra beats.

It's only hormones.

And the heat.

He takes a step forward, then another. I lean back on my hands and keep my eyes locked on his. "Did you need something?"

I swear he's smoldering right now. "Clearly…" He looks down. "I do."

"I'm not a prostitute, Quinn. Sure, you can pay someone to take care of that for you or maybe even use your own hand."

"Too many blisters." He jokes.

"I bet."

He leans down until his face is inches from mine. "You know, for someone who seems to like Ambrose, you sure are blushing a lot."

"Any girl would."

He looks like he doesn't believe me, and I sound like I don't believe me. It's a problem.

Quinn's eyes flash to my mouth before he grins and whispers, "In three, two, one—"

"--Get some fucking clothes on, Quinn!" Ambrose shouts, and then he's diving into the water and pulling Quinn away from me, then shoving him deeper down.

I truly think Quinn might die when Ambrose finally lets him up for air. "Good thing I was a swimmer." He's panting. "Knew you'd be watching. Thanks for joining us."

"Dick!" Ambrose splashes him. "Seriously, such a dick."

"Why yes, it is a glorious dick, thank you, what do you think, Mary-Belle?"

I just shake my head. "That you're both insane and should stop talking about your dicks like trophies?"

"I don't need to talk about mine for you to know how much I treasure it." Ambrose winks.

I feel my cheeks heat and look away.

Yeah, it would be impossible to forget some of what went down between us, and that kiss today didn't help.

Water suddenly splashes my uniform.

"Hey!" I yell.

Both guys have that look in their eyes that says you're about to get taken down. The sudden shift in Ambrose is welcome but also weird, weird that only Quinn knows how to pull it off, how to bring the Ambrose I fell for back.

"Don't." I start to get up, but it's too late. Ambrose reaches for me while Quinn laughs, I splash into the cool water, clothes and all.

When I get to the surface, Ambrose is in front of me, and Quinn is to the side.

"You should probably take off your jacket." Ambrose's lips look almost swollen, like he's been biting down on them. He reaches for my jacket and tugs it off, leaving me in nothing but a white, now see-through, button-up shirt.

"That too," Quinn adds. "I think she needs help, Ambrose."

I'm wearing one of the expensive lacy white bras with a name I can't pronounce. I'm treading water with one hand, trying to undo the buttons with the other, when Ambrose reaches out and, one by one, undoes the buttons. His hands are warm around my waist, he tugs the right arm, then the left free until I'm in nothing but a skirt and, thank God, my black boy shorts normal underwear. My bra floats next to us. What in the ever-loving hell is happening?

I'm pressed against him now; he's at least in swim trunks. I try not to panic that Quinn is just being a creeper and watching all of this or that I'm alone with both of these magnetic men when I feel fingertips on my lower back, a button is undone, then a zipper, and then my skirt is completely off.

But Ambrose's hands haven't moved.

"Sorry," comes Quinn's voice behind me. "I wanted a participation trophy too."

"Guy hasn't won a thing a day in his life." Ambrose's tone is teasing, but I feel a physical reaction take place. He's suddenly hard as steel against me, and I wonder if I'm going to escape that pool with my pride intact.

"And on that note…" Quinn chuckles awkwardly. "…I think I'll just go back into the house and find my own snack…"

I hear him get out of the pool.

My ears are buzzing, and my whole body feels like a live wire as Ambrose's eyes read mine.

"We broke a lot of rules today." He corrects himself. "*You* broke a lot of rules."

"Are you going to punish me then?" I wrap my arms around his neck.

He groans. "Depends."

"On?" I'm dying being this close to him again with all of the memories of our times floating between our wet bodies.

"Will you do it again?"

"I can't make any promises."

"Good." His lips brush across mine. "Neither can I."

CHAPTER THIRTY

Ambrose

I'm breaking all of my mom's rules, all of my rules, all of the rules me and MB established on that damn fridge and then some.

But when someone tastes so good and so right, and you're pressed against their wet body in a pool, what other choice do you really have but to dive in head first?

Her mouth opens to me so beautifully, even though I know I'm being too aggressive, too needy, which isn't like me. Normally I'm the calm before the storm, but this girl makes me lose every perfectly calm thing about myself. I grip her ass with my hands and press her hard against the side of the pool.

She moves her hips against me lazily, making me feel like I'm seeing stars explode before my eyes and inside my body.

I can feel the heat between her thighs with my one hand; her drenched underwear is the only barrier we have. I shove them aside and slide my finger in deep. Her head falls back, hitting the concrete, her hair's plastered to her face, lips parted, beautiful.

"Feel good?" I hook my finger and then pull it out. She squirms on me and unties the front of my shorts. I kick them off.

What are we doing? I mean, really, what are we doing?

The phrase repeats in my head when she grips me and again when I tug her underwear down to join my floating shorts.

This is complete madness.

We aren't even friends, right?

We're just… roommates.

Roommates.

Lonely, needy.

So much more.

She makes me forget about the hallway and find solace and heat in her kiss.

I grip her by the hips and press another kiss to her neck, then slide my mouth up toward her ear. "You want this?"

"Sometimes you need more than you want."

I chuckle. "You tortured men in another life, I'm sure of it."

"Can't I just torture you in this one?"

"If I say please, how hard will you go?" I nip her nose with my teeth and kiss her again. The water floats up by our ears as I try to keep us pinned against the wall.

"Please," I growl with another kiss. "Please… please…"

A loud clap startles us apart. At first, I think my mom's home and she's about to bury our bodies by the first tree she finds. Instead, it's Quinn, looking away from us but pointing at the house. "You might want to turn off the Wi-Fi to the cameras or something… your mom can see all that shit when she comes home."

I almost snort, yeah when, yeah right.

"Yeah, she's gonna bury you under the Oak tree." It's like he can read my mind.

Best friends never forget, I guess.

The mood's broken. Quinn's clearly trying to look anywhere but at a naked MB, and I'm suddenly thrust back into the reality of sleeping with my technical foster sister in my family's pool where neighbors can easily see if they fly a drone over, not to mention the cameras that could be hacked.

I shouldn't care, but I suddenly do.

What would my dad say? That I'm with this girl, the one who saw him last?

It's a conflicted feeling, one I hate because when she's in my arms, I don't think about the pain of losing him or the betrayal in her eyes that day when she said she was trying to save me only to kill him.

Heart attack.

I still don't know the words she said to him, I don't want to know, but I do know that when cornered, she's not one to back down, which means it must have been harsh, it must have been bad, and I can't handle thinking of my dad in his last moments slapping me or being anything but strict with good intentions.

"Hellooooo." Quinn waves a hand at me.

"Yeah, um…" I swim back, leaving MB just floating there by the wall, hurt etched in her eyes. "Quinn, can you get us some towels?"

"Sure." He jogs away.

I look at MB and just sadly shake my head.

She nods like she understands, but neither of us wants it to end like this. I want hallway kisses, pool sex, and someone to laugh with.

I just want someone like her, someone that won't destroy me or anyone around me.

I can trust her, I think.

She cares for me, I know.

But what happens when everyone finds out? It was bad enough we made out at school, and I know I can't stop from pushing the limits every time we're together. What's worse, what happens if Tessa releases anything, and now everyone sees me and MB hanging out with Quinn.

They'll assume the worst.

Everyone will.

Our secret would come out.

My past could permanently hurt the family name.

And MB would be destroyed in the process.

Quinn tosses the towels at me as I get out of the pool. I hold one up to shield MB. She quickly grabs it, averting her eyes like we are in trouble. I grab the other and towel-off real quick while Quinn looks anywhere but at us.

Finally, he clears his throat and rocks back on his heels. "So, pizza?"

"Yes!" MB screams at the same time I go. "Sure."

"Good, because I already ordered it." Quinn smiles. "Let's go to the theater room and forget that I found you both gyrating across one another and eat." He frowns. "Sounded better in my head."

"Did it though? You sure?" I ask.

He rolls his eyes and pulls his long hair back with one hand. "Let's go. It should already be here by now."

MB is shivering next to me even though she has the towel wrapped tightly around her body. She awkwardly reaches for part of her uniform that's still floating in the pool.

"Go." I don't mean to bark. I try to soften my voice a bit. "I mean, I'll grab everything, you're naked... don't worry about it, I'll get your uniform dry cleaned, you can wear the other tomorrow."

She nods, uncertainty in her eyes, it kills me. She turns and walks toward Quinn, the jackass who notices she's cold, and wraps his arm around her, pulling her in close.

The fact that he even has the balls to touch her, knowing that I was the last to taste her, is so damn aggravating. I'm back to wondering if I could drown him in the pool.

I grab the soggy clothes out of the pool, wring them out and lay them on one of the chairs, then text one of the maids that comes in twice a week. Hell, most of the time, I saw her more than my own mom after school.

I let her know we need some things dry-cleaned then I beg her to bring us Starbucks in the morning. She's an elderly retired lady who started working for us because she was bored after leaving my father's company and has no grandchildren, so I'd like to think she at least gained one even though she often tells me I'm a pain in the ass.

> Miss Mable: Ohhhh, and a Starbucks order, Sir? Is that what I call you now?

I smirk down at my phone. It became her nickname after she started binging that show and falling asleep, even though her name is Eva.

> Me: It does have a certain ring to it.

Miss Mable: Cut the shit... and I'll get your damn Starbucks. Just remember to put your clothes IN the hamper, not the floor, not the sink, and not hanging from a tree for your own amusement.

Me: That was hilarious, and you know it.

Miss Mable: Yes, still laughing. Your mom home yet?

I swallow the lump in my throat.

Me: No, but she's been in contact.

I know she can read through my lies. She reads through most of anything.

Miss Mable: Do you need me to bring dinner?

Me: Quinn ordered pizza.

Shit. I should not have brought up Quinn.
I see her typing, then deleting, then typing again.

Miss Mable: ...your Quinn?

My entire body freezes.

Me: Yeah.

Miss Mable: The estranged one your father forbade you from ever speaking to again, that Quinn?

Me: Correct.

Miss Mable: Good for you.

I almost drop my phone. Is she serious?

Miss Mable: Is there a reason you guys made up?

Me: Several actually, the main one being that... the bitch is back, at our school, as a teaching aid.

Miss Mable: I'm calling the principal right now.

Me: No, don't. She has too much on us, and now that Dad's gone, I don't even know how to

begin legal recourse, we paid her off. We have
no proof of that, and even if we did, I can't go
into his office, not yet. Just don't poke the bear.
We graduate in less than a month. It's going to
be fine.

It has to be, right? I look up at the giant house. Dad
would roll in his grave if he knew the past was being dug up.
I wonder what he would do? Pay her off again? Is that what
she wants or expects? Or does she somehow want to try to
sink her teeth into me so she's taken care of the rest of her
life?

*"Look, Ambrose, you're hot, but you know the real reason I
dated you was so I wouldn't have to go to college; besides', Quinn's
rich too and just as good-looking, plus his family doesn't know
about our little… moment. It's better this way, I'm picking him,
and he doesn't want to talk to you ever again."*

"You're a bitch!" I roar.

*"Hey…" Quinn steps between us while we're arguing in the
hallway. "Keep it down."*

"Don't tell me what to do," I growl at him.

*And suddenly, we're chest to chest, his eyes are wild. What
type of shit does she have on him that he's suddenly fighting me
after everything that went down?*

And now they're together.

*Tessa gleams and grabs his arm. "Come on, baby, he's not
worth it."*

"I know." Quinn sneers. "I know that now."

*"The hell?" I say under my breath, just as my phone goes off
in my hand with a snap from Tessa.*

*It's a picture of Quinn from a few years ago, with another
guy leaning in toward him with a smile on his face. The caption*

reads, "Not sure what's going on here, but what sort of friend is Ambrose that he'd out his boy like this?"

"Bullshit!" I scream. "I never sent this photo!"

People around me look afraid I'm going to yell again. Thankfully Tessa had already destroyed her reputation, and since mine was pristine, nobody really believed her, nobody but the one I needed to believe me.

Whatever was once there broke that day, she broke him using me every time, and I had no idea until she left school.

Gaslighting at its finest, I guess.

> Miss Mable: Just be safe. I'll check in more.
>
> Me: Thanks.

"Yo!" Quinn opens the back door. "Are you coming or what? Pizza's getting cold. I also found a shit ton of beer that needs drinking."

"And some things never change," I say under my breath as I clutch my cell and jog across the lawn and cement into the house. The AC is on blast, making my dick feel ten sizes too small.

"Where's MB?"

"Still changing." The animal's walking around without a plate and chomping on pizza like he hasn't eaten all day. "She wanted a sweatshirt."

"Got it." I shiver. "I'm going to grab one and hop in the shower really quick, then I'll be down. Meet you guys in the theater room."

"Yup." Mouth full, he waves the pizza at me and walks in the opposite direction.

I take the stairs two at a time and nearly ram into MB on her way down.

I reach for her arm. She's wearing one of my sweatshirts; it looks so damn good on her. "You're a little clothes thief."

She tucks her wet hair behind her ear. "Yours smell better than mine."

I groan. "I beg to differ."

She scrunches up her nose. "Wearing my thong is a bit far-fetched even for you, Ambrose."

My grin stretches so wide my face hurts. "Damn, ruined that fun surprise."

She pulls her arm back and rubs the spot I touched. I lean over and press a kiss on her right cheek. "Sorry, I couldn't help it."

Her answer is to flick my nipple. "Sorry, I couldn't help it. A little cold?" She looks down.

"I know how to get warm."

"Not this time." Her eyes are sad.

I move toward her until she's pressed against the railing of the stairs, and her breathing picks up. My lips brush her forehead, once, twice. I pull away, and I don't look back.

When I'm in the bathroom, with the door closed, I stand there and stare at myself in the mirror and wonder where it all went wrong and how to make it right again.

CHAPTER THIRTY-ONE

Mary-Belle

The hot Ambrose smell that washes over me almost whooshes into my senses as I step into the theater room. Quinn's already dug in and finished one beer, opening up his second, and he looks probably the most relaxed I've seen him all day.

"You added pineapple to one, right?" I lean across the bar where Quinn's standing with three boxes and the drinks.

He blinks, then blinks again. "Why, of course, I added it to the one with chopped-up anchovies, yummmmmm."

"I like anchovies!"

"They have hair!"

I smack him on the shoulder. "They so do not! That's just what they look like! It's normal!"

"Nothing about a tiny fish on a pizza is normal, Mary-Belle, absolutely nothing. It's not a delicacy, it's a tragedy, like eating spam right out of the can with a spoon."

I scrunch up my nose. "You cook spam."

He shudders. "Some do. Some, however, do not."

"Ewwww."

"Tuna I can get on board with though." He winks. "There's just something about the flavor that I—"

I pinch his ear and twist.

"Ow, ow, ow, ow!" I keep twisting. "I wasn't being dirty! I wasn't! I really like tuna!"

"He really does, in fact, love tuna," Ambrose says, waltzing into the room. "Release the ear."

I imagine he'd say, release the Kraken, the same way, in that same commanding tone, as he sexily walks toward us in nothing but grey sweatpants and a matching hoodie.

What is with gray sweatpants?

I don't look down.

Kind of hard to miss the outline of his dick. I can't tell if it's on purpose or not, but Quinn smirks next to me like I see the game you're playing.

I shove Quinn away and preen a bit when I notice his ear's a bit read where I grabbed it.

"Did you add pineapple?" Ambrose asks.

Quinn curses. "What's wrong with you guys?"

Ambrose ignores him. "I always keep a can of crushed pineapple in the pantry for emergency situations."

I hold up my hand for a high five. He hits it. "I think we'll keep you."

"Aw, and here I thought you were still on the fence."

Quinn raises his hand. "I'm on the fence. Do I count?"

"No, tuna lover, you do not," I say.

"Hairy anchovy eater!" He fires back.

"Whoa…" Ambrose holds out his hands like I'm about to strike. "You like anchovies?"

"Finally! Some respect in this room." Quinn throws up his hands in frustration.

"Yes!" I look between them. "They're the perfect amount of salt—"

"—they. Have. Hair." Ambrose.

Quinn just nods in agreement.

"You guys are idiots." I shake my head. "Are you gonna pineapple me or not?"

"Yeah Ambrose, are you gonna pineapple her, or should I run to the store and—"

"—Stay." Ambrose barks.

"Thought so." Quinn laughs.

I take this time to reach for my phone and google if anchovies actually do have hair. Quinn looks over my shoulder in silence.

I want to smack him.

"See?" I show him my phone. "It only looks like hair, but they're tiny bones that, when cooked, are edible and good for you, so there." I stick out my tongue.

He stares at my mouth. "You really think my focus is on anchovies right now."

I shut my mouth so fast I nearly bite my tongue off. He leans in, his eyes darting to my mouth. "Should I fight him for you?"

"Why fight someone who's already won?" I counter.

He puts a hand to his chest. "Brutal, I think I'm even more turned on."

"Necessary, and stop hitting on me before I kill our friendship and put anchovies in your locker to seal the deal."

Quinn's quiet. He leans in and whispers, "And if I have no self-control and can't stop?"

"Find some." I pat him on the back hard.

His cough turns into a laugh. "Small but scrappy."

Ambrose comes back into the room with a bowl of pineapple, and all is made right in the world… all except the fact that his ex-best friend and my only friend keeps flirting with me. I can't tell if he actually means it or if he's just testing the waters.

And I don't hate it—he's a hot guy, no girl would hate it, but I want Ambrose.

Great, I'm that girl, caught between a guy that's most likely willing and one who's going to push me away the minute he gets what he wants—again.

The boys start talking about different pizzas while I quietly walk around them, grab a plate and add on two pieces of pepperoni, then reach across and grab the bowl of pineapple and douse it on heavily. I think the guys are still deep in conversation, but when I look up, they're both staring at me as I lick my fingertips.

Ambrose looks like he's seconds away from grabbing my other hand and helping me out, then moving on toward the rest of me, and the fire in Quinn's eyes is anything but decent.

"What?" I lick my lips.

Ambrose curses under his breath and actually looks away while Quinn continues to stare. "You have more sauce on your thumb."

"No, I don't, I—" I look down. I do have sauce on my thumb.

Ambrose shakes his arms a bit and goes across the way. "I'll just put on a movie."

He's turned the other way when Quinn reaches for

my hand, swims his finger over my thumb, brings it to his mouth, and sucks.

My lips part.

"What sounds good to watch?" Ambrose calls.

"Something distracting," Quinn answers back, looking over his shoulder.

He licks that same finger again, then lowers it and runs it down the front of his obvious erection. His dick is literally trying to burst through the fly.

"Pizza? Good." He nods. "Sauce? Better."

And then just casually walks off.

I stand there like an idiot until Ambrose finally asks if I need help or something.

Yes. Yes. I need help.

Because even though I want to drown both of them, I'm finally realizing maybe it's me in over my head, dying for a breath of air.

CHAPTER THIRTY-TWO

Ambrose

I try to ignore the way he looks at her, and it kills me; it feels like history is repeating itself. How many times was Tessa hanging out with us in this very room, cock teasing both of us only to lead us into hell weeks later, only to betray us to the point of no return?

I can forgive a lot of things, but I will never forget or forgive the fact that even after that night, Quinn started dating her exclusively as if it wasn't a big deal that she filmed us doing… that.

I've never been more embarrassed in my life than when Quinn's dad and hers came over for dinner and showed my dad the video and then gave him an ultimatum, all because I was a stupid horny piece of shit and had no clue how diabolical she could really be.

The next day a check was cut, no questions were asked, and all I felt was shame.

It made me double down on trying to be perfect. I played my role at school and at home... I resented the man who didn't even for once ask what happened or why but decided to speak with his checkbook instead of his son.

He didn't look at me the same after that.

And the one time we did talk about it.

I hang my head in my hands, sit on the couch, and try not to look too distressed as I think about the words.

"You gay?" He took a sip of whiskey.

"If I was?" I said right back. "What then?"

He looked away. "My son isn't gay. No one in this family can be anything but—"

"—Perfect." I nod. "Yup, I got it, but what's so bad about being gay? What if I was? Who the fuck cares?"

"Watch your language!" He snapped. "No son of mine—"

"—Wow." I nodded. "No son of yours is allowed to be anything but what you want them to be, not what you need them to be."

I stood and tried to walk out.

Dad grabbed me by the arm and pulled me in close. "But you aren't right?"

I was so disgusted I almost puked. "Why would it matter. I would still be your son."

"No," he whispered. "You wouldn't."

"Message received," I said. "Message. Fucking. Received."

"What did I say about language?" Dad stood head to head with me, chest to chest, and I just wanted to push because I was so offended, so pissed that he would say those sorts of things.

What century was he even living in?

"Yeah," I finally said. "I'm gay. Deal with it."

I wasn't. But I was too pissed to think.

He slapped me across the face so hard I fell to the ground, my hands collided with the chair, one of my fingers broke on impact, and still, he stood over me.

Mom came in minutes later only to hear Dad announce to her that I was gay and I was dead to him.

"But he has a girlfriend," Mom said.

Dad looked down at me. "That true?"

"Whatever." I pretended that it didn't matter when I got up and went to my room.

I pretended that I wasn't crying when I texted Tessa and asked her to delete the video, and I pretended that it was all okay that my dad was just overreacting when I texted Quinn.

He came over and was promptly turned away by my dad because he wrongly assumed that Quinn was my boyfriend.

That was the day it all ended.

When I admitted to something that shouldn't be a crime and wasn't even me—and when Quinn went to the dark side and started dating Tessa the next day.

I clear my throat as the movie turns on. MB is sitting between Quinn and me. Quinn's on his third drink, I'm on my fourth, and MB just sits there like it's not weird she's between us.

I take a deep breath and wait while Johnny Depp appears on the screen. No clue why I chose Pirates of the Caribbean. I think I was too distracted by the fact that Quinn was so close to MB and looking at her like a tasty snack.

I get it.

She's beautiful, but that doesn't give him the right to hit on her. Part of me wonders if he's serious, and the other part wonders if he's just trying to get back at me after I cut him out of my life all those years ago.

He hasn't brought it up.

Neither have I.

But I know we both feel it, this awkwardness of what went down, how it ended, and why it broke.

She's sitting between us like nothing's wrong, like it's normal, though I do see her fidget a bit and wonder if that's because she's uncomfortable.

I adjust my body and lean in closer, and her breaths come faster. Quinn's looking straight ahead at the movie and starts popping in Mike and Ikes like it's his life's work.

"Be right back." MB jumps to her feet and scurries away like she's afraid of candy. Quinn looks over at me while popping another into his mouth. "Still hate me?"

"Pretty much."

He laughs. "She's cute."

"She's mine."

"Caught that," he says. "But what if she chooses different?"

"What if I kill you?"

"That's super aggressive." He looks down at his hands and puts down the box of candy. "I'm not okay anyway."

Not what I expected. "What? What do you mean?"

"I miss my best friend. I know what I did was shitty, but everyone has their reasons."

I roll my eyes. "What? You wanted sex, so that was your reason?"

He's quiet. "You have no idea, what I wanted, and what I did to protect us."

Chills run down my spine. "Protect us? We already paid her family off. What more did you need to do?"

"Give in," he finally says, then looks at me. "I had to give in… trust me, I would have rather written a check."

He gets up and grabs another drink, then another. By the time MB is back from wherever she went, Quinn is pretty much wasted, he's leaning on the armrest with his cheek and closing his eyes more than opening them.

"He okay?" MB asks.

The movie is halfway through. I just sigh and get up and pour myself and MB shots, we each take two, probably not the best idea, but I'm done, so done.

I get up and take another, then another. Quinn gains his second wind, and suddenly, he's grabbing a shot with us.

MB kind of stumbles toward me.

"Just like old times, yeah?" Quinn slurs. "Us with one girl, fighting over her, grabbing our dicks like we're so hard." He bursts out laughing. "And does it even matter in the end?"

"Stop," I say, taking my shot.

"No, it's true." He grabs MB's arm and pulls her against him. "Wanna make out? We used to share. Did you know that? One time we were filmed, but we shared more than this." He crushes his mouth against hers.

I shove him so hard he stumbles back onto his ass. "Quinn. Go to bed. You're drunk."

"I'm high too." He pulls out his vape pen. "Surpriseeeeeeeee."

"Go," I say again. "This isn't fair to her."

He seems to sober, then gets on his feet, still swaying, and walks out of the room, slamming the door behind him.

"Sorry," I whisper. MB seems out of it, so I grab her hand and bring her back to our seats and sit, then grab her a bottle of water.

She sways a bit, takes it, and starts chugging it like her life depends on it. The room is blurry, and I'm starting to crash. She grabs one of the blankets and lays down on the couch, motioning for me to come sit, the movie's still playing around us, but I see like four Johnny Depp instead of one.

"Not the best idea," I mutter. "With school in the morning."

"Let's skip…" She moans, "Too tired to think hard."

She smells like sunshine, or maybe I'm just so drunk I'm hallucinating, but I pull her into my arms, covering us both with the blanket, then press my mouth to her neck and just breathe her in.

She wiggles closer to me until there's no space between us. It's one of my favorite moments. Her eyes meet mine, and for a minute, I think she's going to pull away or come to her senses or maybe even kiss me. Instead, she just tucks her body into mine and whispers. "I miss you."

"Hating me is smarter than missing me," I say like a fucking philosopher.

"Maybe I'll just be dumb then."

"Can I be dumb with you?"

"Do you know how to act that well?"

I laugh. "You really are drunk."

"And dumb," she adds again.

"So dumb." I hold her tighter. The last thing I remember is the smell of her perfume and her little hands clinging to me as she drifts off to sleep.

CHAPTER THIRTY-THREE

Mary-Belle

I wake up to a pounding headache in the back of my skull and a sexy beast of a foster brother lying next to me, one arm behind his head, the other underneath mine, cradling me close to him. The blanket's still covering my body but not his. He'd taken off his shirt sometime in the middle of the night, but he was still wearing his sweats.

"Something died in my mouth last night." He groans and sits up.

"That's one of the most romantic things you've ever said to me." I barely have a voice and am so parched that I'm going to need to brush my teeth with a gallon of toothpaste and then follow it up with a gallon of water and four ibuprofen to even feel human.

"I try." He holds out his hand after getting up, looks down, and curses. "Ignore my dick. It's just thinking... hard."

"Very hard by the looks of it." I tilt my head. "Almost overachieving, aren't we?"

Ambrose actually looks somewhat embarrassed. His cheeks flush a light pink before he starts to move away from me. "Come on, let's go get ready for school."

"Noooooooooo." I'm stumbling at his side, suddenly freezing, and I really need to wash what I'm assuming are dried-up bits of mascara and liner from my face by the feel of it. Gross.

Ambrose flicks my nose. "Come on, Cinderella, I think the pumpkin exploded on your face."

I stick out my tongue as he leads me into his bathroom and hands me a new toothbrush. I don't even ask questions, I just start brushing and brushing and brushing. He does the same, then turns on the shower like we get drunk every night, then go to the same bathroom and get ready.

Doesn't he have to pee?

Well, I guess with a raging boner, he'd end up decorating the ceiling, so maybe not now.

Moaning comes in from the hall. Quinn appears in the doorway, looking how I feel, his eyes are swollen. "Why is it so bright?"

"It's called daylight." Ambrose snickers.

Quinn flips him off. "Give me a toothbrush. It feels like roadkill rotted and died in my mouth, then came back to life only to take three more possums with it, stab them in the chest, and allow them to rot as—fuck, I think I'm still drunk. Did any of that make sense at all?"

I finish brushing my teeth, at least he seems happier this morning. "Only the first part."

"Shit." He grabs a new toothbrush from Ambrose,

brushes his teeth twice, uses mouth wash then leans against the counter. "Did you guys even finish the movie? Did they capture Jack Sparrow?"

"Never." Ambrose finishes brushing his teeth as well.

"But the rum was definitely all gone," I add.

A laugh escapes from Quinn, forcing him to grab his head with his hands and brace himself. "It hurts."

"Everything hurts." I agree. "But Ambrose won't let me skip school."

"Come on, Mom, let us skip!" Quinn whines.

Ambrose tosses Quinn a clean white towel. "I have lacrosse practice; even though we aren't in season, we still have to work out, the coach is ruthless, and if I don't get to school by noon, I can't play, which means coach will be all up my ass."

Quinn peels off his shirt and tosses it onto the floor. "What? Like they actually need the captain and starting senior in order to win?"

"These be crazy times." Ambrose agrees.

I point toward the door. "I'm just gonna go... get ready, and pray that banging my head against the wall will make my headache go away."

Quinn frowns. "Just hop in the shower real quick. Is it hair wash day? Because I hear that's a thing."

"It's a thing," Ambrose confirms. "She usually goes about two days before I start smelling her from her room."

"Ahhh, the curse of the dry shampoo." Quinn nods, crossing his arms over his lean chest.

I sidestep him. "I can just shower in my bathroom."

"Don't waste water." Quinn shrugs. "It's nothing I haven't seen before, and it's not like I'm going to stare with Ambrose standing next to a blade and a plunger."

"What an intriguing way to die, so many creative strategies." Ambrose leans against the counter.

"Ummmm." I look between the two of them.

Quinn rolls his eyes. "It's not weird, you're the one making it weird, and we have to hurry, so I vote no hair wash day, get in, get out, grab a towel, so nobody sees your bits, and then get changed."

He turns around so his back is facing me, but Ambrose doesn't turn; he just looks into the mirror and smirks at me like he's daring me.

It kind of makes me want to punch him in the face or at least threaten to kick him between the legs. Instead, I quickly peel off the sweats, my eyes locked on his through the mirror, and get into the shower. His hands ball into fists. I kind of like the idea that he's having a hard time and that I'm weirdly exposed. I drop the clothes to the ground and shakily step into the shower; all Ambrose does is watch me wash myself while gripping the sink. His muscles are stretched tight across his back like he's physically holding on, so he doesn't turn around and come into the shower.

I wash my face and body, then quickly grab the towel that's hanging on the rack and jump out, shivering as the cold air hits my wet body.

Ambrose makes a strangled noise in the back of his throat while Quinn simply checks his phone like he's bored. I'm taking so long.

I'm just about to dry down my front when Ambrose's hands are suddenly grabbing the towel from me and patting me dry with it. He's visibly trembling as he moves the towel down my arms and breasts, stopping at the curve of my hips, gently he brings it between my legs and closes his eyes as he moves the towel down to my feet.

When he stands up, he turns around, pulls down his sweats, and jumps into the shower without looking back.

What was that about? I frown, then realize how different this time was from the last time we were in the shower, almost like he wanted to take care of me instead of take advantage of me. I'm still frowning as I wrap the towel around me and start to walk out of the bathroom past Quinn.

He grabs my elbow gently and leans in. The shower's loud enough that I know Ambrose can't hear Quinn's low whisper as he leans in and says, "I think it's only fair that you give me a chance too, you know, what if you prefer me to him? What if I'm better for you?" His grin is teasing, but I can tell there's a bit of truth to it. He's always flirted, but I also know there is a serious line he won't cross, and it makes me wonder more about their past.

A shiver runs down my spine. "What if you aren't?"

"Don't knock it until you try it." He winks and lets my elbow go, and I nearly sprint back into my room and grab one of my other uniforms neatly hanging in my closet.

I barely have any time to do my hair, so I toss it up in a bun, throw on some makeup, put on my black boots, then run downstairs to grab a protein bar.

Quinn is wearing a new uniform, maybe one of Ambrose's? And sitting at the counter with a cup of coffee while Ambrose is grabbing stuff out of the pantry.

"Ready," I say.

Quinn looks up, and his eyes heat. "I like the messy hair."

I stick out my tongue. He just smirks. "Is that a promise?"

"Quinn." Ambrose chucks a protein bar at Quinn's face. "Could you not hit on her when I'm standing right here?"

"Hey, she's the one that was luring me with her tongue. I just responded."

"I don't want to go to school." Ambrose breaks the silence. "I mean, I really don't want to go."

"We need a warning word or something for when that witch gets too close."

Quinn pops to his feet. "Witch works."

Ambrose laughs. "Yeah, saying that to her face sounds like a stellar plan."

"Probably wouldn't be the first time." Quinn adjusts the collar of his white shirt.

Anxiety slams against my chest until it feels too tight to breathe. Are people going to be talking about Ambrose and me kissing in the hallway? I haven't seen anything on snap or insta, so I'm assuming they just, for the most part, ignored us.

Something still feels wrong—off. I can't shake the feeling that something bad's going to happen, and it freaks me out more than Quinn's constant stares.

I take a deep breath. "Just stick together, and you two..." I point between the two of them. "...less hostility, keep your friends close and your enemies—"

"--getting drunk and sleeping over at your house." Ambrose finishes. "Yeah, message received."

Quinn looks away, a dark expression crosses his normal amused face. He runs his hands through his long hair and bites down on his bottom lip like he's trying to keep himself from saying something; instead, he takes a breath. "Whatever, let's just get the rest of the week over with."

He storms out of the house and slams the door. Ambrose curses, making his way over to me to hand me a protein bar. "Sorry, he's just... Quinn."

"It's fine; I know it's not me."

"No, it's definitely me." Ambrose smiles and leans down like he's going to kiss me, he's so beautiful my chest aches. A shiver runs down my spine when I think about him toweling me off.

"Why'd you dry me?" I ask while he's still staring into my eyes. "In the bathroom?"

"Too weird?" He laughs. "Too far?"

I shake my head. "No, not at all; I was just curious."

He tucks a piece of fallen hair behind my ear. "It was instinctual."

"To dry me?" I laugh.

He drops his hand. "To take care of you."

The front door cracks open, and Quinn pokes in his head. "Let's goooooo, we're going to be late. Talk about your feelings later!"

His yelling jolts me out of the urge to lean into Ambrose and press a heated kiss to his mouth.

He takes a step back, then another, putting purposeful space between us before turning and walking out of the house, grabbing his leather bag and swinging it over his shoulder in the process.

I take a few seconds to gather more air into my lungs, then follow suit.

Between these two guys and the anxiety at school and I already feel like puking, and I'm thinking the hangover has less to do with it as we drive quietly to school, the three of us not making eye contact once.

When Ambrose pulls into the parking lot, things look pretty normal. You know if walking into hell on a daily basis is normal.

"Stick together as much as possible," I remind both of them before opening the door and getting out. I start walking, and Quinn and Ambrose follow, flanking each side. Students are staring a little bit, but they always stare at Ambrose and Quinn—me too, to be honest, since I'm the fresh meat they can't quite figure out.

The smell of sweaty bodies, cafeteria food, perfume, and cologne assault me when I open the metal door to the hallway. People are looking at their phones, talking, and then they're looking at us and talking.

My phone goes off in my hand, and I'm afraid to look down. Students start laughing and gasping, then they're pointing, and I'm ready to bolt.

"Just keep walking," Ambrose says.

Quinn looks down at his phone and stops walking, nearly walking into a group full of sophomores, all wide-eyed and staring at us like we're about to be thrown into prison.

"Shit," Quinn mutters under his breath.

Ambrose stops walking and looks at his screen, then up at Quinn, then grabs me by the hand and tugs me toward our lockers.

Both guys shield me from everyone pointing, and now I'm thinking it's worse than I can possibly imagine.

"Don't look." Quinn tries to grab my phone from my hand. "it's not a big deal."

I jerk my hand away, nearly punching Ambrose in the face, and look down at my alerts.

There's a random text message from an unknown number. I open up the text and drop my brand-new phone onto the ground. It cracks on impact, just like my heart.

"You didn't hear this from me, but little foster sister

has quite the reputation with the foster dads she barreled through. Check out this news article from the last town she lived in. What a slutty cunt, bet she's sucking both their dicks."

Tears fill my line of vision. It's the news article where I accused my foster dad of rape.

I was twelve.

Who would send this to everyone? It's not like it was a secret, but it feels like shit even seeing my innocent face there, and the fact that nobody in that family would vouch for me, the wife hated me, the kids thought I was shown too much favoritism, and the case was eventually thrown out, the only reason it made the news was because I called the cops on him in the Wal-Mart parking lot after he threatened me in the minivan for not spreading my legs for him again and that I needed to stop asking for it.

I'm shaking. I'm mortified. And I'm angry, but I'm afraid to move; it hurts to breathe. I lean back against the locker and try to even my breathing as much as I can when Ambrose pulls me into his arms and rubs my back. "Ignore it as much as you can, chin high; you have my family to protect you. People always want to hate you when you have it all, do you understand?" His words are falling on deaf ears.

"You don't know," I whisper. "You don't know."

"He knows," Quinn chimes in behind me. "Trust me when I say he knows." Ambrose tenses.

People are starting to gather around us; I feel Quinn move away. Is he abandoning us?

And then, the sound of the fire alarm goes off as water sprays down from the ceiling, and people start screaming and running.

I turn around and see Quinn casually standing next to the handle and shrugging. "I was hot."

"Yeah, the flames basically swallowed us all whole." Ambrose agreed. "Thank you."

"But…" I look between them. "Quinn's going to get suspended now!"

"Who? Me?" Quinn points at himself. "Look, I know Ambrose is a big deal, but so am I." He winks. "Now run along while I go turn myself into the principal's office. Sometimes she has bubble gum suckers."

"Get me the blue one," Ambrose calls after him.

"I'll get you two!" Quinn salutes us and runs off while Ambrose walks me outside the school.

The fire department comes, and everyone's so focused on the sirens and missing classes that they're not even looking at their phones.

I know it's only a temporary thing—people forgetting and focusing on something else, but it was what I needed before I broke down in the hall.

Ambrose wraps an arm around my shoulder. "You doing better now, sis?"

I scrunch up my nose. "Gross."

"Agreed." He laughs. "I can totally see your nipples through your white shirt, by the way."

I elbow him. "You can't call me sis, then say that with your next breath, you weirdo!"

"But I did make you laugh." He points out. "If you're feeling generous, I'd be more than happy to let you slide your breasts across my chest a bit to warm up; I can even offer a hot mouth, a bit of biting just to make sure you still have sensation."

My cheeks heat, I try to scowl but smile anyway. "There will be no rubbing or sucking."

He pulls a sad face. "At least let me down easy. Instead, you just shove me off the horse and trample me to make sure I'm dead."

I give him a light shove. "And yet, somehow, I think you're going to power through."

He laughs, then looks over my head. "There's the hero of the hour; little shit better have my sucker."

"What is with you and sucking?"

"What is with you and not sucking?" He looks genuinely confused.

Quinn finally makes it to us and tosses Ambrose two suckers and one for me. "Sorry, they were out of the pink. By the way, I can totally see your nipples through your shirt—"

"—What is wrong with you two!"

"What?" Quinn frowns at Ambrose. "What did I say?"

Ambrose winks at me and unwraps his bubble gum sucker, then shoves it into his mouth, and suddenly, all I can think about is, well... sucking.

My eyes lock on the way his mouth pops it in and out, tongue swirling.

"Shhh." Quinn leans in. "He's auditioning for a porno."

"Ass." Ambrose shoves him, and Quinn shoves back. "So what did the principal say."

"You mean when I told her I slipped?" Quinn starts sucking on his own sucker, and I'm surrounded by hot guys licking things. Ahhh! "She asked if I needed to see the nurse."

"Ohhh, that's why you got two suckers." Ambrose nods.

Quinn stares down at me. "I was a very good boy."

"Did she give you a sticker too?"

He literally pulls up his sleeve and shows me a heart sticker; I want to roll my eyes but laugh instead. "Thank you for your sacrifice."

He bows. The bell rings, and teachers start ordering kids to go back into the classrooms. I suddenly wish I could just stay outside in the parking lot with these two confusing guys watching them lick suckers while imagining the ways one of them used to lick me.

It's going to be a long day.

CHAPTER THIRTY-FOUR

Ambrose

School moves by at a snail's pace. By the time I have practice, I actually want to skip and just check in on MB, especially because she's probably with Quinn. Would it kill her to make friends with some of the girls?

A few girls on the cheer team walk by and wave; I have to force myself not to cringe. Did they just get back from a makeup tutorial?

They all look like they're either thirty or fifteen, no in between. I wave, sigh, and grab my shit from my locker.

The smell of her perfume fills the air around me. I smile and turn, only to realize it's Tessa.

What the hell?

She's wearing the perfume I gave MB when she first moved in? The same brand? What are the coincidences, and why the hell is she even ruining the smell of the girl I like too?

"Can I help you?" I grit my teeth. "I have practice in like one minute."

"I was just thinking." Tessa crosses her arms in a stupid attempt to get me to look at her boobs. It's painful not to blurt out go to hell, you ugly bitch, but I manage it. "Does the school know the history of that girl you took in? I saw the text, doesn't exactly look good, especially now that your dad's gone. My condolences, by the way."

How she manages to actually look sad is terrifying in a very real way.

"I'm sure he knew, and even if he didn't, she's part of our family now. So drop it."

I rush by her and wonder if it makes me a bad person that I'm praying for her to trip on her high heels, chip a tooth, and then somehow impale herself on a pencil.

"Yeah, I kiss my brother like that too."

I ignore her and stomp down the rest of the hall with my shit and hope to God she isn't going to use that against her or us.

I'm furious by the time practice starts, even Xander gives me a wide berth, and he likes pissing me off when he knows I'm in a mood.

I'm a midfielder, and I'm ready to literally chuck the ball at his face when my coach blows the whistle for some running drills.

I point my stick at Xander. "You got lucky, bitch."

Coach blows the whistle again. "Ambrose, laps!"

"Shit." I throw my stick onto the ground.

"Two miles," Coach yells again. "And Xander gets to go with you."

"Fuck." Xander curses under his breath and kicks the

grass. "Thanks Ambrose, real cool."

I don't apologize, I just start running the route that will take us around the school, down the street, and back. We'll have to do it twice.

I'm annoyed, but maybe a run is good as long as Xander doesn't open his mouth.

"…so I think I have an STD." Is the first thing he says.

I nearly trip over my own feet. "What? How?"

"Sex, bro, lots and lots of sex." He bursts out laughing. "Wow, the expression on your face was worth it. What the hell is wrong with you today? Trouble in perfect paradise?"

He matches my stride. "Yeah, you could say something like that; with Tessa being back, I'm not exactly thrilled to see her face haunting our halls."

"Fuck her." He snaps. "She chose Quinn anyway; let it go."

"I have. It's not that; she's just evil."

"Most women are," he grumbles. "Oh, and I don't really have an STD. I wrap it tight, bro."

"Doesn't matter sometimes, bro." We fall into silence until he opens his giant mouth again, as per usual.

"So what's your sister's deal… like, did she really come onto her foster dad? Because that's some messed up shit."

I hold the anger in and up my pace. "It's not true. He was trying to take advantage of her; you've seen her, she's beautiful."

"I mean, yeah." He laughs. "But girls like that are the ones you fuck, not the ones you keep. Imagine if you took her home to your mom, oh hey mom, this girl was in foster care, fucked her father, has zero possessions and probably zero education, oh and I got her pregnant, surpriseeeee!"

"You assume a lot," I said through clenched teeth. "And she's not uneducated. She's rich, and let's get one thing straight, she's not my sister."

He barks out a laugh. "Be honest, you tap that?"

"Hell no!" I yell as sweat pours down my face.

"See? Even you wouldn't touch it." He needs to shut the hell up. Fast. "I mean, I wouldn't blame you if you did, I know you guys were super close when she first got here, but that's not a good look man, just creeping across the hall to fuck the girl your parents took in. Even I wouldn't go that far, though I'm not her brother, so—"

"—Do you have a point to the words coming out of your mouth, or do you just like to hear your own lower intelligence?"

"What was that about the kiss yesterday, then?" he finally asks the question I was dreading.

"I like making out."

"She totally came onto you." He grunts. "Which just proves my point, that article, probably all true, once a slut always a slut—"

I hold out my leg, and he trips right over it and skids across the grass. "Son of a bitch, Ambrose!"

"I slipped."

"I'm going to kill you!"

I sprint around toward the parking lot, he's hot on my heels—he's just as fast as I am.

I see Quinn and MB in the parking lot leaning against my car with McDonald's—they must have grabbed food before coming back for a ride.

My life would be so much easier if I could keep every idiot away from her. I'm too focused on the way she's laughing with Quinn to notice that Xander's right behind me. He tackles me to the ground and punches me in the stomach; since I still have my helmet on, the jaw is out. He does it one more time before I throw him off of me, undo my helmet and throw it on the ground.

"You want to get the shit kicked out of you?"

He undoes his helmet and throws it at me. "Let's go!"

I lunge for him.

He snickers and sidesteps me. "Pretty pissed off about a girl you don't even like. Was it something I said?"

I yell and knee him in the stomach, then toss him onto the ground, straddle him and start beating the shit out of his face.

I don't know who pulls me off of him until I see MB to my left, eyes wide.

My hands are bloody, and Xander's nose looks like it might be broken, along with a cut lip.

"Yeah, that's right, let your gay-loving friend pull you back from a real fight." Xander sneers. "Hey, how is your brother, Quinn? Still sucking dick?"

Quinn gets to his feet, walks over to Xander, and punches him in the chin. Clearly, Xander wasn't expecting it. He stumbles back.

"Pathetic, that all you got?" Xander shouts. "Come on! I'll take both of you!"

"Three," MB yells. "Take all three of us." Without warning, she does this insane roundhouse kick that catches Xander in the head, sending him to the ground.

He's out cold.

Stunned, I look from him to MB, then to Quinn. "Where the hell did you learn that?"

"First foster mom." She leans over Xander, who's moaning and trying to sit up. "Good luck getting any girl to sleep with you with that face, oh, and I mean the one you had before the blood."

"Daddy loving, bitch," Xander says under his breath.

I jump to my feet, Quinn's right next to me, fists clenched, eyes wild.

A teacher comes running. Oh great, I immediately notice Tessa's tight black shirt tucked into her equally tight black leather skirt. We can't catch a break, can we?

"What happened?" She has a certain gleam in her eyes that grossly makes me wonder if she likes the blood and violence. Would I be surprised? Not at all.

"I um, fell." Xander gulps.

Her eyebrows shoot up her forehead. "You fell, and that explains the blood on all of you?"

"We all fell." I jerk my head in his direction as if to say I won't nark even if I do want to murder him with my bare hands.

"Uh-huh." She nods, then clasps her hands together and looks over at MB. "And you? Did you push them, or did you somehow magically fall as well?"

"I'm the witness of said, um... falling."

Tessa checks her watch and sighs. "Fine, I guess since technically it's no longer school hours, I'll let this slide by, but no more falling." She makes air quotes and then looks MB up and down. "Aren't you just precious? I would have never known."

MB flinches; her eyes fill with tears.

"Okay well, if that's all..." Tessa waves goodbye, her heels pound against the concrete, while Xander curses and starts running back toward the practice field. By now, it's probably over anyway, he's brave for letting coach see him all messed up, and I hope he doesn't tell him the real reason we're both bloodied up. The last thing I need is to sit out a game or lose my captain position on top of everything else.

I wipe my nose, then my fat lip. Perfect, I probably look like shit.

"You good?" I ask Quinn.

He shrugs. "It is what it is." He looks defeated though. "Is it cool if I come over again tonight? I need to go grab some clothes and make sure my parents know I'm alive."

I nod, no words necessary because as much as I want to make him "trip" as well for wanting what's mine—I would never turn him away after Xander said what he said.

He exhales roughly, shoves his hands in his pockets, and walks off, getting into the Maserati and peeling out of the parking lot.

MB is still staring after him, even with the car gone. "Is he going to be okay?"

"Yeah well, lots of fun memories have been kind of thrust on both of us these last two days, and that's another one he's been trying to forget."

"His brother being gay?"

"Nah, his brother being dead," I whisper. "Nobody really talks about it in his family, the funeral was small, and most kids at school aren't even aware. It's none of their business anyway."

MB gasps next to me. "What happened to his brother?"

"Overdose." I shake my head. "He was away at NYU and, from what we can gather, was recreationally using, and whatever pill he took was laced with fentanyl, killed him almost instantly." My hands flex and tighten into fists. "He was like the coolest guy on campus when he was here; he slayed the ladies, then one day just realized that wasn't who he was. Quinn and him got in a lot of fights with other people, but eventually, things calmed down. Some people are still giant dicks though."

"Like that one who fell?"

I laugh. "Yeah, like the one who fell, let's go; I gotta get my shit from the locker room."

As expected, by the time we make it back, practice is ending, coach is doing his typical pre-game prep talk. He gives me one look once he dismisses us and crosses his arms. He's a burly guy with a shaved head, two whistles just in case one breaks, and played collegiate lacrosse. His eyebrows rise. "Let me guess, the second half of the zombie apocalypse practice squad?"

"Coach, we just want to prepare. You always teach us practice makes perfect, right?" I smirk.

He looks heavenward. "Don't let it happen again. You're the leader; act like it, even if Xander's talking shit, got me?"

"Got you." I nod as he turns away. "Oh, and coach, we're taking auditions for the rest of the zombie team if you're interested."

He stares me down, blows his whistle, then yells. "Fifty pushups, practice makes perfect, right?"

"Fuck."

"Twenty-five more." He blows his whistle.

MB snickers next to me.

"You think that's funny?" Coach widens his stance.

"Er, um, no, I'll just go wait... over here."

Coach literally stands over me, sunglasses and all, staring

down like a prison guard while I finish all my sweaty pushups. When I hit the last one, he grunts, grabs his iPad, and says, "See you for Saturday's game. If you dress up like a zombie because you think you're a comedian, it's death by burpees."

"Got it." I'm breathing hard and ready to pass out from the practice, but I do feel good. I get up on shaky legs, realizing my arms are ready to fall from my shoulders.

MB walks over. "So that was sexy."

"Me teasing coach?"

"Oh no, not that, him making you work out for opening your giant mouth." She grins. "I like him."

"No." I point my stick at her. "Off limits. Plus, he's married. Sometimes we pray for his wife before practice, light a candle, you know every little bit helps."

She shoves me hard. "Yeah okay, zombie apocalypse trainee who fell."

"So much blood; you don't know zombies like I do."

MB grins and pats my sweaty back. "So, does that mean I get to be on your team?"

"Gonna have to ask Quinn, there's this very serious vetting and orientation, I mean, I won't get into specifics, but you have to prove your worth."

"My worth?" Her eyebrows shoot straight up. "I just did a roundhouse kick, I'm worth more than Quinn at this point, and you combined."

I nod and hold out my hand. "You're in."

She shakes it and then pulls me close, so close I can see the small flecks of yellow in her brown eyes. "That was easy."

"Zombie work is hard work."

"Says the expert."

"Got a patch and everything." I grin.

She just shakes her head, releases my hand, and laughs. "Let's go back to the house and eat some food. Anything from your mom?"

"Mood killer," I grumble.

"But seriously…"

"No." I swallow the lump in my throat. "Nothing."

All it does is remind me that my dad's dead, my mom abandoned me, and the girl that started it all is someone I love but shouldn't.

I take a deep breath and a step away from her because what if she leaves me too? I've tried to protect myself from falling.

I failed.

Fuck.

CHAPTER THIRTY-FIVE

Mary-Belle

The first thing I do when we get back to the house is put on one of Ambrose's lacrosse sweatshirts, a pair of white shorts, and super comfy pink socks that match nothing I'm wearing and put my hair in a ponytail with a leopard scrunchy.

I'm clearly trying to impress him. I almost laugh to myself as I walk back down the stairs and search the house for both guys. They said they were going to make nachos. I see no nachos, but I do smell them.

I follow the smell into the movie room. Johnny Depp is running around like a drunk chicken on the screen, and Quinn's pointing out that he too, would look great in eyeliner.

"Test me, bro." Quinn crunches down on a chip. "I bet you anything that if I wore eyeliner, I'd look like fucking Jared Leto and Jonny Depp had a love child."

Ambrose stares him down. "That's the weirdest thing I've ever heard." He pauses. "You're more Johnny Depp and Leonardo DiCaprio."

"Aw bro, that came from the heart. I felt it."

"Thanks for noticing." Ambrose holds out a chip. They touch nachos and then smile.

"Do you two need alone time?" I grin at them both. "I feel like I just came in on a super special moment."

They scramble to their feet like I'm the queen of France. Ambrose grabs the plate of Nachos. "My lady."

I roll my eyes.

Quinn grins. "Saved you a spot between us, and yes, while the moment was special, it's even more special with you here."

Ambrose kicks him.

"Ouch!"

"Ass."

"Why!" Quinn throws his hands up and then winks at me. Sometimes it's easy to forget how handsome he is only because I think I fell for his words before his looks. He's one of those guys that, even if he shaved his head and wore his sweatshirt backward and smelled like feet—you'd somehow still find him endearing.

Maybe if I didn't have Ambrose, I'd want Quinn as more than just a friend.

I shake my head at the two of them and make my way over to the couch, lean over and take a bite from Ambrose's nacho, spicier than I thought but gooey with hot cheese, black beans, lettuce, and some tomato.

I nod. "Good, very good."

"Glad we have your approval." Ambrose laughs. "But

you have some cheese right here." He points to the corner of my mouth. "I can take care of it, don't worry."

Before I can do anything, his finger taps the side of my mouth and comes back with cheese, he sucks his finger deep, and I nearly die when his lips make a popping sound afterward, like my body remembers what it was like to have those lips on me—everywhere.

"Easy," Quinn grumbles. "You don't need to give her a heart attack."

Ambrose's face falls.

Crap.

Quinn instantly realizes his mistake and sits down. "So, Pirates four, let's do this."

I try not to deflate as Ambrose wordlessly sits down and looks straight ahead like he's not even watching the movie.

Quinn moves his hand to my thigh and shakes his head slowly.

It's too raw.

I know this.

Everyone freaking knows this. It just sucks; it's not like I had a gun and shot his dad. All I was doing was protecting the boy that saved me, the boy I loved, standing up for him, and while we haven't fully talked about it, I figured that things were better now.

They felt better.

I take a deep breath.

"Why?" Ambrose finally asks without looking at me. "Why did you go to his office? I was fine; I was dealing with it; I'm used to it. Why did you go?"

"Aw hell," Quinn grumbles and presses pause. "Maybe we should play a game? Drink? Go for a swim—"

"—You could have just stayed in your room." Ambrose isn't going to let this go, is he? "Why did you have to make me hate you? Why did you take him from me?"

I can barely breathe; my throat closes from anxiety, I'm sure… I mean, not literally but figuratively. "Regardless of what you want to believe, Ambrose, the only reason I went was because of you."

"Because I was upset?"

"Because you were heartbroken!" I yell. "Because I love you!" He flinches like I slapped him. "Because it was wrong! Because I've been hit before, and it hurt even though it was by a stranger, and this is your father because…" Tears stream down my face. "…b-because you deserve better."

Quinn reaches for my hand and squeezes it while Ambrose just stares straight ahead, his jaw flexed; he's clearly clenching.

"Never… have I ever…" He starts. "Had someone care about me so much—other than Quinn."

Quinn releases my hand. I think he's as stunned as I am; we're both quiet.

"Never have I ever…" Quinn says. "Gotten a hug from my mom."

My jaw drops.

Ambrose squeezes his eyes shut. "That's cold."

"That's mom," Quinn says simply.

"I think we need something stronger than nachos for this game."

"Agreed," Quinn whispers.

Ambrose gets up and walks off, I'm sure in search of his feelings and vodka or something comparable.

I know he'll be back though, he's processing, and one

thing I've learned about him is that he needs time, so I turn to Quinn and wrap my arms around his neck.

I hug him. "Sorry, I'm late."

He hugs me back. "Silly girl, you're right on time."

"I like you," I whisper. "I like having you as a friend."

He pulls back and tilts my chin toward him with his fingertips. "Did you have to kick me while I'm down?"

I can't help but smile. "I think you'll be fine."

"I'm always fine." He leans in and rests his head on my shoulder. "But I could be finer."

"More fine?"

"Shhhh, you're ruining the moment."

"Yeah okay, Jacob."

"Quinn, the names Quinn."

"Oh right, but you're totally the Jacob in this scenario, congrats, you're the werewolf; he's the vampire."

He gently shoves me away. "I wanted to be the vampire."

"And yet you aren't."

"I bite harder."

"See? Werewolf."

"That felt like trickery somehow."

I just mess up his thick gorgeous hair. Ambrose meanders back into the room with a bottle of Gin.

"Wow, night two, let's not get too crazy." Quinn jokes.

Ambrose pours three shots for each of us and stares down at the glass. "Never have I ever wanted to kiss someone so bad."

"Bro!" Quinn exclaims. "If you want it come and get it."

We all laugh, and so goes our game for the next hour, confessing, laughing, while Johnny Depp drinks rum in the background.

"…Never," Quinn whispers while Ambrose snores next to us on the other couch. "Have I ever wanted my friend's girl more than I do now…"

I smile over at him and grab his hand. "I'm not that special."

His eyes lock on mine as he takes his shot. "I beg to differ."

"Just kiss already," Ambrose grumbles. "Kiss her, you idiot, God, I hate this movie sometimes." He's in and out of watching the next one on Netflix.

"Damn." Quinn laughs. "And here I thought I just got permission."

"You would only need mine, not his," I say.

He pauses. "Can I kiss you?"

"No…" I almost feel sad saying it. "…but you can give me all the hugs you want."

"Thought so." He pulls me into his arms. "Can I have a few minutes, just like this?"

"I'll set a timer." I joke.

"Please…" his voice changes. "Don't."

My heart cracks a bit as I whisper. "Okay."

CHAPTER THIRTY-SIX

Mary-Belle

I wake up hours later to Quinn's snoring from the floor and notice that the place Ambrose was lying on the couch is empty. Maybe he's going to the bathroom?

I stumble down the hall in search of water when Ambrose comes out of the bathroom.

We stare each other down.

He looks ruffled and sexy with his hair poking out in every direction, and his full lips look so sexy I want to cry.

He gives me a sleepy grin. "Sorry, had to pee, and bonus didn't have an erection, so I was actually able to, thanks to not sleeping next to you."

"Boo." I give him a thumbs down. "I was going to grab some water."

"Can I come with?"

"Sureeeee." I hold out my hand.

He stares at it for a few seconds, then takes it in his as we walk down the hall toward the kitchen. It's dark and quiet, but it doesn't feel lonely the way it used to.

Is it because Quinn's here with us?

Is it because Ambrose and I have finally talked about everything?

Or is it because wherever this boy is—is my home?

I go to the fridge and open it, grabbing a bottle of water. Ambrose comes up behind me and closes the fridge with his hand, I never really paid attention to hands, but his fingers are beautiful.

Even though they can do insanely wicked things.

I shiver and stare at our little list of rules.

"How did you and Quinn become friends anyway?" I'm staring straight ahead, making small talk even though I'm genuinely curious.

"Well…" Ambrose pulls me back against him. "He kind of just forced it on me, sat next to me in Math, told me he was a numbers guy. I didn't believe him, a bet turned into me buying him a burger, and we both complained about parents that gave us shit. I later found out that his dad was one of my dad's lawyers for a few projects, and my parents approved of our friendship because we're both rich as fuck."

"Until they didn't, right?"

He's quiet, and then. "Until they thought he was my boyfriend, pretty much."

I start to trace the different letters on our agreement. "Why didn't you deny it?"

"Because they were being pretentious cunts," he says. "And insulting. And I was pissed. I shouldn't have to ask them who I can love. Parents' love should be unconditional. I guess in a perfect world, there would be, but in my dad's world, there were rules, and that would count as breaking them."

I nod. "That's sad."

"Very sad."

"So why did you guys have the falling out?"

"Because at the end of the day, he chose her over me; he says he had no choice, his hands were tied, but part of me wonders if it wasn't just because he wanted something that I did, we'd always been competitive. I saw it as a challenge, I think he saw it as a threat. Who really knows? She's the worst, at least, we both know that now."

"She really is."

Nerves wrack my body as I reach for the marker still taped to the fridge. "Are we going to be okay?"

"Why wouldn't we be?"

I start to write. "Friends for life."

He takes the marker and writes. "Ride or die."

I laugh. "Friends at school too, and friends for life, no matter what."

"Always." He writes below it. I can tell he's hesitating or thinking about adding something else. He slowly raises the marker to the top and adds Quinn's name in with ours as if to say, it's a pact for everyone, rules for everyone.

Friendship rules.

I smile when I see it, then hold out my hand for the marker. Ambrose passes it over. His fingertips are warm, sexy, and comforting in a way that they shouldn't be for something so simple.

I write. "Never have I ever had a boyfriend."

I hand it back to him.

"Be my girlfriend, circle yes or no." His writing is adorable.

"Hmm." I grin at the paper. "Should I wait until first period tomorrow to circle?"

"And keep me in suspense?" He laughs. "Do you like torturing people?"

"Yes."

"Figured."

With shaking hands, I circle yes, then turn in his arms. He rests his chin on the top of my head for a few brief seconds before pulling back and lowering his head, pressing a slow kiss to my lips.

I'm suddenly lifted onto the kitchen counter and realize that this is the moment things become real. This is our moment.

Our chaos.

Our frenzy.

Our imperfect perfection.

CHAPTER THIRTY-SEVEN

Ambrose

My fingertips greedily slide up her sides, lifting her sweatshirt over her head and tossing it to the side. It lands in the sink.

I truly don't give a fuck.

I just need to taste more of her, I need to take my time, but my body is so not on board with that idea.

"I need you." I sound like a total simp, but I don't even care. It's been too much recently, and I just want her; I need her so desperately that I feel tears prick the back ok my eyes like a total loser, and then I just, I do lose. I lose to her. I lose it all. To her lips, the way they press against mine, pulling, taking.

I'm starving for her.

I only want what she gives.

I'll kill for more of this.

My hands move to her hips. I fit perfectly in this space, the way she moves against me without even realizing that we already have this rhythm between us, something so natural and pure that I can only just keep kissing her and begging for more in my mind.

Her tongue wraps around mine, and then she pulls back and bites me in the fucking lip.

I walk her into the living room, still gripping her like a needy little shit.

I slam her against the couch and laugh. "Was that fun?"

"You tell me."

"I'm out for blood."

"I'm out for you." She grips my head, and I come down and think to myself, yeah, you wanna play, I'll play. I shove her against the cushions then toss them away, my hunger so big for her that even if she wants to run away, I'll chase, every fucking time.

She's mine.

Mine.

My teeth scrape against her neck.

She laughs like it's funny.

I grip her ass.

More laughter.

"Girl came to play," I whisper.

She flips me onto my back in a way that I wasn't expecting as I fall onto the ground, her straddling me. "Oh, I'm sorry. Did you want mercy?"

I put my hands behind my head. "Yes."

She lowers herself on me and grins. "I'm gonna make you my bitch."

"Fuck yes." I grip her by the hair and kiss her harder, harder until I can't even feel my lips anymore. The table next to us shakes. MB grabs me by the neck and pulls me against her; I didn't expect her to be so aggressive, but I like it, and my body realizes it really soon.

We needed this.

Her.

This.

Touching.

Being together. Knowing that even in pleasure and pain, we have each other, and we have this, we've always had this explosive passion between us. I'm so hard I can't function, or at least my body's telling me that as I rub myself against her, as she reaches into my jeans and grips me so hard, I think I might die.

I kiss her neck, then lick up toward her chin. My teeth dig into her chin before kissing her on the mouth and tugging at her lips. Fuck she tastes good.

She shoves me back.

"What?" I ask.

A lean leg lifts, and her foot presses against my chest, down, down, down, oh hell, I'll go deeper if that's what she wants, down into the seven circles of hell as she presses me harder against the floor.

"I need you." Is all she says as her top comes off her body thrown to the side, discarded like it's a disgrace. I peel my shirt over my head, and it joins hers.

Her hands reach for my jeans and jerks them open.

"Here for it," I say. "Also, can you make that really sexy face again just now because damn, I think I just orgasmed."

She laughs and slaps me against my stomach.

I grip her fingertips and slowly kiss each one. "I really like you."

"I really, really like you," she says back.

"We doing this?"

"Yeah." She nods. "We are."

"Should have never stopped," I whisper, tugging her by the neck and pulling her mouth to mine, kissing her deeply; our tongues don't know what to do but touch, slide, suck, hold. I feel like I'm drowning, and I accept it, like breathing in the water, knowing you might die.

I'd suffocate in her.

She smiles against my mouth and shoves my jeans down. I kick them further. Her shorts are next, and her thong follows, crashing against the ground.

And then we're naked against each other.

Skin against skin never felt so good. She's soft and hard, strong and beautiful, there are so many things I want to say, but all I have right now is my body and the hope that I can make her feel as good as she makes me feel. She's so perfect in a beautifully imperfect way.

I want to see her scars.

I want to trace them with my tongue.

I want to tell her they're beautiful no matter what she thinks.

"Mine," I say again. "I'm never letting you go."

"Good, because that would be awkward." She laughs.

I capture that laugh with my lips and tumble us towards the other couch, our legs bang against furniture and the tables, and then it's just us and the moonlight from the window. I always wanted someone to hold.

Now I have her.

I can't breathe without her.

I take a deep breath and stare down at her. "Stay by me forever?"

She nods, and a tear slides down her cheek. I capture it

with my finger, taste it and look down at her. "I want to lose control with you."

"Good," she says. "Because I've lost everything to you, and my only hope is that you'll let me save you the way you saved me."

I grip her thighs with my hands. I spread them wide, so wide, she gasps and then thrust into her like a savage. Her eyes roll to the back of her head. "Like this?"

"It has to be like this," she cries. "Like this,"

I shove harder, her hips brace higher.

"Tell me you hate me," I say. "Then tell me you love me."

"I love every part of you." She moans, then pulls at my hair. It hurts so good I nearly come. "Yeah," I yell. "Like that, we have to lose it together, lose everything."

She flexes her hips.

I quickly grab a condom I conveniently stashed in the potted plant on the table and put it on. I didn't plan it, but I wanted to plan just in case and take care of her, of us.

It takes no time for me to drive between her thighs.

I'm dead.

This is my heaven.

It might be others' hell.

But not now.

"I'm not letting you go."

"Did you think I was running?"

"Did you not realize I would chase?"

Her eyes well up with tears as we move in sync.

"Mine," I say, capturing her lips as I gently slide into her this time. She's still so tight I almost stop, but her legs hook around me, pulling me in.

I think I might like to die this way.

I'm completely hers.

I thought we were having sex.

No, she's fucking me.

I'm just here for the popcorn.

Because, damn.

I roll my hips.

Her moans aren't helping as she meets me with every thrust, and then I'm gone, dazed, confused, fucking her so hard that I can't see straight while she kisses me and tugs at my hair.

"Aghh." She jerks back. "I'm--"

"—Same." I finally grunt out.

And then it's just us again.

Staring at each other.

Wondering where to go from here but knowing there has to be a trail, a sign, something.

I have no words.

But I do have my mouth. I have my body.

So I kiss her again. I hug her, then press another small kiss against her neck and whisper. "Perfect."

CHAPTER THIRTY-EIGHT

Ambrose

I can't believe you've never done that before…" I laugh, tickling MB awake and probably annoying the shit out of her.

"It was late!" She ducks under the covers and mumbles. "Why are you waking me up so early anyway?"

"Ice cream on your nipples, classic."

"So cold."

"So tasty," I say quickly. "And I'm not the least bit sorry."

"Yeah, I could tell. Even when you bit me, you were all, oh sorry, my jaw slipped."

"It happens!"

"No, it really doesn't." She pinches my leg.

A throat clears, she looks out from under the blanket, and I look over my shoulder. Quinn's standing there in nothing but the jeans he was in the night before, shaking his head.

"Please, at least tell me you used a condom because I really can't become an uncle this early in life; I have dreams too."

I throw a pillow at him. "Always wrap it up."

"Always." Quinn nods, then goes to the fridge.

When he gets there, his hand freezes on the handle as he reads the list.

He doesn't move.

"Is he okay?" MB asks. "He's not moving."

I nod. "It takes Quinn longer to process human emotion."

"Cool list." He finally says, not making eye contact with us. "Also, you spell my name with one N."

My eyes widen.

He looks over his shoulder. "I'm kidding. Also, yes, thank you, I had a fantastic night by myself while I kept hearing moaning and groaning and things like more Ambrose, thank you Ambrose, you're a god Ambrose, do it again, ouch that hurts, just kidding bite it harder."

MB ducks back under the blanket while I burst out laughing; she peeks her head back out. "I do NOT sound like that!"

"Sureeee." Quinn winks and tosses us two water bottles, "But also get dressed, school time, and not to be the bearer of bad news after such a wonderful sexual experience where I'm sure Ambrose did his due diligence and actually found your clit... but there's another weird text that was sent from an unknown number."

Why did last night have to end this way? With us waking up to more bad news? "Do I even want to know?"

"Why fight over incest? Check this out." It was a picture of Mary-Belle kissing Ambrose in the hallway, followed by another of her next to Quinn smiling.

"Great, just another day in Hell. What else is new?" I grumble and pull MB against me. "We can skip today."

"No more hiding." She sits up, wrapping the blanket around her. "If they want to talk shit, let them. I know who I am, and you guys know too. Let's just get it over with. It'll be worse if we stay home."

"I agree with the smart one," Quinn says. "Skipping won't make it better. If anything, it just proves them right."

Ambrose sighs. "How can I even begin to protect—"

"—Don't," MB says. "Finish that sentence. I get that you want to protect me, but I've been protecting myself for a very long time. When I need your help, I'll ask; until then, just stand by my side."

They're both quiet.

Quinn speaks first. "Damn, that was hot as fuck."

"Back off." Ambrose points a finger at him.

Quinn holds up his hands. "Easy boy, I wasn't going to lick her and claim her."

"Sure you weren't," I say. "Now turn around because I'm super naked, and the last thing you want is to start school with low self-esteem because my dick's so big."

"I've seen it, not impressed." Quinn shrugs. "Mine, on the other hand—"

I cover MB's ears with my hands and glare at Quinn. He just grins and walks out of the room, the little shit.

I don't know why but I honestly feel good about the day, I check my phone again once I shower and get ready, and I still have zero messages from my mom. It's like she's just disappeared into thin air.

Losing a parent to death is one thing. Losing another by choice... it hurts.

It hurts that she hasn't even checked in to make sure we're both alive. What sort of parent makes that choice? Last year she was by my side, making sure I was okay after all the drama with Tessa, and now? Now I'm wondering why she even cared when clearly the only thing she cared about was what it looked like to everyone else.

At the time I thought it was me, she was worried about me, she said as much, but now I know the truth.

Everyone lies.

And both of my parents were embarrassed.

I take a deep breath as I drive everyone to school, I don't really say much, but it kinda feels like none of us need to. The windows are down, music's blasting, and for the first time in forever, it feels like old times with Quinn, just letting the warm breeze hit our faces. MB is in the back, sunglasses on, smiling to herself.

Everything is perfect.

Perfectly imperfect, and I love it. So what if things are messy with my mom?

I have a new family.

A new perfect, one I'm okay with, one I'd die for.

I pull into the usual parking space and immediately see Tessa standing outside the school building like she's waiting for us—well, she's going to be waiting a really long time.

As luck would go, all of our phones start buzzing. When I look down, it's a news alert.

"DA John Andrews is in critical condition with a gunshot wound. Update soon."

I freeze.

That's Tessa's dad.

He's evil to the core, but I would never wish that on

anyone. Quinn and I share a look while MB just stares at her phone like she's seen a ghost.

"That sucks," Quinn says.

"You okay?" I ask MB.

"That man." She shakes her head. "Nevermind. Don't worry about it. That is sad."

I frown and get out of the car. MB follows with Quinn to my right.

"Let's go." I grab MB's hand, and we walk to the doors.

"I need to talk to you." Tessa's voice cracks as her eyes search between all of us, finally falling on the phone still in my left hand like she knows I know. "It's important."

I don't want to give in; Quinn shakes his head slowly.

"Please." Tessa reaches for me; I jerk back, irritated she would even think she has the right to touch me. "It's like, life or death, Ambrose, I wouldn't ask, but—" A tear falls from her cheek, sliding down past her jaw and onto the concrete.

Fuck.

I turn to Quinn. "Take care of MB. I'll be right in."

I can tell he wants to say something, but he puts an arm around MB and leads her protectively into the school while Tessa motions for me to walk through the parking lot.

We get to her Jeep; she gets in the driver's side, and I get in the passenger's side.

The doors lock, and I assume that it's for more privacy, but she starts the engine.

Frowning, I put on my seatbelt. "Are you helping me skip school or what?"

Her smile seems almost sad. "Something like that."

We pull out of the parking lot, and immediately I feel

sick to my stomach. Something feels almost too calm, too normal.

"Music?" She asks, turning up the dial while Imagine Dragons plays in the background.

I lean away from her, and for whatever reason, I call Quinn and keep the phone on next to my right side. "What's this about?"

"Has he told you yet?"

"Who?"

"Quinn." She takes a sharp left. "About getting me pregnant? About ruining my life? His dad ruining our family after the payout because of that stupid harmless video?"

I shake my head. "Your dad was embezzling money from his own law firm and got caught. As far as the video, that was complete shit. You don't just drug two underage kids and get away with it. As for Quinn getting you pregnant…" I feel like I'm going to be sick. "No, I didn't know; he didn't tell me."

"He was ashamed of us."

I'm silent because, in my head, I'm thinking he felt like he had no other choice, no wonder he stayed with her.

"Dad said to keep him close since I had dirt on you guys, and surprise, on top of that, the golden child gets me pregnant after having really shitty drunken sex one time."

Bile rises in my throat. "Is that what you needed to tell me?"

She makes a hard right, then another, hitting the accelerator like she's trying out for NASCAR. I hold on for dear life and look down. Quinn's still on the line. I try to switch to text but don't want her to see.

So I keep her talking.

"Your dad was a piece of shit, by the way." Tessa hits the accelerator again through a red light. "He said if I ever talked to you or Quinn again, he'd make me pay, and when I showed up at your house again to tell you about the baby, he offered me more hush money and asked if it was yours. The funny thing is, I never told Quinn… it could have been yours, or it could have been his, kind of like fucking Russian roulette. In the end, both of your parents paid me more than I deserved, but my own fucking father took it since he was so deep in, then killed himself this morning after making a few bad investments."

"I'm sorry, Tessa." I don't know what else to say… she isn't in her right mind.

She slams her hands against the steering wheel. "It wasn't supposed to be like this, Ambrose! I was supposed to teach! I was supposed to come back and fall in love! You were supposed to love me first! Not second!"

"You drugged me, forced yourself on me, and you think I loved you?" I ask. "Maybe at one point I could have, but you took advantage of me."

"You knew exactly what you were doing!"

"You slipped something in our drinks!" I yell. "No, I had no clue what I was doing! I was a fucking virgin, Tessa!"

She starts to laugh, and it's not the normal laugh that comes bursting from her lips but something evil, like a monster. "Oh please, you wanted it, I could tell. Every day you flirted with me, every party you drank with me, you wanted it so bad, I just forced your hand a bit."

"A bit?" I repeat. "A bit? You literally sent both of us to therapy after that. We could have put you in prison!"

"Shut up! Shut up!" The Jeep makes a jump and barrels down the next hill. I'm starting to freak out.

I don't know what to do. The truth is important but more important than my life?

We fly down the road, passing cars on the left and the right, nearly running into a semi.

"I see how she looks at you," she whispers. "She loves you, but she doesn't deserve you, either of you." Tears stream down Tessa's face. "I do. I deserve something good after everything I've been through."

"You do." I lie. "You deserve all the good things."

"Liar!" she shouts, clenching the steering wheel. "I want to die."

"NO!" I shout. "Tessa, you have so much to live for. Think about this."

"I have." She grits her teeth. "Since the cops left at five this morning. I've thought about it a lot, and the only way this should end, our tragic love story, you, me, Quinn… it ends this way."

"Tessa!" I scream, then make sure my seatbelt's on.

Quinn starts yelling through the phone, then MB.

I say a quick prayer, then try to grab the steering wheel as the Jeep careens toward the dock by the lake.

She suddenly lets go of the steering wheel, but we're still going fast. She turns to look at me, her smile sad, her eyes crazed. "It's all your fault for being perfect."

The Jeep hits the water so hard that I lunge forward then try to unbuckle my seatbelt; it sticks for a few seconds as we sink.

Chilly blackness covers me as I try to get the window down. It's past halfway, enough to escape out of, when I turn and see Tessa choking on water. I undo her seatbelt and grab her, trying to pull her out with me.

We're completely immersed when the Jeep hit's something hard, jolting me so far into the back of the car that all I see is Tessa's floating body and darkness.

I start to choke.

Arms wrap around me; they're not large. I see a woman with dark hair and frown, struggling to hold my breath.

I'm in and out of consciousness as something pulls me from the car and the water.

When I blink up, all I see is sunshine.

And my mom.

I see my mom.

So I know. I must be dead.

She no longer exists.

How sad that in my last moments, I saw the last person who abandoned my perfect life.

I reach for her and feel the stinging sensation of tears forming and falling down my cheeks.

"I still love you," I whisper before closing my eyes for good.

It's all my fault, after all, for trying so hard to be what everyone wanted me to be rather than myself.

I should have loved more.

I should have protected my friend before my family.

I should have told MB it was okay, that it wasn't her fault the very second my dad died.

Should have, should have, should haves suck.

CHAPTER THIRTY-NINE

Mary-Belle

"He's still out." Tears stream down my cheeks. I've never been more freaked out than when Quinn pulled me aside and had me listen to the conversation Tessa and Ambrose were having.

I don't know why, but I immediately called Ambrose's mom, and weirdly enough, she had just left the airport and was driving home and saw them go screaming by.

She hung up on me.

And that was it.

I could have never known the ramifications of that one phone call. I stare at him in the hospital bed, and I know, I'm convinced, he's going to blame me again.

It's going to be my fault again.

His entire perfect life fell apart the minute I walked in that door. The minute I walked into his life—mine began—his ended.

I'm shaking and don't even realize it. I know I need to go to the house and pack up my things. I haven't asked yet, but I'm hoping Quinn can at least take me in for a few days while I try to finish school and find a job. I have some money saved from Ambrose's mom, but this is where it ends.

I don't need Ambrose telling me that to know it's true. It's been eight hours and twenty-nine seconds, thirty—of waiting for Ambrose to wake up post-surgery.

He doesn't know yet.

I wonder if he'll feel it though, if he'll know that his body is different, that he needed something only a mother could give?

Quinn wraps a strong arm around me while we sit on the small couch in the depressing hospital room. He has no idea the thoughts running through my head, the things I'll have to eventually say out loud, the things I will need to give up.

It's hard to even look at Ambrose lying lifeless, knowing what I know.

Quinn pulls my legs into his lap and runs his hands through my hair. I don't have the energy to fight him, and part of me wonders if he knows I need comfort.

It's soothing. I steal a glance at Ambrose. All he did was try to be a friend; even though that horrible woman didn't deserve it, his heart was still in the right place.

She literally raped fourteen-year-olds as a senior and has the balls to try to kill him because her life is so horrible?

So what? Everyone goes through shit. Everyone. That doesn't justify ruining everyone else just because you aren't happy or don't get what you deserve.

And now he has nothing.

I think back on my black trash bag full of crappy things over my childhood.

I think I cherished those more than she cherished anything her family ever gave her.

I turn against Quinn's chest; I can't stop shaking or thinking about the last few hours.

Quinn clings harder. "I didn't want Ambrose to know about the baby. I was afraid he'd be pissed, but mostly, he's always been this insane high school god with everything ahead of him. My dad wanted me to play sports, but I was more into math and playing video games; I figured, hey, if they need shit on us, why can't it be me? Why can't I be the father in his place? No need for a paternity test since we both slept with her. It wouldn't be fair to him, but he thought—" He starts to choke up like he needs to get this out for him, me, and Ambrose. It helps soothe the ache in my soul. "He thought I chose her over him when I chose him every time. I chose my best friend."

He's trying to comfort me, to share his story so that when Ambrose wakes up—I don't sob because of mine—ours.

A tear slides down my cheek, I wipe it away and look up at Quinn. "You did more than enough."

"No." His eyes fill with tears, but they don't spill over; it's like he's holding them in. "I didn't protect him enough. He's been under pressure his entire life; while my dad already gave up on me, his never did… I was always so fucking jealous. I guess we all have our journeys. Our own stories. I just never saw his ending this way."

I think back on mine and get closer to him. "Yeah, we do."

"Maybe had I found you first… right?" Quinn jokes, his eyes are sad though, and it kills me because I know he's being honest and that it hurts his soul the way it hurts mine

271

because, in another life, maybe I would have loved him. In this one, I still have love, but I look over at Ambrose, and I ache.

I don't ache for Quinn.

I ache for Ambrose.

And I'll ache for him for an eternity. I need to walk out of that room before I don't have the strength to leave. When I disappointed Ambrose the first time, it nearly destroyed me.

Now? There won't be any more pieces left to salvage.

Quinn holds me tight, then rubs my back. "Sorry, too soon? I was just kidding, you know."

No, he wasn't.

I laugh despite the fact that my boyfriend is currently a few feet away from me. "Who knows, he may get amnesia and never want to see my ugly face again."

"You're not ugly." Ambrose groans. A chill runs down my spine as if to say it's time. "And I'm right here."

I fall out of Quinn's lap and stumble toward Ambrose. "You're awake." I try to keep myself from bursting into tears as I make it over to Ambrose. His head's bandaged. No airbags deployed in the car for whatever reason—we are waiting to find out why—so he hit the front really hard and got scratches along his jaw with a lot of bruising down his arms and chest.

But that's the least of his worries right now.

I swear I can see the scars on his body from the surgery, the ones he probably feels but doesn't yet know about.

"Ambrose." I choke out, holding my breath for a few seconds.

One. Goodbye.

Two. I'm sorry.

Three. Believe it wasn't my fault.

Four. I love you.

"I'm awake, not talking in my sleep, and why does everyone look so morose?" Ambrose groans again and sits up.

He stares at Quinn, not me. "I love you too, bro."

Quinn bursts into tears and walks over to Ambrose, then pulls him in for an embrace while I watch. These guys. Ride or die. I love them. I love it.

I've never had that.

And now I've lost it.

"I'm sorry," Quinn says, holding Ambrose close. "I'm so fucking sorry, I had no idea, and when I finally figured it out, I realized what was happening. I—"

"—Not on you." Ambrose pats him on the back. "I got in the damn car."

"Because you're a good person," I whisper. "You always have been, always will be."

"Oh yeah." His smile's teasing. "The guy who slept with his foster sister on, like what? The first day?"

I just shake my head. "Maybe she wanted it."

"She asked for it."

"Too far. Now you get slapped."

He bursts out laughing. "I was kidding!"

"Not funny." I stick out my tongue. "Plus, you're a horny little thing, with your tiny little—"

"—Hey now." He sits straighter. "You know very well that my dick is in good condition."

"Should I leave?" Quinn asks.

I needed the comedic relief; for whatever reason, it gives

me strength, seeing them together, seeing the smiles despite the grief he's about to undergo.

"Nah…" Ambrose says. "Stay."

The word feels final between all of us; I try to regain composure and then realize that maybe it was always supposed to be like this.

The three of us.

Together.

But not forever.

I smile over at Ambrose, his eyes search mine, and then he suddenly starts to pale even more. "What's wrong?"

"Nothing." I lie and kiss his forehead. "I'm just going to step out really quick." A tear slides down my cheek. "I love you."

He frowns. "You're coming back, right?"

One day. "Sure." I wink. "I'm just super tired. It's been a long day."

"Oh." He frowns over at Quinn. Quinn gives him a confident smile. I haven't told him yet either.

The doctor in charge chooses the worst possible moment to walk in. He takes one look at Ambrose and says nothing, then grabs his chart. "You're one lucky man."

Ambrose looks at me, then Quinn. "I am."

"How's the back feeling?"

"My body?" Ambrose seems to think about it. "It feels fine, why?"

"Morphine." The doctor smiles, "I'm glad it's working. At first, you woke up screaming mid-surgery; some patients do that."

"What, surgery?"

The doctor clears his throat, which is never a good sign.

I start to back away toward the door. "You were in a very serious accident once the car hit the water…" His voice lowers. "A woman jumped in to save you. According to the EMTs, you were trapped, and something was stabbing both of your kidneys, we think maybe metal from the dock. An investigation is ongoing, but you were in full kidney failure."

Ambrose sits up and groans. "But you fixed it? Right? Who was the woman who saved me? I need to thank her, am I going on dialysis or—"

The doctor holds up his hand. "The woman has sadly passed."

I suck in my tears and try to keep strong.

"But…" The doctor looks over his shoulder. "She was an organ donor, so you'll make it through perfectly fine. We were able to give you her kidneys at her request before she passed."

Ambrose squeezes his eyes shut and leans back against the hospital bed. "Can I at least ask who made that sacrifice?"

The doctor looks over at me in confusion; I give him one silent nod. The tears spill down my cheeks.

The doctor sighs. "You were her next of kin—it was your mother. This young lady back here called her before you crashed, and she happened to see the accident. She was able to save you in your last moments but sadly lost her life in the process."

"M-my mom?" Ambrose stares at the doctor, it looks like he's going to puke. "I have my mom's kidneys? She saved my life?" He's quiet and then whispers, "She's dead."

The room falls silent.

Quinn reaches for Ambrose, and I can't take it. I can't look at him, so I turn and look at the perfectly white wall and wonder how this all happened.

How.

I have no idea.

She saved him.

At what cost to him, though?

He's an orphan, just like me.

And he'll blame me, as he should. After all, I'm the one that called her. I'm the one that spent the last moments of his father's life with him, just like I spent the last few seconds of her life with her.

"Love him," she whispered.

"I know, I know." I hold her hand.

"Didn't mean—"

"—It's okay!" I yelled. "You're going to be fine!"

"Doctor, need to save—"

"—No." I shook my head. "No, it's fine—"

She started to code, then miraculously opened her eyes and stared at the doctors and surgeons.

"Save him."

It was all she needed to say.

Paperwork was brought, she was able to actually sign it, and then...

She coded again.

And she was gone.

Ambrose starts to cry. I know Quinn will be there for him, and I'll be there in spirit.

I leave the room.

I'm numb as I walk to the parking lot, and then I just keep walking.

I walk three miles to the house that gave me a fresh start. I walk through each of the hallways and memorize the way they always look so stark and perfect to me.

He'll have Quinn.

He'll have money.

But I can't bear to let him have me knowing that it's my fault. I ruined everything that was perfect in his life without even realizing it.

The words of my previous foster parent before Ambrose's aunt sink in. They finally sink in.

"You're a curse! You ruin everything! My marriage is over because of you!"

She yelled so much that day; she blamed me for tempting her husband, she blamed me for him losing his job, she blamed me for everything.

And now I wonder if she's right. If the reason that nobody ever kept me was because I'm unkeepable. I'm the person that stays for a season, only to be kicked out the very next.

After all, aren't the last three people who tried to love me dead?

It's better this way. There is no actual logic to my choice other than I can't see any other option.

But sometimes, life isn't logical. Sometimes things just happen, but when you see a pattern, the only way to change it is to change yourself.

I go into Ambrose's room and grab a piece of paper and one of his black markers. I almost smile at how impeccable his room is for a high school boy; he even made his bed.

So perfect, isn't he?

I draw a black heart and then sign it: Love, MB. I'm sorry for everything.

I leave it on his bed and then walk into my room. I leave the makeup. I leave the fancy clothes and purse. I gather what I came with—just that.

And I put it all in a fancy new trash bag, then take the money his mom had given me.

The credit cards, purse, and keys go on the kitchen table.

Old habits die hard, so I grab a few protein bars and a bottle of water.

And I take one last look at the perfect house, with the perfect people and perfect lives.

What is perfect anyway?

Was it this?

Is it him?

Me?

Is there even a definition?

Life is messy, dirty, and beautiful, like a tidal wave of sorrow followed by someone telling you to fight to survive until the sunrise.

I've yet to fully see mine.

But one day, one day, I'll find it.

After all, the story isn't over until the end, right?

I nod to myself and open the front door, shut it, and start to walk again.

I let it go.

I let him go.

And I've never felt more broken.

CHAPTER FORTY

Ambrose

"**W**hy isn't she back yet?" I ask Quinn.

Quinn looks down at his hands. We've been waiting an hour, and I've cried most of it. I have a funeral, another one to plan, and I'm worried sick about MB.

"Did Tessa make it?" I finally gain the courage to ask.

Quinn nods. "She's a couple rooms over, most likely going to get arrested for reckless driving and possession."

I nod. "At least that explains her erratic behavior."

My throat's scratchy from trying to hold back tears, and I'm sick of seeing detectives come in and out of my room asking me the same questions over and over again, not to mention the fact that I'm most likely front-page news right now.

My mom came back to me.

Only to leave for good.

I'm bitter, sad, and thankful, and then I go back to being bitter again. I loved my mom. She loved me in her own way, and in the end, she gave me the perfect gift.

Funny how a month ago, I wanted to sit outside and have my freedom thinking that my life was so bad.

And now I'm an orphan.

Alone.

Money doesn't do shit. I'll inherit millions of dollars, but what does that do when you're alone in your giant home at night? It doesn't keep you warm.

It makes you a target.

So you isolate and isolate some more—self-preservation and all that. I just... I can't imagine it, and I can't wrap my head around it, nor do I want to.

I just want MB. I want her to tell me we'll figure it out like she did when mom left.

I want her to tell me it's okay to cry and that cuddling on the couch during Pirates of the Caribbean is a totally normal way to deal with trauma.

I want her.

And she's not here.

"Maybe check your find your friend app?" Quinn suggests. "I'm not a creeper like you, so I never added her, but I'm sure you probably have seventeen trackers in her bag."

I smile despite still feeling wet tears on my face. "Is this your way of trying to cheer me up? Being a dick?"

"Is it helping?" he asks.

"A little." I sigh. "And she turned off location services."

He frowns. "Did you try texting?"

I show him my phone. "I've sent a few. I just thought

she was giving me a minute, but now I'm worried, and she's all—" I choke up. "All I have is her and you, but you're being a dick, so I really need to find my forever right now."

His face falls. "I'll find her."

"How? Magic?"

"Money." He shrugs. "Same thing."

I almost laugh. "Okay, Tony Stark."

"Avengers assemble." He winks. "Will you be okay by yourself for a few minutes?"

"Are you asking me if I'm going to slit my wrists?"

He sobers. "I'm being serious."

The elephant in the room is literally holding a sign that says. "You know because you lost your dad and mom so close together and nearly died from a psycho ex-girlfriend who raped you as a freshman, but yeah sure, how's your day going?"

We're both quiet, except for the hum of the machines around us and the smell of antiseptic, medicine, and bleach.

I look up at him, really look at him, and I can't take it anymore. It's like the world shatters around me, and all I can see is him.

Quinn's on my bed before I can stop him, and I'm in his arms. He's holding me so tight it almost hurts to breathe, but I want to shout that I need the physical pain.

I need it, so my heart doesn't feel like it's breaking.

My world doesn't feel like it's fallen from the stars only to crash into infinity.

"I love you," he doesn't whisper it. The words are forced, his lips against my neck, the graze of his teeth against my skin. "I. Love. You." He holds me tighter, his arms nearly choking me from my neck down. "And so does she. It's going to be okay. You're my best friend. The best."

"I don't deserve those words."

"But you do." He hits my shoulder with his fist, and then he pulls away. I think he's going to stand up. His eyes search mine. "Too bad there's this wonderful girl between us. I could probably rock your world."

"You could try." I wipe my tears, and he hugs me again. "I love you too."

"I know, man, I know." He rubs my back. "And I'll find her."

I don't trust my voice, so I just nod.

He gets up and gives me one last look. "Keep your phone on, try to sleep, enjoy the morphine."

"Sleeping sounds nice." I lean back against my pillows.

He opens the hospital room door and looks over his shoulder. "Ambrose, it's going to be okay, maybe not right this second, but it will."

"You think so?"

"Yeah well, you've got a kickass best friend and girlfriend, plus you're actually not horrible at kissing, so the world is your oyster."

I laugh at that. "Yeah, thanks needed that morale boost."

He salutes me. "Anytime, now nap while I find our girl."

"Our girl?" I repeat with a smile.

"Ours." He nods. "Always been ours. Maybe all the haters are true; maybe we really do share."

"In this case, I'm okay with it," I say. "Find her."

"Consider her found."

The door clicks shut, and I try calling her again, only to have it go to voicemail. "Please find her, Quinn. Please."

My eyes flutter closed, and the last thing I see is her smile and then her tears.

I wish I could wipe them away, only to realize I'm crying again as a tear slides down my cheek to my pillow.

I always wanted to be left alone.

And now I am.

Fuck.

CHAPTER FORTY-ONE

Mary-Belle

I'm eighteen. I can't go back into the system, and I still need to graduate. Will my tuition still be paid for? Do I even want to risk going back, or should I try to get my GED?

So many thoughts haunt me as I walk down the hot street; the pavement feels like it's melting into my old black slides.

I look down at them just as I stumble—the right one breaks right by my left toe, I have a bad habit of stretching them out when I'm sitting—and now I'm going to need duct tape to revive them.

Of course, it would be today of all days. I almost laugh because, again, of course.

I could use the two hundred dollars I saved up from Ambrose's mom to go to the dollar store and buy some flip-flops, but I have no idea how close that is, and I need to save for food and shelter.

I turned off my phone for a minute, afraid that Ambrose would be sending me angry texts, afraid I'd answer and that he'd maybe be the amazingly decent man I've come to know and tell me to come back to him only to deal with guilt every day of my life.

I don't know why today, of all days, the universe decided to have the hottest day from hell, but I keep stumbling down the sidewalk with my black trash bag.

How perfect, this ending, just like the beginning. I'm brought back to my first foster home, sweaty and gross, walking into an air-conditioned home, hoping that I could at least have water and getting it.

I'd never had ice before in my water, everything was tap, and then I had ice, and I thought, wow, this is how rich people live, with tiny ice cubes and air conditioning.

I don't know how long I walk, but it starts to get dark, and I'm seeing part of the city from Ambrose's private suburb, the night sky is lit up. My phone isn't on still, I wonder if he's okay, I feel stupid that I'm acting like this, but I don't think I can take much more heartache, and I don't think I can trust myself in his life when all I've done is ruin it.

At the end of books and movies, you always see the girl either rescue herself or the guy rescues her. He comes in panicked, worried—but what they don't tell you is so often it's not like that.

So freaking often, it's loneliness and despair, it's bitterness and agony.

It's not Disney.

I'm not Cinderella, even though for just a small moment, it kind of felt like a fairy tale. Maybe I'm too old to believe in them anymore because they aren't something to believe in when all you have is yourself.

A horn honks, then honks again. I know it can't be Ambrose; he's still recovering from major surgery, but for one fleeting moment, my heart skips a beat, and I imagine him pulling over in one of his fancy cars and saying.

"Need a ride?"

I smile to myself. What a great fantasy, what a great dream. Maybe if I just stand still and let the wind blow against my face, I can have those moments of peace. I can build my own ending.

A tear slides down my cheek and onto the concrete in front of me.

I look down at my broken slides.

That first day with Ambrose in the bathroom.

Him kissing me in the kitchen.

Eating all the food.

Him taking me as I am, as I was, as I will always be.

The pool.

Quinn.

My hands start to shake.

I turn to the left. I'm on a bridge that leads right into downtown.

It would be easy. A voice whispers and taunts me to just take those memories and moments and keep them forever in my dreams, an eternal sleep.

I have perfect hope for the first time.

"That sounds nice," I whisper to myself as I look out at the river; the sound of the water almost cools me down for a minute. "It's dark, peaceful, deep… maybe if you fall into its depths, you'll be set free."

My hands shake as I drop the trash bag and grip the edges of the railing. I wouldn't. I couldn't. But is this what people experience when the lights fade? When they've lost everything they were living for or suddenly realize it was all a lie, or maybe they were the problem all along.

I've been tempted by Ambrose.

Even Quinn.

I've been tempted by hope.

Dreams.

Tempted to steal away and give.

Right now, I'm tempted to take one step, one more grip. I'm tempted to do something I can't come back from because something so against my character, something that would destroy everything, almost makes sense.

It should have been me in that car.

Me in that accident.

My sacrifice.

Is that selfish?

I stand up on my tiptoes, brace myself against the bridge, and then lean over it.

A few seconds go by.

I count to ten.

Strong arms embrace me from behind. The smell's familiar.

"Don't you dare." The low voice rasps in my ear. "Do you even realize how long I've been looking for you?"

What a perfect ending I want to say, "Do you even realize how long I've been waiting?"

Great dialogue.

Great scene.

I almost laugh.

And then the arms embrace me harder, and I look down at the friendship bracelet Quinn always has on his left hand. It's old, from some seaside town in Oregon, something Ambrose gave him forever ago; he joked he'd wear it until it fell off and his dreams came true.

I asked him why his dreams would come true when the bracelet left him.

He never said why.

But right now, he's holding me. I can smell him, breathe him in. I lean back against his chest, and with shaking hands, he pulls the ragged strings of the bracelet loose with his teeth while still holding onto me.

It loosens. I stare down at the whitish-brown strings that are braided together with one small rock in the middle. The rock isn't even pretty; it's this grayish-blue-looking thing that's held together by nothing.

"Dreams come true when you let them go," he whispers in my ear. "You hold them in the palm of your hand for so long that it's all you can feel against your skin. It imprints onto your body in such a way that you don't even realize it." I don't know why, but I start to cry. "What nobody tells you is that dreams can very easily turn into nightmares when they linger too long, when they imprint in your soul, when you can't see past them and only focus on them, they become bigger, and they shift." He briefly lets me go, grabs the bracelet from his hand, and dangles it over the water. "Sometimes dreaming means letting go, not holding on. I was going to wear this until my dream came true and you know what's so funny about that? My focus was so straightly focused on getting my best friend back, on fixing things, on things being so fucking perfect that I forgot what it meant to be a friend, what it meant to truly be there. I let my dream become a nightmare, and I used this as a symbol of what I needed to accomplish, like some trophy I'd get when I finally did it. I never needed it, and neither do you. You're perfect the way you are, Mary-Belle. You have a boyfriend who loves you despite the hatred you feel for yourself sometimes. That's what true friendship is. True love isn't in the pretty—it's born out of the ugly, so if you want to let go… take mine."

He puts the bracelet in my hand.

Hot tears stream down my cheeks, and my throat hurts so bad I feel like I really might die as I grip the bracelet.

"Let go," Quinn whispers. "I'll help you."

"And if I can't?" I ask.

"You always can. It's not if you can. It's if you *will*. Sometimes, we hold on to things because we're afraid if we let them go, we'll have nothing left to worry about. Anxiety can be your best friend or worst nightmare."

"Does he hate me?" I ask.

"Who could hate you?" he says. "We love you."

"We?"

"We," he repeats.

I sink back into him, and I release the bracelet into the river, I watch it fall, and I feel myself falling with it.

I didn't jump, but I fell with it, down into the darkest depths of that river. I left it behind, the dream of perfection, of being enough of making people proud, of finding love, of losing it.

I drowned in its depths.

And it was me who set me free.

CHAPTER FORTY-TWO

Ambrose

Two Weeks Later…

I've finally been discharged from the hospital, Quinn and MB have taken care of all the funeral preparations for my mom, but MB still refuses to see me.

Quinn said to give it time.

One second was enough.

I love her, I miss her, I need her.

Tessa's possibly getting charged with child pornography, no shock there, and all I keep thinking while I'm sitting bored out of my mind at home is that I miss MB and that she's staying with Quinn.

I want to hate him, but he's done so much for me—him and his family.

I know sometimes his dad can be a prick, but he's a smart prick, and he's taken care of the will and everything else, but

I'm lonely. And I feel like an idiot because the first day I'm back, all I do is stare at her closed door and wish it would open.

I can't even go to the bathroom without staring at that stupid shower like I've completely lost it. I don't blame her, and I think she knows it. Quinn says she's getting there, but how do you get back from that sort of trauma?

I don't blame her, and yet I do, because she didn't trust my love, my loyalty—and then I think back on my dad's death and go, okay, but do you really blame her for thinking this way?

I don't have to finish school since the accident, but I want to go, I want to see her even though I don't even know if she'll talk to me, but I have another week of recovery.

I'm lonely in the giant house I used to boast about but hate at the same time.

How many days did I roll my eyes at my mom or dad, and now I have nothing.

I stare down at the black suit I have to wear for the funeral and don't even know how I'm going to make it through any sort of speech for my mom.

The eulogy should be done by her son, right? But what if you have no words anymore? What if they're stolen with each breath you take.

I've written nothing.

I feel everything.

Senior year was never supposed to be like this. I was and am a rich asshole complaining about a life I actually get to live.

And they're buried in the ground.

I take a deep breath and reach for the suit on my bed.

I hear footsteps and imagine it's a ghost. How great would that be?

A total cherry on top.

A knock sounds on my door, and Quinn appears with MB behind him. They're both in black. MB has a pretty black dress on that hits her at her knees and caps her shoulders. She looks regal, and I miss her so much it hurts.

Quinn's in a full black suit, and he looks like he hasn't slept in days, probably because he's been helping me since I have nobody.

Nobody but him.

I might fall apart right now.

I know I need to learn to face the dark, but I'm terrified I'll never look back at the light.

At least, that's what it feels like in the heaviness of my own room as I stare at the suit.

"Hey," Quinn whispers. "Thought we'd come make sure you didn't need anything."

"Loaded question." I finally answer, then look over at MB. "Are you okay?"

Tears fill her eyes. "I'm good."

I nod. What else can I do?

Quinn, I can tell, is torn between two worlds, one where I'm his best friend, one where she's his, one where that's my girlfriend and foster sister living with him—and finally, one where we both love her.

Eat shit, Shakespeare.

"Guess I'll just get changed." I don't move.

But Quinn does. He grabs my black shirt from the bed and starts to slowly unbutton it—MB moves behind me and tenderly pulls my shirt over my head and tosses it to the ground.

Not the sexy times I imagined—no, this is more like a holy cleansing.

I'm motionless as Quinn puts the shirt on me, and MB buttons it up.

Quinn sighs, then pulls my sweatpants down to the ground as gently as he can. I step out of the ADIDAS pants and swallow the rock in my throat as he hands me the pants.

I shake my head like I can't do this, man.

He nods his head like, yes, you fucking can, and you will.

I step into the trousers while he pulls them up, and then his hands are grazing my hips. He tugs me against him and presses his forehead against mine. "You will do this, do you understand?"

I say nothing.

His hand grips my chin; his eyes are a blazing heat of fire that has me almost stepping back. Who is this strong person? And why can't I be more like him?

"Put on your pants," he whispers. "All you have to do is put on your pants, and then you're going to take a step, then another, then another, and you're going to get in my car, and we're going to drive."

I finally nod.

MB grabs my jacket and helps me put it on, then wraps her arms around my waist, resting her cheek against my chest, Quinn comes next, holding us all together with his arms, and it feels right, the way it should be like we were always supposed to find each other despite the tragedy that led us here.

"You've got this." Quinn slaps me on the ass.

MB laughs.

And I almost laugh too, but then I lock eyes with MB, and all I want to do is kiss her, and I want Quinn to see just because I want him to be part of everything we have.

Are we a couple, or are we now just finally whole in our grief and trauma?

Life, oftentimes, doesn't make sense, so why does this?

The three of us.

I wonder if they'd freak out if I said I'm never letting them go, neither of them, that I don't care what people say about us, about what happened in the past or could happen in the future.

"We'll be late," Quinn finally says. "You're going to do great, Ambrose. Just speak from your heart."

"I love you," I blurt.

They both turn and look at me, MB's lips tremble, and Quinn reaches for me.

"Both of you," I say. "I love you."

Quinn grabs one of my hands, and MB grabs the other.

Together forever.

We walk slowly down the stairs, and I realize that maybe I had it all wrong—this.

Is.

Perfection.

CHAPTER FORTY-THREE

Mary-Belle

He looks beautiful. His brownish blond hair's falling longer against his chin, and his coloring is good despite still recovering from his transplant and walking slower. I can tell he's trying to hold his head high, Ambrose.

I haven't let go of Quinn's hand. He's taken care of me not because we're in a relationship but because he knows I need a place to stay away from Ambrose before he makes his choice.

I stare straight ahead while Quinn rubs his thumb over my skin back and forth back and forth.

I turn toward my left and whisper in his ear. "I'll love you forever, I'll like you for always…"

It's a joke we've had ever since binge-watching Friends when Joey does his special reading, and I know he needs to relax right now; he's worried about Ambrose just like I am.

He lowers his head and smirks. "…As long as I'm living, my baby, you'll be."

Normally we both laugh, but today's different. Today he kisses my hand and squeezes it.

I don't know if Ambrose sees, but suddenly he's up at the Catholic Church where the funeral is being held.

We have standing room only. After all, he's royalty here in this town. He's worth nearly seven hundred million dollars—at eighteen.

He owns everyone.

He has everyone's secrets.

The weight of what he has—must be damning, and yet still he holds his head high. "I didn't prepare anything."

People start whispering.

He holds up a hand. "Not because I didn't want to, but because I didn't know what to say. How do you put into words the tragedy and gift I've received? My mom was a beautiful and ambitious woman. She was a great mom sometimes, a horrible mom other times. Some days we fought, other days we hugged." He looks up and smiles. "She used to always say that love was interchangeable with money, that if you had enough money, love would happen, and then one day she came into my room, held my hand, and said, love is as endless as it is short, it's your choice alone how long it lasts." He sighs. "She left the room and didn't mention it again, and my dad died a few months later. I saw a shift in her, in the stress of our lives of trying to be something we were never meant to be in order to keep up. So, while I'm thankful for my family's legacy, I'd like to say, right now, I would rather be imperfect, I would rather show my flaws to the world. I would rather be the person people accuse and point fingers at than the person who has the constant stress of standing still while chaos ensues around me—knowing I'm the one that caused it and must keep it quiet. My mom taught me that in such a short sentence and moment, and my best friends showed me that all that matters is it's not over yet, that they'll douse the flames every single time because, at the end of the day, it's about connecting with people, it's about making the world a better place, it's about selflessness when even at your most tempted moment, all you want is to choose you. Choose someone else.

Do better.

Shut up the voices in your head and become what you envision for the world. I loved my mom and dad; now, my burden's heavy." He moves to the side of the stage. "So, as the heir to my family legacy, I've chosen to donate two million dollars to Hearts For Home, an independent foster care business that helps place kids in good homes."

Tears start streaming down my face.

"…Three million dollars to domestic and sexual abuse victims with our city's largest organization, Keep Me Safe."

Quinn starts shaking next to me.

I grip his hand harder.

"And finally…" Ambrose smiles. "Another five million…" People gasp. "…to the local college fund for people who need help getting an education, and in the future, I'll be doing more and more donations. I don't want the money, I don't believe in how it was earned, and I don't believe in keeping all of it. My parents did the best they could, and I vow to do better. I love you, Mom. Thank you for your gift, fly high, and thank you for this…"

I frown.

What's he talking about?

He pulls out a letter, one I've never seen.

Ambrose smiles down at it. "You know what's funny? I didn't want to go to the reading of the will at all, I kept this letter for a week, and I finally read it this morning after some friends came and helped me… so now I'm going to read it out loud… and maybe then you'll understand."

He clears his throat.

The room is so silent you'd think that we weren't even allowed to breathe.

"Ambrose," he starts. "If you're reading this, something tragic has happened, and what I've been told for the last year and a half has actually come to fruition. Stress has been hard, and my heart isn't the best. I hide it from you the best I can. Your mom tried as well because we wanted you to focus on school, thinking it was easier to appear perfect when the world was crashing down around us. You might be alone, but you won't always be. Money cannot be your family, but you can use the money to give family to others. My greatest regret, I'm sure, will be that I worked too hard to build an empire—and lacked. Son, time is the only thing in this world people wish they could obtain. It's the only thing you can't take more of or give back. It's structured purposefully to make us cherish what we have and regret what we don't."

Ambrose smiles down at the paper.

"Time."

He smiles again. "Time."

"Time." He repeats again. "Exactly thirty-seven seconds passed that I will never get back while writing those last few words. I've made mistakes, I hurt you in ways that I'll never be able to take back, just like time, and it was all out of fear of you finding out, fear of losing it all, when I now realize as my hands shake, as I stare at the door and realize that I might not make it that far—it was you and your mom, my most treasured possessions, the doctor had said if this happens again even an ambulance won't save me, you see son, when your heart fails you—it often times does not beat again no matter how many times you will it to keep going. I will always have regrets, and the biggest ones I have are the minutes you'd come into my office and beg me to play catch, but you see, I was too busy."

Ambrose pauses and looks over at me. "I don't know why I'm writing this and adding a letter to my will. Maybe it's because I just hit you because of my own frustrations. My own failings, but I'm sitting here at my desk wondering where I went wrong and realize that I valued money over time. I valued perfection over chaos. You may never see this letter, I hope to God you don't, that I do better and that this is just anxiety, but instead of reaching for my phone, I wanted to reach for you. I love you, son, and I'm proud. Make the world a better place, and when I see you again. Know I love you. I always have. I always will."

I don't know what to say; I think back on that night when his dad pointed toward the desk after I ran in there, ready to raise hell.

All his dad kept saying was keep, keep, keep, Ambrose, and when the EMTs came, I ignored his points at the desk and just sat next to him.

I held his hand.

And realized I'd killed him.

But I didn't.

It wasn't out of shock.

He was sick.

Ambrose stares across the room at me and nods once as a tear falls from his cheek. "I'll do my best to not be perfect."

"What a wonderful fantasy…" I whisper. "Imagining you can be perfect."

"What a beautiful nightmare…" Quinn says next to me. "Owning your dreams."

I turn to him. "What do you mean?"

"They go hand in hand," he whispers. "You have to own them both—to have it all…"

The service ends, and I wonder what's going to happen, but I don't have to wait for long. Ambrose makes his way toward us after about an hour. Everyone's down the street at his home—my old home.

He smiles at me, and it feels real.

I don't know if I should run toward him or away.

"I've been waiting for you." He nods at Quinn. "Thank you."

Quinn lets go of my hand. "All in a day's work of being the sidekick."

"You were never the sidekick." Ambrose shakes his head. "Some might say you were the main character who just got lost because the bat signal was complete shit."

"Probably your fault."

He pauses, then laughs, "Yeah, probably."

Quinn gives Ambrose a slight punch in the arm and then leans in and presses a gentle kiss to my lips.

A month ago, I'm sure it would have started a fight.

Today, I'm thankful because I know what that kiss means. I once heard a song where the lyrics said it's time to rise again.

And it is.

It truly is.

I give him a hug, and I wonder so many things… but for now, I need to not fall apart, and I need Ambrose the way he needs me.

He pulls me into his strong arms. "Stay."

I still against him. I have no words to give him, no courage, only myself, and I hope it's enough.

Rise.

Just lift your head, show him your eyes—give him your soul.

I nod against his chest.

And I don't know how long we stand there, holding each other, but it's long enough that I feel him getting strong again, I don't know how or why I feel it, but I do.

"I won't let go." My lips move against his chest, against his shirt. "I won't leave you alone, Ambrose. I just knew we all needed time."

"Time," he replies. "What a wonderful gift."

"And horrible curse," I say.

We both turn toward the casket and stare.

CHAPTER FORTY-FOUR

Ambrose

I'm exhausted." Quinn collapses against my couch and tugs at his black tie. "Why didn't you tell me your great aunt kisses people on the lips like twenty-four-seven?"

"She's European?" I laugh.

He scrambles back from me. "No! That accent is fake as shit. I won't believe it, I won't. Her lipstick tasted like cake though, so I mean, not a total loss."

MB walks by him and kicks his legs off of the table. "Feet off, and it was MAC. MAC always tastes like cake."

"Yeah okay, Mom." He sits up. "But, really? It does? How do you know?"

MB smiles. "I lick my lips, dumb-dumb."

"So you guys seem comfy." I laugh for the first time in a few days, and it feels really fucking good. "Like the bickering couple, everyone admires but also wants to punch in the throat?"

MB glares at Quinn. "He's messy."

"She's loud!" he yells as if he isn't breaking the sound barrier. "She's constantly singing in the shower. Look, I love you, but you are NOT Adele!"

"I COULD BE ADELE!" she shouts, then stomps her foot, God, she's adorable.

"Wow." I scratch my cheek and lean back against the chair. "Sounds like things have been fun for you two."

They glare at each other. Are they going to cross swords at dawn? Should I be worried?

Quinn finally crosses his arms. "She's all right, I guess."

"He's fine." She winks over at me.

"Glad my best friends can get along." I stand. "Movie night?"

Quinn jumps to his feet. "Hey, it's been a rough time for you. You should at least rest, you aren't fully healed and—"

I don't know why I do it; I truly don't. I just grab him and hold him against me. I hug him so tight that I'm sure I'm breaking my own bones.

He hugs me right back.

And then MB is right there between us, and I kiss her, then he kisses her, and then I'm like, what the hell is going on, and I just go with it; my emotions are everywhere, they're out of control.

MB pulls back and looks between us. Quinn's stunned. His eyes are wide as he looks between the two of us.

"Fourteen." MB nods her head. "You were drugged. You were a freshman in high school, what a horrible sexual experience."

Quinn laughs awkwardly. "Yeah, well... we don't remember all of it, but yeah..."

I mean, what else is there to say?

Tessa's gonna most likely go to prison. The video will never see the light of day again, and it was a mistake, one we covered up because, hello, gotta make everything look great and perfect.

How pathetic.

How sad.

It almost makes me want to blast it and flip off the world, but I realize the repercussions. We were underage too, so that definitely would not be okay.

MB looks between us. "You need new memories."

"I have them," I say.

"No." She frowns, sucking in her bottom lip and putting her hands on her hips. "You need happy ones between the two of you."

Silence ensues.

I look down at my shoes.

Did that just fucking rhyme?

I don't even know what to say.

"We did go fishing that one time." Quinn pipes up lamely.

I roll my eyes. Like, really, bro? Really? "Yes, and we caught nothing."

We also got super high, but I leave that part out.

"Bad bait," we say in unison, causing MB to just laugh and shake her head.

"What?" I reach for her and realize too late that Quinn does the same thing, me for her hand, him to rustle her hair. She frowns between the two of us and starts to laugh.

Quinn leans in and whispers, "She's lost it. We've made her lose it."

"Her eyes look wild," I add. "Definitely mad cow disease."

"I thought she hated beef?"

"Food. She loves all food," I add. "But yeah, she's definitely not—"

She grabs my hand, then his, and presses hers between it. I suck in a sharp breath. I'm afraid to look at Quinn. Maybe he's afraid to look at me.

"It's okay, you know," she whispers. "To love lots of things at the same time." Her eyes shine. "And it's okay to have a do-over."

Quinn's hand shakes as he leans over to me. "Definitely mad cow."

I nod.

MB laughs. I smile because it sounds so pretty, her laughter, her joy.

"Rules," she finally says once she's done laughing. "I'm his girlfriend," Thank God she's pointing at me. "And I'm your do-over." She points at Quinn.

"I'm confused." Quinn raises his hand.

She grabs it and kisses it, then pulls him in for a kiss and wraps her arms around his neck.

I think we're both too stunned to move. I'm jealous as hell, then I think about what he went through, what we both went through, and I think that's the gift the universe deserves to give him.

Damn.

Good.

Just good.

MB is the best of us all, so a mere kiss? Yeah, my best friend deserves to know that love, that tenderness, the feel of her against him, and I can't believe I'm even smiling, but I am.

He's been to hell and back—so have I—why not have a small slice of heaven?

MB pulls back and looks over her shoulder at my stunned expression. Then I realize it's more shock because I'm smiling, and I know he just touched her lips, but those are mine, so I pull her in for a kiss as she releases him.

"New memories, huh?" I pull away, mouth wet. "What did you have in mind?"

"Movie room." She laughs, and we follow like she's completely hypnotized us, maybe she has, or maybe she just has the right answer to our problem, the problem that's separated us for years.

Our shame doesn't have to stay that way.

"I mean, obviously," Quinn says behind her, his hands linger around her hips; she leans into him, then into me, and then somehow, we have her sandwiched while I press an open-mouthed kiss to her lips.

I've never really thought about it, but opening up to someone, breathing them in, how personal can you really get?

Sex is sex, but kissing, kissing is literally opening up your soul. It's connecting on a level where you are literally facing someone and saying.

Here I am.

Here you are.

Own me.

Take me.

Love me.

Sex, well, sex, you don't even need to kiss or make eye contact. It's animalistic in its basic form for pleasure or to procreate.

But this, this feels—otherworldly.

Her lips are sweet and wet. I taste and devour as my tongue lingers on her lips only to touch hers, test it, remember it.

Quinn groans behind her, and a hand grips mine—his. I grip it right back while I press her against his chest, deepening the kiss.

I pull back. "A do-over."

"A better one. Let's be honest… she's the worst."

I lock eyes with Quinn, and he nods at me, then looks away. "I know this isn't like… I mean, I'm just saying no pressure. Clearly, I need to find my own person and—"

"—Don't be a dick." I interrupt. "My girlfriends giving us something Tessa never did."

Quinn swallows. "It's perfect."

And I almost laugh because, yeah, us three, totally perfect, in a mess of tangled kisses, do-overs, bad decisions, followed by really fucking good ones.

Ones that feel so good I don't even know what's happening even when my best friend's hand slides by mine, even though I know what he's doing.

It really is the best.

She moans.

"…but honestly, kiss her again after this, and I'll kick your ass…" I say as we walk toward the theater room.

He laughs. "Noted."

"No penetration," I say under my breath.

"Kill joy," he whispers.

MB turns and glares at us. "Talking behind my back when it was my brilliant idea to take away your trauma, hmm?"

"Sorry," we both mumble.

Quinn shoves me.

I shove him back.

MB bursts out laughing. "I'm kidding."

"Yeah." I nod. "Um, but really like, we weren't really aware of what went on in that video when it was happening, so we haven't really done this."

"And you think I have?" she asks once we're in the dark theater room.

"No!" Quinn yells. "It's just, like, you know… logistics."

MB turns to us, completely serious. "Logistics, whatever do you mean?"

"Yes, please describe; details would be preferable." I nearly choke on my words to keep from laughing as Quinn raises his hands, lowers them, then raises them again like he's getting ready to teach a class.

"Okay, I'm gonna stop you from embarrassing the hell out of yourself," MB says. "It is what it is. You have a bad memory from something that should have never happened to you." She turns to me. "That's my boyfriend over there, who I love." Quinn smiles. "You're one of my best friends, something I never thought I'd have."

I nod.

"And," she continues. "Back in the day, a very wise therapist told me to erase with new things, so that's what we're doing, no fighting, no contracts, no goals, no jealousy, no more nights like these, just… us, in this moment, right now. Healing."

I don't even realize I'm reaching for her, but Quinn does it at the same time. I'm kissing her mouth, he's kissing her neck, and with a tangle of hands and mouths, we fall against the couch. Quinn's pulling his shirt over his head, and I'm working on mine while she's moaning into my mouth.

I taste her excitement, her fear, and our new memories.

Us.

Quinn kisses down her naked back, and his hands move to her hips.

I nod and keep kissing her while his fingers dip between her thighs, I didn't expect him to go that far or be willing to, but somehow it's like I'm outside of my body as he locks eyes with me, almost like he's saying, love her. I have this along with, let me have just this.

Just. This.

He doesn't realize I overheard his conversation in the hospital room, about the possible baby, about him taking over when I couldn't.

About him protecting what he thought was my perfection, so why not give it back in the most primal way possible?

She bucks against his hand.

His eyes close.

And I kiss her again. I hear the sounds of his fingers, every breath of air that she inhales and exhales, and every time I know she's close to the brink of losing it.

Her moans and gasps are like a breath of prayer on my lips. Our tongues tangle while Quinn gives her pleasure, only to suddenly pull back. I know he's turned on, fuck I'm turned on, and I would have never even known this was a future scenario; I'm so hard I want to strip every inch of clothing I have on my body and take her as hard as I can.

Her eyes open; she looks between us and smiles. "Guess it was always us three, just like everyone said…"

"Shit." Quinn rubs his palm down the front of his slacks. "Yeah, it was us."

"Us," I repeat and reach for her. MB grabs me and

kisses my mouth, then his, then mine again until we're both pressed against her, rubbing our hands everywhere, from her hair to her face.

"This must be what it's like to be worshipped," Quinn whispers against her neck.

MB reaches for the front of his pants and presses her palm down. "Yes."

He groans, then jolts back, horror on his face.

I'm still trying to figure out why he's freaking out, even though this is definitely not something we do when he turns around and gives us his back.

"Too hot to handle, Quinn?" she asks.

"Consider…" He clears his throat. "…my memory fully restored with this one as I embarrassingly tap out and make my way to the bathroom, where I will one hundred percent cry in the corner while you guys do your thing."

I laugh; I can't help it. "Bro, how long has it been?"

"Clearly too long." He grumbles and then groans and looks away. "PS gonna have a serious talk with my cock right now."

"That's weird," I say.

"So is kissing your best friend's girlfriend, but here we are." He looks over his shoulder. "Best tongue I've tasted in—"

"—Go." I point toward the door.

Quinn laughs and winks at me. "Let's be honest. It would have never worked out between the three of us. First of all, my dick is so big you'd—"

"—GO!" I yell.

MB bursts out laughing. "Come back when you can, Quinn. We can watch more pirates."

"Come," he repeats. "Now, why is that familiar?"

I throw a pillow.

And then MB is on top of me as the door shuts, she's all over me, actually, and I realize that while he gave her pleasure, he's the only one who reached it.

It's not weird when I cup her, almost like his only job was to blot out what happened, get her ready, and experience pleasure for the first time in a while in a safe space.

I'm okay with it.

I'm okay.

I have her.

She has me.

And we both have him.

Weird but true.

"You okay?" I ask as I peel away her remaining clothes and discard them on the floor along with mine.

MB grabs my face, pulling me down to kiss her, and we tumble onto the floor. The heat from her body presses against mine; her skin is soft as I straddle her on the floor. This is my future.

Her.

My best friend.

MB grabs my hair, tugging me forward until our bodies are sliding against each other, and I know there's no going back.

She's already mine, but right now, it's different.

She was mine because I wanted her.

Tonight she's mine... because there's no secrets between us, no lies, no more hiding—it's raw, emotional, physical, spiritual.

Perfect.

Damn, It's so fucking perfect.

Soft fingers touch my cock, and I nearly have the same problem that Quinn does as I try to keep my body from responding. My tip teases her entrance. I tell myself not to explode.

I keep the fireworks at bay, just barely enough to inch closer inside her heat, and then she grabs me by the ass, and I lose all sense of existence. I slam into her, fucking her against the floor, her head hits the red leather bottom of the theater chair, and she says nothing, just hooks her heels around my ass and pulls me deeper.

Deeper.

Deeper.

Deeper.

Until our motions are a reaction to being too close, too deep, too everything. Her hips rise up, mine push down, yin and yang.

She kisses me while I finish inside her knowing she's already there if the lack of friction between us is anything to go by.

"Perfect," MB whispers against my sweaty neck.

"The Perfects." I correct. "Us."

EPILOGUE

Ambrose

Everywhere I walk now, or drive, or eat, people stare, they point. I'm still on TV along with my "stepsister," who I'm now openly dating.

It's a weirdly imperfect world I now live in and one I wished for, not knowing what I was wishing for.

MB visits my parent's graves and leaves flowers, and she's been cooking on a daily basis, trying to fatten both Quinn and me up, who told his parents post-graduation he was moving in with me—us technically to help support.

Our new life can wait.

The perfect college—has to wait.

My life is on hold for the first time since I was born.

And I'm weirdly okay with the wait because I have my two best friends with me.

Maybe we'll start a company.

Maybe we'll go fishing for ten days straight.

My parents worked hard to make it possible for me to do

that, and I have to thank them every day for providing for me despite all my complaints so that when shit hit the fan, I could sit and stare at a wall or cry.

I keep my dad's office pristine, and one day, I hope to sit in that chair and do better.

To work just as much as I play.

To love my kids even when they crap their pants and draw on the walls with permanent marker—and I hope to God that it's Mary-Belle being the one yelling at me for letting them get away with everything.

God, I hope so.

I love her so much.

I turn in bed and look over at her; she's spread out like she owns the King-sized thing and slightly snoring.

She's amazing.

She saved me.

I lean over. "You're snoring again."

"Eat shit," she whispers hoarsely.

Yup, that's my girl, my future wife—and on one perfectly imperfect day—I'm going to get down on one knee and ask her to be mine forever.

The door to my room pushes open. "Dude, you'll never believe who just got an even heavier prison sentence."

I jolt up. "Tessa?"

MB freezes next to me.

Quinn comfortably sits on the bed. "Yeah, the girl I just started seeing from the coffee shop." He nods. "You know the hot barista with the really cool bracelets from overseas?"

I nod. "Yeah, yeah, makes the best cappuccinos."

"That girl." He snaps his fingers.

"Does she not have a name?" MB asks.

"Lexi." Quinn and I say in unison.

MB groans. "So you still call her that girl?"

"Focus!" Quinn snaps his fingers. "I was in a panic. Okay, so Tessa apparently had more videos of other guys from our school."

I feel myself start to feel sick. "Seriously?"

"Yeah, none came forward, but it's like almost every single investor in her dad's company, she was basically sent out to like… you know…"

I shudder. "Were they underage?"

"All of them." Quinn nods. "It was front page news, anyway, I didn't mean to mess up your morning sex routine."

MB throws a pillow at him.

He dodges it.

And then dives into bed between us. "Ahhhh, memories."

"GO FIND THE BARISTA!" I yell.

"Already did. She's in my room." He winks. "Oh, I told her she could move in but that my parents might be weird about it."

I frown. "Your parents?"

"Yeah, you two, hey ps, this really gorgeous sexy, talented barista's gonna be bunking up with me across the hall, cool?"

"Get him," I growl.

MB jumps.

Quinn runs.

And chaos ensues.

Perfect.

Fucking.

Chaos.

Totally imperfect. Forever.

Want to see Quinn get his Happily Ever After?
THE UNPERFECTS — coming in 2023

IF YOU NEED TO TALK TO SOMEONE, HERE ARE SOME RESOURCES THAT ARE AVAILABLE ALL DAY, EVERY DAY.

Please know you are not alone.

988 Suicide and Crisis Lifeline

The Lifeline provides 24/7, free and confidential support for people in distress, prevention and crisis resources for you or your loved ones, and best practices for professionals in the United States.

If you or someone you know is having thoughts of suicide or experiencing a mental health or substance use crisis, 988 provides 24/7 connection to confidential support. There is Hope.

Call or text 988 or chat 988lifeline.org

Línea de Prevención del Suicidio y Crisis

Lifeline ofrece 24/7, gratuito servicios en español, no es necesario hablar ingles si usted necesita ayuda.

1-888-628-9454

Lifeline Options For Deaf + Hard of Hearing

For TTY Users: Use your preferred relay service or dial 711 then 988.

Veterans Crisis Line

Reach caring, qualified responders with the Department of Veterans Affairs. Many of them are Veterans themselves.

Dial 988 then press 1
Text: 838255
veteranscrisisline.net

Substance Abuse and Mental Health Services Administration (SAMHSA)

SAMHSA's National Helpline is a free, confidential, 24/7, 365-day-a-year treatment referral and information service (in English and Spanish) for individuals and families facing mental and/or substance use disorders prevention, and recovery.

1-800-662-HELP (4357)
TTY: 1-800-487-4889
Text your zip code to: 435748 (HELP4U)
samhsa.gov/find-help/national-helpline
findtreatment.samhsa.gov

The National Sexual Assault Hotline

RAINN (Rape, Abuse & Incest National Network) is the nation's largest anti-sexual violence organization.

800.656.HOPE (4673)
Online chat: online.rainn.org
Español: rainn.org/es

The National Domestic Violence Hotline

We answer the call to support and shift power back to people affected by relationship abuse.

1-800-799-SAFE (7233)
TTY: 1-800-787-3224
Text "START" to 88788
Online chat: thehotline.org

love is respect

loveisrespect's purpose is to engage, educate and empower young people to prevent and end abusive relationships.

1-866-331-9474
TTY: 1-800-787-3224
Online chat: loveisrespect.org
Text LOVEIS to 22522

FOSTER + HEART

Our mission is to ignite the hearts of our community
to foster + meet the needs of children in foster care.

Check out the amazing things that
Foster+Heart has planned!
fosterandheart.org

WANT MORE RVD?

Did you enjoy The Perfects?
Then check out these other New Adult Romances!

Cruel Summer Trilogy
New Adult, Angsty Romance — Trilogy
Summer Heat (Marlon & Ray's story)
Summer Seduction (Marlon & Ray's story)
Summer Nights (Marlon & Ray's story)

Wingmen Inc.
New Adult, Romantic Comedies — Interconnected Standalones
The Matchmaker's Playbook (Ian & Blake's story)
The Matchmaker's Replacement (Lex & Gabi's story)

Bro Code
New Adult Romance — Standalone Novels
Co-Ed (Knox & Shawn's story)
Seducing Mrs. Robinson (Leo & Kora's story)
Avoiding Temptation (Slater & Tatum's story)
The Setup (Finn & Jillian's story)

Seaside Pictures
New Adult, Angsty, Rockstar/Movie Star Romances —
Interconnected Standalones

ACKNOWLEDGMENTS

I'm so thankful to God, my family, Jill, Tia, Nicole my agent, Nina, and all my readers. I'm too tired and on deadline to write this, haha, no but seriously. I wouldn't be where I am without you guys and without the amazing readers who continue to support me!

I know this book is different than the ones I've written over the past 12 years but thank you for giving it a chance.

You guys are amazing.

Love you all, join RRR and follow me on TikTok and Insta at @RachVD

ABOUT THE AUTHOR

Rachel Van Dyken is the #1 New York Times, Wall Street Journal, and USA Today bestselling author of over 100 books ranging from new adult romance to mafia romance to paranormal & fantasy romance. With over four million copies sold, she's been featured in Forbes, US Weekly, and USA Today. Her books have been translated into more than 15 countries. She was one of the first romance authors to have a Kindle in Motion book through Amazon publishing and continues to strive to be on the cutting edge of the reader experience. She keeps her home in the Pacific Northwest with her husband, adorable sons, a naked cat, and two dogs. For more information about her books and upcoming events, visit www.RachelVanDykenAuthor.com.

ALSO BY
RACHEL VAN DYKEN

Eagle Elite
New Adult, Mafia Romance — Interconnected Standalones
Elite (Nixon & Trace's story)
Elect (Nixon & Trace's story)
Entice (Chase & Mil's story)
Elicit (Tex & Mo's story)
Bang Bang (Axel & Amy's story)
Enforce (Elite+ from the boys' POV)
Ember (Phoenix & Bee's story)
Elude (Sergio & Andi's story)
Empire (Sergio & Val's story)
Enrage (Dante & El's story)
Eulogy (Chase & Luciana's story)
Exposed (Dom & Tanit's story)
Envy (Vic & Renee's story)

Elite Bratva Brotherhood
New Adult, Mafia Romance — Interconnected Standalones
RIP (Nikolai & Maya's story)
Debase (Andrei & Alice's story)

Mafia Royals Romances
New Adult, Mafia Romance — Interconnected Standalones
Royal Bully (Asher & Claire's story)
Ruthless Princess (Serena & Junior's story)
Scandalous Prince (Breaker & Violet's story)
Destructive King (Asher & Annie's story)
Mafia King (Tank & Kartini's story)
Fallen Royal (Maksim & Izzy's Story)
Broken Crown (King & Del's story)

Standalone K-Pop Romances
New Adult, Angsty, Rockstar Romances — Standalone Novels
My Summer In Seoul (Grace's story)
The Anti-Fan & The Idol

The Dark Ones Saga
Paranormal Romance — Interconnected Standalones
The Dark Ones (Ethan & Genesis's story)
Untouchable Darkness (Cassius & Stephanie's story)
Dark Surrender (Alex & Hope's story)
Darkest Temptation (Mason & Serenity's story)
Darkest Sinner (Timber & Kyra's story)
Darkest Power (Horus's story)
Darkest Need (Tarek's story)

Players Game
New Adult, Sports Romances — Interconnected Standalones
Fraternize (Miller, Grant and Emerson's story)
Infraction (Miller & Kinsey's story)
M.V.P. (Jax & Harley's story)

Ruin Series
Upper Young Adult/New Adult, Angsty Romances —
Interconnected Standalones
Ruin (Wes Michels & Kiersten's story)
Toxic (Gabe Hyde & Saylor's story)
Fearless (Wes Michels & Kiersten's story)
Shame (Tristan & Lisa's story)

Seaside Series
Young Adult, Angsty, Rockstar Romances —
Interconnected Standalones
Tear (Alec, Demetri & Natalee's story)
Pull (Demetri & Alyssa's story)
Shatter (Alec & Natalee's story)
Forever (Alec & Natalee's story)
Fall (Jamie Jaymeson & Pricilla's story)
Strung (Tear+ from the boys' POV)
Eternal (Demetri & Alyssa's story)

Seaside Pictures
New Adult, Angsty, Rockstar/Movie Star Romances —
Interconnected Standalones
Capture (Lincoln & Dani's story)
Keep (Zane & Fallon's story)
Steal (Will & Angelica's story)
All Stars Fall (Trevor & Penelope's story)
Abandon (Ty & Abigail's story)
Provoke (Braden & Piper's story)
Surrender (Drew & Bronte's story)

Covet
New Adult, Angsty Romances — Interconnected Standalones
Stealing Her (Bridge & Isobel's story)
Finding Him (Julian & Keaton's story)

The Consequence Series
New Adult, Laugh Out Loud Romantic Comedies —
Interconnected Standalones
The Consequence of Loving Colton (Colton & Milo's story)
The Consequence of Revenge (Max & Becca's story)
The Consequence of Seduction (Reid & Jordan's story)
The Consequence of Rejection (Jason & Maddy's story)

The Emory Games
New Adult, Laugh Out Loud Romantic Comedies —
Standalone Novels
Office Hate (Mark & Olivia's story)
Office Date (Jack & Ivy's story)

Curious Liaisons
New Adult, Romantic Comedies — Interconnected Standalones
Cheater (Lucas & Avery's story)
Cheater's Regret (Thatch & Austin's story)

THE PERFECTS CONTAINS:

Death of a Parent
Date Rape—flashback to an incident in the past
Car Accident
Foster Care System
Discussion of Past Food Insecurity
Bullying
Cyber Bullying/Sexual Harassment
Organ Donor/Donation & Transplant
Mental Health: Depression, Brief Thoughts About Suicide

www.rachelvandykenauthor.com